for Lindsay

The Skull Chronicles II

The Red Skull of Aldebaran

D.K. HENDERSON

With love & blessings

D.K. Henderson xxx

Lyra Publishing
England

Copyright © D.K. Henderson 2013

The right of D.K. Henderson to be identified as the author of this
work has been asserted by her in accordance with the Copyright,
Design and Patents Act 1988

Cover design by Manor Cottage Studios
www.manorcottagestudios.com

Cover photo of skull by Penelope Thompson-Griffin

A CIP catalogue record for this book is available from the British
library

ISBN: 978-0-9571952-64

For all my much loved friends. Thank you so much for all your encouragement and support. I couldn't have written this book without you.

The Skull Chronicles II

The Red Skull of Aldebaran

PROLOGUE

Below the surface of this planet Earth they wait, the physical expression in our world of those who watch us from above. In caves, or buried beneath long-deserted sacred temples, or hidden in the care of ancient spirits, patiently they rest.

Some are known to a few, to those whose time-old lineage permits them to know of such things. Most though are forgotten, awaiting the time when they will once more see the rays of the sun. Awaiting the dawning light of a new age of consciousness.

Those who brought these treasures to us watch and wait also, as they have watched and waited since the beginning. Once, in times long forgotten and on a world that no longer exists though its soil is that upon which we walk today, they were known to us, were known to all. They came freely, walked freely, amongst us, brother alongside brother, sister alongside sister. For in those times we knew that we were one, knew that even if their homes were far away, out amongst the distant stars that lay like glittering dust on the rich dark canvas of night, our origins, our source, was the same.

And then the time came, as they knew it would. The time of great forgetting. Still they waited serenely, as they do today, in expectation of the new dawn when the tide of consciousness turns and we begin to remember once more.

That time is upon us. We are waking up to the truth of their presence, one by one, degree by degree.

They are helping us in our remembering, bringing us signs of their existence which, when our eyes begin to open, we see clearly. The skulls too are there as they always have been, watching over us, guiding us, leading forward those of us who are ready to walk with them. Powering this awakening. Assisting in our spiritual and energetic evolution as they have done for the last two hundred and fifty millennia. Touching us with their love.

As we move now forwards into the era of transformation, the skulls are intensifying their power output to match the quickening pace of change and our new level of existence. Igniting, or perhaps that should be re-igniting, our higher levels of consciousness and understanding. Preparing us for the day when we will welcome them once more openly into our presence. United, as it was before in the time of Atlantis. When that day arrives, when all thirteen skulls sit together once more, so it is foretold, the people of the stars will once more walk and live alongside the people of this planet Earth.

CHAPTER 1

'She still sleeps beneath the black pinnacle, deep buried in the sand.'

'What?' Cathy's forehead wrinkled in confusion as she looked across at me. I was curled up in an armchair on the other side of the living room, concentrating on my magazine.

'What what?

'What did you just say?'

I peered back at her over the top of my reading glasses. 'I never said a word.'

'Yes you did. Something about someone still sleeping under a black something.'

What was she going on about? Now it was my turn to look a bit bewildered.

'No, I didn't. You must be hearing things. I'm too busy battling this bloody Sudoku and it's driving me nuts.'

'Honestly, Gemma, you did speak. And it didn't sound like anything much to do with Sudoku to me.'

I leaned forward towards where Cathy was sprawled on the sofa, and pointed accusingly at the small empty glass on the floor beside her. 'How much of that sloe gin have you had?'

'Less than you!' she retorted indignantly. 'You did, you know.' Cathy was adamant. 'Say something I mean. Quite loudly too. It was something about someone sleeping. I wish I could remember exactly what it was but I was miles away and it didn't really register.'

'I know. You already told me. Something about someone still sleeping under a black something. Why on earth would I come out with something like that? I haven't a clue what it means. I still think you were hearing things.'

'Oh I don't know. But I definitely heard it, and you definitely said it. Otherwise how would I be able to repeat it?'

'She still sleeps beneath the black pinnacle, deep buried in the sand.' What the...? This time I had heard it too. What shook me up most though was that it had been my voice uttering the words – and I had no idea where they had come from or why I had spoken them. I stared wide-eyed and open-mouthed at Cathy, fear lurching up inside me. 'Cathy,' I was struggling to keep calm, forcing my voice to stay level – and losing the battle – 'why did I just say that?'

'That's it! That's exactly what you said just now.'

'Well I didn't intend to. I haven't a clue what it means. It didn't even feel like it was me speaking.' I didn't understand what was happening and to say it was scaring me was an understatement of some magnitude. 'But... it came out of my mouth! Cathy,' I could hear my voice rising as the fear inside me surged forwards towards full-blown panic, 'WHAT THE HELL JUST HAPPENED?'

By now Cathy was sitting bolt upright looking excited (maybe I should mention here that as well as being my best friend, Cathy is a psychic whizz and fount of knowledge on all things spiritual and esoteric), a curious expression spreading across her face as understanding slowly dawned. 'I think,' she said slowly, 'that you've just channelled someone. Or something. The skulls maybe?' She wasn't put off by my obvious scepticism. 'Well, why not?'

'Because I don't do that. Does anyone?'

'Yes. Lots. Although most of them keep quiet about it in case they get labelled basket cases.' Yes, just like I would. She leaned across and squeezed my hand reassuringly. 'Look, the skulls have been contacting you through your dreams for a long time now. Well, that's a form of channelling in itself. But because it's happened while you've been asleep you haven't been resisting it. You've willingly accepted their messages. You've done what you've been asked to do. Maybe this is the time they want to step it up a notch? You know, make it more direct. Maybe now they want you to let them speak through you. To use your voice to relay their words.'

Honestly? That freaked me out even more. 'You're saying I've been possessed? Oh, come off it. That's just horror film stuff and nonsense.' I was NOT going there.

'No, not possessed. They aren't taking over your body or your mind or…'

'No, just my vocal chords.'

'That's exactly it. They're just using your voice as a transmitter. You know, like when a radio picks up a signal and sends it out as sounds we can understand.'

'No way!' I wasn't having any of that. I was *not* going to be anyone's radio transmitter. 'Anyway,' I was puzzled, 'why now? It's never happened before.'

'Who knows? Perhaps they feel you're ready to take the next step. Look, just think about it for a minute. You were in the perfect place. With your conscious mind preoccupied with solving your puzzle, the other, more intuitive part was open and receptive to them coming in.'

'Well they can damn well go out again. Come on, Cathy. You know that I'm really happy to do what I've been doing, receiving these stories in my head and writing them down. I've got my head around that. I can cope with that. I enjoy it even. But anything more? Not a chance.

'They've probably picked up already that you aren't ready for this. Your reaction would have given them a big clue. It might be worth spelling it out to them clearly though.' She paused. 'Don't shut the door on it for good, Gemma. I tell you, if it was me I'd be beyond excited. To be able to channel verbally like that? It's something I've always wanted to do.' She was almost bouncing up and down in the sofa, her eyes sparkling at the idea. Then, with a sigh, she brought her thoughts back to the question in hand. 'What do you think it means?'

'How on earth do I know? I'm still dealing with the fact that something has just hijacked my brain. Frankly, right now I don't give a toss what it means.'

Cathy was finding it hard not to burst out laughing. 'Poor you. It was a bit of a shock, wasn't it? You look so indignant...' She couldn't hold her amusement back any longer; the rest of her sentence was lost in a gurgle of stifled giggles. I scowled, which only made things worse.

'Oh come on, Gemma. You have to admit that things have been getting weirder and weirder ever since this business began. This is simply one step further down the weird path. Why not just run with it and see where it goes? It's got to be somewhere pretty exciting and unbelievable. And don't you dare leave me behind.'

A weak smile signalled my surrender. 'OK. But no more freaky speaking. I mean it.' I was determined to forestall Cathy's enthusiasm for buying me into this whole new scenario. 'I'm happy to carry on the way things have been going but no-one is going to use me as a ventriloquist's dummy. Do you hear?' I tilted my head until I was looking up at the ceiling and repeated my last words in a tone that brooked no argument. 'Do you hear me? No dummy!'

'That's telling them!' Cathy laughed. 'Right. Down to the important stuff. What does it mean?'

'I have absolutely no idea. I can only think it has to be linked to the skulls. What else could it be? But other than that... This could be another case of wait and see.'

'Somehow I get the feeling that you won't have to wait too long to find out.'

As usual, Cathy was right.

CHAPTER 2

Callum's latest email had intrigued me. It was concise and cryptic: *'Hot on the trail of you know what. Can't tell you more now, will be in touch soon.'*

His words chased themselves round and round in my head. It was too mysterious. What was he talking about? Was 'you know what'…? Could he possibly mean one of the skulls? No, that was just crazy. Much as I wanted to believe in the reality of it all in the way that he did, I was still finding it impossible to find a way past my scepticism. In spite of all the pretty bizarre things that had been happening for some time now, the possible implications of that email were just too off-the-wall for my rational mind to accept. Or was I just reading too much into it?

I wanted to know more and my chance to find out came more quickly than I expected when a second email pinged in only a day after the first. Again it was brief but this time to the point: *'Flying back to the UK on 28th Aug. Essential we meet up. Lots happening. Progress! Will ring you from my hotel when I get in. C.'*

28th August? That was just over a month away. Why the delay, I wondered. Well, I wouldn't hold my breath. The last time I had received an email from Callum asking to meet up, I had heard absolutely nothing more about it. If he had information to share though…

Callum: the tall, slim, grey-eyed and long haired maverick archaeologist and skull hunter who believes that all the information I am getting through is one hundred per cent genuine and accurate. A dangerously charming and flirtatious man whose eyes melt me into a little puddle.

I could try to fool myself that the flush I felt hot on my face and the increase in my pulse rate were due to excitement over Callum's mysterious news. I would be lying. The prospect of seeing him again sent my emotions and, let's be brutally honest here, my whole body into a complete tailspin. My logical, sensible mind was doing its best to hold my infatuation (because let's face it, that's exactly what it was) in check – and failing miserably as the rest of me leapt on it, wrestled it rudely to the ground, and squashed it flat.

GOR-KUAL: The Red Skull

Part I

THE FINGER OF THE GODS, 1

CHAPTER 3

Nihu peered warily at the object that lay half-hidden in the dark shadows. She couldn't distinguish it clearly, only that it was smooth and rounded with a polished surface that was evident even in the gloom. It hadn't been here on her previous visit, of that she was certain. So how was it here now? Where had it come from? Who had left it here? And why?

Few came to this place, and seldom. It was an inhospitable place: a high dry, plateau of stony, infertile ground in the midst of which a soaring column of black rock pierced through to the sky like a Titan's spear point – the Finger of the Gods. This black rock was hard, durable, the remnant of long ancient volcanic activity. Over the hundreds of thousands of years since it had exploded from far beneath the Earth's crust, the softer rock around it had been eroded to leave behind a single, sinister black finger that towered over one hundred feet into the air and was visible from a vast distance away. Since the people had first arrived here they had considered it sacred, a world between worlds.

It was indeed a sacred and special site, a magical site where the energy lines of the Earth converged to create a vortex of power. Unlike many of this planet's other energy hubs however, the Finger of the Gods' forbidding atmosphere did not welcome idle visitors. No-one would come here by choice. No-one that is except Nihu. Nihu loved it. Loved its solitariness and uniqueness. Loved the barren isolation of the high land from which it emerged. Loved its natural power as it stood tall and unmovable, withstanding all that assaulted it.

She peered more closely. Despite her irresistible fascination for this place, the girl was still fearful of the spirits that lived here and of their capriciousness. The rock towering above her leant at an angle of over forty five degrees and looked as if at any moment it could topple over and smash to the ground, crushing anything beneath. It was an irrational fear – the pinnacle had been here like this since times before memory – yet still it remained steadfast within her. She knew from experience that the spirits were quick to anger and that once they were roused anything could happen.

'What do you see, child?' It was her grandfather approaching, his footsteps silent upon the stony ground.

'There, Grandfather. Do you see it?'

The old man peered in the direction of the child's outstretched arm. His fading eyesight registered nothing unusual. 'I see nothing, Nihu. Where do you look?'

'There. Beneath the Finger of the Gods. Do you know what it is?'

The old man looked more intently, straining his eyes to see what his granddaughter had noticed. His sight was not what it had been, he mused sadly to himself. At one time, and not so very long ago, his vision had been as keen as that of the vultures that soared over these hills and valleys. Now he found it difficult to see much beyond a few paces. By concentrating hard, however, his focus cleared a little and he saw what appeared to be an unusual reddish coloured rock tucked in the narrow gap where the slender finger pierced the ground.

'I'm going to get it.' Gathering her courage, Nihu dropped flat on her stomach and wriggled into the narrowing gap at the very base of the rock where the object lay half buried. She stretched out her arm to hook it and draw it closer, squirming backwards to bring it out into the light.

*   *   *   *   *

Mesmerised they sat cross-legged on the rough ground, as they had done without moving in the hours since the object had emerged into the sunlight. It lay in front of them, mysterious and out of place. When Nihu had wriggled back out from beneath the rock pillar and shown her treasure to Grandfather, she had been holding in her hands a skull, but unlike any they had ever seen before. This was not the skull of a once-living man or woman. It was instead carved from a deep brick red rock streaked with veins of creamy bone white, and polished so that it shone like the glassy surface of a still pool under the sun's fierce rays.

Since she was little more than an infant Nihu had been cared for by her Grandfather, the wise man of the village. He had taught her well, so that when the time came she could take his place, though she still had many years of training ahead of her before she would attain the knowledge and skills to become a worthy successor. Even now, at only twelve years of age, her intuitive and extra-sensory abilities were so well-developed as to be second nature, and the moment she had touched this mysterious object she had understood that it was special, a gift from the gods. Grandfather nodded as he picked up her thoughts. This would indeed be a powerful talisman, and his little Nihu had found it.

At last, reluctantly, unwilling for these moments to end but knowing they must, Grandfather rose. 'Come Nihu, it is time to show this to our people.'

She got to her feet, ready to return to the village. But as she looked up she froze, the skull that still lay on the ground where they had set it for the moment forgotten. Standing before them was a man, dark-skinned like themselves, but whereas their people were short and wiry, this man was tall, far taller than anyone they had ever seen before. Thin arms and legs that looked barely strong enough to hold his weight were just visible beneath his shimmering, bronze coloured robes, while his long, regal face, set with eyes the colour of jet, looked like it belonged to a world other than this one. His raven black hair was tightly braided and twisted into knots that lay close against his strangely elongated skull, and he stood smiling and relaxed under the hot afternoon sun.

*   *   *   *   *

It was evident that he had been waiting for them to look up and see him, for as they met his gaze he gave waved his hand in acknowledgement. 'Greetings, my brother. Greetings, little sister.'

With a jolt of surprise Grandfather realised that he was speaking to them in their own tongue. How had he learned this? He had little time to wonder; the stranger was speaking again. 'I have been waiting for you, and now you are here. It is good to meet with you at last.'

Grandfather was confused. He couldn't understand. How had this man been waiting for them? He had not known himself that he would be coming this way until Nihu had asked him to bring her here to find some stones for her rituals. Nonetheless they had evidently been expected; this man was here waiting for them.

'I do not understand, stranger. How could you be expecting us when we did not know ourselves that we would be passing this way?'

'It was told that you would come, and you came. I am overjoyed that it is so,' the thin man replied. 'I see that you have found the gift we have brought to you and to your people. It is a gift beyond all price. Beyond all value. I am Urdh, emissary of those who watch over you. I offer it to you on their behalf.'

He bowed his head to Grandfather once more. 'You are wise, my blessed friend, wise with the wisdom of your years and of your experiences. You are skilled in speaking with the realms that lie beyond the physical world in which you live. You have a heart filled with love, and the desire to see all prosper, and this gives power to your wisdom. I have come to you because we have foreseen that you will honour our gift and respect its power. You are to be its guardian. Use it with all the grace and love that you hold within you.'

'But I am old, not worthy of such a responsibility.' The old man's voice shook, feelings of inadequacy for the task he had just been assigned rising up from deep within him. 'I do not have many years left. Surely you would wish for someone younger, stronger, more deserving?'

'Grandfather, true strength does not lie in youthful looks or a firm body, but in compassion and understanding. You will watch over this treasure for many years to come and, when you are no longer able, its guardianship will pass into the hands of this dear child, your granddaughter, for she bears your qualities. You will teach her your wisdom and your knowledge. Teach her well. Take now our gift to you – Gor-Kual, red skull of Aldebaran.'

With those words, he stepped forward and swept the skull from where it still lay on the coarse grey sand of the plateau, offering it with both hands to Grandfather in a gesture of respect that nevertheless that would not accept refusal.

As the skull settled into Grandfather's hands he almost dropped it, surprised initially by its weight, and then by the fierce pulse of energy that pounded into his palms and rushed up his arms. He had sensed the great power held within this object during the recent hours that he had sat gazing at it in the company of his granddaughter. Just how powerful however, he had not understood until this moment. Nihu had not commented when she had laid her hands on it and, young and inexperienced though she was, she was already skilled in reading energy. Could it be that this man's simple touch had activated it to another level?

'Not activated, awakened from her sleep,' the stranger replied to Grandfather's thoughts as if he had spoken them aloud. 'She is ready to teach and guide you, if you will listen.'

'Teach us what?' Nihu was curious. She had learned long ago that all objects held their own energy and power, and that they shared this willingly with those who wished to use it. This though was something more again.

Amongst her people, as they were amongst many others, skulls were revered, held as sacred objects of immense importance and magic. The skull was the cradle of knowledge, intelligence, understanding and wisdom, the point where spirit entered the physical body through the portal at its crown, its form the perfect amplification chamber for these forces. Through a skull a wise man such as her grandfather could access the knowledge of the ancestors, of the spirits of the natural world around them, and of the gods themselves. But this skull was different. This was not the legacy of a formerly living soul; it had been created from cold stone. And yet... It felt somehow alive, as if its own heartbeat pulsed within. Nihu's young mind was struggling to make sense of it all. How could that be? Was this skull really a living entity that could speak by its own will, possessing its own independent thoughts and feelings?

'Indeed she is, little one.' Urdh smiled at her, again hearing the unvoiced words. 'She was created with the gift of consciousness and carries within her the divine essence and life force not just of those who fashioned her but of the entire universe. She is a sentient, intelligent being, one who holds you in great love, wishing only to help you to flourish and grow. Care for her, love her in return with the love you hold for your grandfather and your people. Use her knowledge for the good of all. That is all that we ask of you.

'She will teach you of worlds beyond this one and of those who visited you from those worlds, as the stories of your campfires tell. She will teach you of the movement of the cosmos, of its importance in your lives, and how to read the passage of the stars. She will teach you how to increase the fertility of your fields, the abundance of your crops, and the joyfulness of your lives. She will teach you how to heal all that which is not whole, and to create miracles in your lives using nothing but your natural, inborn abilities.

'Know also however, that while her power is strong, it can be abused by those who are determined to do so. Power is power, neutral in its essence; its consequences, for good or ill, are determined solely by the intent of those who use it. Do not let this misuse befall your people. Take care of the thoughts and intentions you hold, let them come always from your heart and a place of love, remain conscious, and work with her for the purpose she has been given to you.

'Before many cycles of your moon have passed I shall return, bringing others of my kind, for it is our greatest wish that our peoples become close friends. We shall visit you often in the times to come if you will welcome us amongst you. For now however, my all too brief time with you has come to an end and I must leave.

'Grandfather, hear well what I now say. Gor-Kual has a gift for you. Do not resist it. Until we meet again my friends, farewell.'

With these last cryptic words, the air around Urdh began to shimmer with a silvery light. Nihu and Grandfather watched in astonishment, mingled with not a little fear, as his body grew hazy, then transparent, and began to dissolve before their eyes. Within a few seconds he was gone, the place he had stood only moments before now empty. Nihu ran to it, staring first at the spot, then back at Grandfather with wide, question- and fear-filled eyes. 'Where did he go, Grandfather? How did he do that?'

'I don't know, little one. It is evident that he has knowledge and abilities far beyond that which we hold. Maybe he was a god, come to bless our people, for I believe that in receiving this skull in some way we truly have been blessed, although I admit freely that its purpose and consequences still lie beyond my understanding. Come now, Nihu, we must return to the village and share this news with the others.'

CHAPTER 4

'Argggghhh!' The pain in his eyes was excruciating, as if someone was prising them from their sockets with red hot pincers. He was completely blind, could see nothing but a solid crimson fog, and was curled up into as tight a ball as his aged limbs would allow, aware of nothing but the agony in his head. Unaware even that he was screaming.

'Grandfather! Grandfather!' Nihu was kneeling beside him, terrified. She had never seen him like this, in truth had never seen anyone like this, and did not know what to do. Tears rolled slowly down her young face as she watched him helplessly in his torment. What was happening to him? Why was he suffering like this? Was he possessed? Being punished by an angry god? Or was he succumbing to some terrifying, unknown affliction? Her little body shook from head to toe in distress as she watched this beloved man writhing in relentless agony in front of her eyes.

Within moments gentle, strong hands were on her shoulders, lifting her up and guiding her from the hut out into the warm, velvet dark night, away from the nightmare within. Others rushed to help Grandfather in his suffering. The whole village had been woken by his cries and many had hurried to his aid. A woman's soothing arms held Nihu tightly as she sobbed inconsolably, wrapping her in a soft blanket, rocking her gently, reassuringly, until her tears lessened and she lay quietly. All the while Grandfather's screams continued to fill the night, those who tended to him helpless in the face of his pain.

Then, as suddenly as it had begun, it ended. An unnerving silence settled momentarily over the village. The women who had hurried to help Grandfather came out of his hut, confused and frightened.

'Is he dead?' Nihu struggled out of the arms that held her and rushed towards them. 'He can't be dead!'

One of the women shook her head. 'No, Nihu. He's not dead. He's sleeping. Like nothing happened.' She was completely bewildered. 'I don't understand it. One moment he's rolling around in agony, the next sleeping like a baby.' She looked at Nihu and smiled a shaky smile. 'Go with Mhana tonight, Nihu. I'll stay with your Grandfather and watch over him until the morning.'

'No, I…' Nihu did not want to leave him alone.

'Come.' Mhana, the woman who had led her from the hut, took the child's hand. 'Tala will look after your Grandfather. He is in good hands. She will come and get you if anything happens. Come.'

Tala looked down at Nihu and nodded. 'I promise.'

So Nihu let herself be led to Mhana's hut where, exhausted by the events she had just witnessed, she too soon fell into a deep sleep.

* * * * *

The following morning, just as the sun was rising, a loud shout burst forth from Grandfather's hut, followed by a peal of joyful laughter. Tala sat up abruptly, woken by the sound; she had drifted into sleep at her bedside vigil as Grandfather continued to snore peacefully and evenly, no trace of his former torment remaining. Now however, she was immediately wide awake again, peering at him, anxious for his wellbeing. She need not have worried. The old man was beaming at her, his face lit up with joy, his eyes bright and sparkling. There was something different about him, about the way he looked, but in that moment she could not grasp what it was.

His gaze shifted to the entrance to his hut where the morning sun illuminated clearly the world outside, then back to Tala once more. Amazement and delight showed in his entire body. 'I can see. Tala, what miracle is this? I can see. I came to my rest almost blind, and I wake this morning with eyesight as clear as it was when I was a young man.' Another joyful laugh burst from his lined lips. 'It's a miracle,' he repeated as the people of the village, woken by his shout, clamoured around the hut's entrance. 'Pado, I can see you. Hayati, I can see you too...'

He stopped, bewilderment clouding his face as he took in the situation. 'Tala, what are you doing here? Why do you sleep in my hut this night?'

'Don't you remember?' Tala's voice faltered as she recalled the horrific scenes that had taken place during the darkest hours of the night.

'Remember what? There is nothing to remember. I came to my hut virtually a blind man, I slept, and now I wake this morning to find you here and that I have the vision of an eagle.'

'Grandfather?' Nihu had pushed her way through the crowd and was standing in front of the old man, tears prickling her eyes. 'Can you really see?'

'I can indeed, little one, though I am at a loss to explain what magic has happened here.' Grandfather clambered stiffly to his feet, took her hand and led her outside. The eyes of the village followed them in silence, dumbfounded by what was taking place. Grandfather glanced around, his joy in his newly restored eyesight written all over his face. Nihu was still unsure, and he sensed her doubts. 'There, Nihu. Do you see?' He pointed towards the ribbon of water that glittered silver in the morning sunlight. 'There is a hawk on the top branch of the tree that stands at the bend of the river.'

Nihu peered intently. Her clear child's eyes could certainly see a bird in the tree, which had to be at least two hundred paces distant, although she could not make out what sort of bird it was. She stared at Grandfather. Only yesterday he would have been unable to see the bird if it had landed on the ground less than thirty paces from him.

'You *can* see. Was it the pain, Grandfather? Did the pain heal your eyes?'

'What pain, little one?' Grandfather knelt in front of her, looking into her troubled eyes. 'Why do you speak of pain? There is no pain.' He gazed at her in concern as the tears, still not far from the surface, glistened once more in Nihu's lashes.

'In the night, Grandfather. You were screaming.' Her voice cracked and she sobbed out her next words. 'I didn't know what to do. I was so afraid.' The old man folded the child in his arms and held her, reassuring her, until her trembling eased.

'I know nothing of any pain, little granddaughter. Perhaps you should tell me of what happened in the night, for it seems that strange and powerful forces have been at work here. But do not allow yourself to be upset, for pain does not touch me now and if, as you tell me, it did then, I have no memory of it.'

So Nihu and Grandfather walked hand in hand along the bank of the river and she told him the story of what had occurred. After much talking and contemplation both agreed that this must have been the gift of which the stranger, Urdh, had spoken.

'Why would it bring you such pain, if it was truly a gift?' Nihu was struggling to understand.

'Urdh told me that I should not resist...' Grandfather was deep in thought, allowing the answers to bubble up from deep within. 'Perhaps in some way I was resisting, even though I didn't know it. Perhaps it was this fighting it that caused the pain.' He smiled at the child sitting beside him. 'Do not upset yourself further, my granddaughter. I do not remember experiencing the pain. It happened, and from what you say I clearly felt it and suffered as it was happening, but it has been erased from my memory and so has left no scar upon me.'

'Why would you fight something that was going to make things better?'

'I don't know, little one. Maybe because we are always afraid of that which we do not understand, or because we resist that which will change things even when it is for the better? Whatever was fighting in me must have come from a place so buried within me that I did not know of its existence.' He paused, deep in thought. 'Why has Gor-Kual been given to us, Nihu? Why us?'

CHAPTER 5

It was a question that held Grandfather in its grip and would not let him go. Each day for many months following her appearance he would sit with the red skull for hour upon hour. Walk with her. Absorb her energy. Yet she remained silent, did not speak to him, nor to any other of the villagers as it had been promised she would.

They created a small shrine for her in a clearing above the river bank, where she could gaze on the rushing water and hear its song. It felt right to them that she live there though no-one could have told why. Whenever she was not with Grandfather, it was there that she would rest. None of the other villagers would touch her. It was not forbidden to them, indeed Grandfather did all he could to encourage them to spend time with her. It saddened his heart that they simply did not have the desire to do so, even if many came regularly to bring offerings of food and flowers.

To his burning disappointment, for his deepest wish was that his granddaughter would feel the same attachment Gor-Kual as he himself did, Nihu too steadfastly refused to have anything to do with her. It was a disappointment he kept to himself because he saw that Nihu was still very afraid of Gor-Kual and the power she held, was still scarred by the memories of the skull's first night in the village and Grandfather's subsequent suffering. Try as she would, Nihu could not erase the images and memories from her mind, or trust fully in the benevolence of the red skull.

Another bitter disappointment and sorrow for Grandfather was the continuing absence of Urdh and his fellow travellers. The promised visit had not manifested, nor had he received from the red skull any of the teachings that Urdh had spoken of: teachings about the stars and his peoples' origins, or knowledge that would help ease the burden of their daily lives. Gor-Kual remained stubbornly silent, communicating with no-one. Soon the villagers forgot these promises and carried on as they always had. Gor-Kual became simply a part of the village in the same way that their livestock and the natural world around them were part of the village. The offerings became a habit, a daily ritual that was undertaken purely because it had been done for some time. Amongst all of this, Grandfather and Nihu did not forget.

Silent and uncommunicative as she was, Gor-Kual was nonetheless exerting a steady and constant influence on the community, though it was an influence so subtle that no-one noticed it. Even if they had, it was unlikely that anyone would have attributed the changes they were experiencing to the red skull. There was no reason why they should.

These changes were real enough however. They did not come about in huge leaps as had happened with Grandfather's eyesight, but in slow, almost imperceptible steps so gradual that it took some time before they became noticeable. Little by little people were becoming healthier, fitter and stronger. Hearing, eyesight and the other physical senses grew sharper and clearer. Skin and other minor problems cleared up completely and did not return, while more serious afflictions were greatly eased. Stiffness in the joints and muscles of the older members of the community melted away and those elders became as strong, agile and flexible as villagers many years their junior. Eventually these changes were so evident that they could no longer be ignored. None though was prepared to attribute them to Gor-Kual and her presence amongst them. None that is but Grandfather and Nihu.

For no-one will see that which he or she does not wish to see, and the people of the village did not wish to see the power of the red skull. On some hidden, inaccessible level they recognised it, and they were afraid of it. So they laughed down any attempt by the old man and his young granddaughter to persuade them otherwise.

CHAPTER 6

'Gemma! Gemma? Have you seen this?'

I was sitting peacefully finishing a leisurely breakfast when Cathy burst unceremoniously into my kitchen, not taking the time to knock, her dark red curls bouncing around her face as she waved a piece of paper at me excitedly.

'I don't know, Cathy. What is it? It must be pretty special for you to be out and about so early.'

'Sorry, I know. It is a bit early. But this is something you just have to take a look at. I saw it on the web, printed it off and dashed over here straight away. It was too important to wait,' she finished, by way of explanation. 'Anyway, never mind what time it is,' she thrust the sheet of A4 into my hand, 'what do you think of THIS?'

As I read, Cathy watched my face intently, wanting to catch my reaction. She wasn't disappointed. I could feel my jaw drop more and more the further down the page I got. At last I stared up at her, disbelievingly.

'It can't be right. Where did you get this?'

'Like I said, off the internet. Some obscure news site I found a week or two ago that carries all kinds of mysterious stories that don't make the standard channels. Now you see why I had to come over? You had to read it for yourself. You wouldn't have believed it otherwise.'

She was right. If she had just phoned I'm not sure I would have believed her. And with no web access here at present – to my irritation, it had been down for three days already and *still* the company couldn't find the problem – I couldn't have looked it up to confirm it for myself.

'Well, what do you think?' Cathy's eyes flashed excitement and impatience at me, eager for me to say something.

'I'm gobsmacked. I don't know what to think. If I hadn't read this with my own eyes… But…' I looked through the lines of print once again, this time reading it out loud, just so it would sink in.

MYSTERY TREASURE DISCOVERED IN NORWAY

A group of scientists working close to the Finnish border in northern Norway has made an incredible find: a mysterious gold object that as yet no archaeologists have been able to identify.

The object is of a strange design, shaped like an 'f' and a 'j' attached at 180° to each other from a small centre circle. Its purpose and origin remain a complete mystery. The gold is of a purity that cannot be attributed to any previously known source and at around 10cm in length this is an object of considerable value.

It was found lying under a thin covering of ice on what is believed to be a former river bed not far from the Norwegian/Finnish border. This area has only recently been freed from the grip of the ice that has covered it since the last ice age, probably due to global warming and the thaw of the glaciers that had covered it. To have been beneath the ice, scientists are speculating that this object must have lain there undiscovered for at least 50,000 years, which throws into disarray all formerly accepted timescales for human civilisation and the birth of such advanced skills. To say the experts are baffled is an understatement. Where did it come from? Who dropped it? What was its purpose? Could such an advanced civilisation have existed so long before conventional wisdom says it was possible, and if so, who were they?

Archaeologists at the University of Oslo…'

'Coincidence?' I asked hopefully. I didn't really believe it, but I didn't want to believe the alternative explanation either. Cathy snorted.

'Coincidence my ar… my foot!' she stated bluntly. 'I don't buy that and neither do you. The question is – what are you going to do about it?'

'Do?' I looked at her as if she had gone mad. 'I'm not going to do anything. What do you suggest? I go up to those Norwegian scientists and say "Hi guys, I know exactly what that thing is. It's a key to the caskets containing the thirteen crystal skulls that are hidden around the Earth. Oh and by the way, it doesn't come from Earth. It was brought here about a quarter of a million years ago by the same aliens who brought the crystal skulls to us. How do I know? Oh, it came to me in a dream."? Come off it, Cathy. I'd be laughed off the face of the planet.'

'Hmmm. I get your point. But Gemma, once your book is released – when's that, a month or so's time? – people will read it anyway.'

'Maybe. But that will be them drawing their own conclusions, not me stepping forward and deliberately shoving my head above the parapet inviting it to be blown off. I wrote a novel. If people want to see it any other way... Well, that's their choice.' I plonked a fresh cup of coffee down in front of each of us.

'It's scary though, Cathy,' I said quietly. 'When I started I thought it was all made up stuff that I was writing. I'm not so sure it is any more. I keep finding more and more validation. First Callum's email and now this? To tell the truth, I'm getting a bit apprehensive. It's getting a bit too real for comfort. Where is it all going to lead? Perhaps more importantly, do I really want to deal with wherever that is? I mean, I hadn't really thought about it properly until just this minute, but this article has really brought it home to me with a crash. What the hell am I getting myself into here, Cathy?' I could hear the unease rising in my voice. 'Do I really want to go there?'

'Only you can decide that.' Cathy leaned across and gave me a hug. 'I'm sure it will all be fine. If the skulls are really as powerful as they seem, then they will look after you. Anyway, if you decide you don't want to do it, you don't have to. If you are that worried, forget this book and write something completely different instead.'

I appreciated Cathy's support and knew she was talking sense. At the same time, deep inside me I knew without a shadow of a doubt that, despite the fear and trepidation I felt, I would carry on. I would carry on because more than anything I wanted to know what on earth was going on and what it all meant.

Not for the first time I wished I could talk to Joe about all of it. As a lifelong crystal skull fanatic, it had been him I turned to when all this spooky stuff started happening in my life. He had introduced me to real-life crystal skulls and we've been really good friends ever since. Or at least, we had. I think the world of Joe but I hadn't seen him or heard from him in months, not since we'd had that major bust-up over Callum. Yes, I really wished I could speak to Joe. But I didn't know where he was, and he still wasn't answering my emails.

GOR-KUAL: The Red Skull

Part I

THE FINGER OF THE GODS, 2

CHAPTER 7

Nihu wandered across the stony plateau, not noticing where her feet were leading her, entangled in sorrowful thoughts that could not be shaken loose. There had to be something she could do.

Under Grandfather's guidance Nihu had developed into a skilled healer and intuitive and now, as almost twenty four years had passed since her birth, she was ready to take over from her Grandfather and step into the role of village Wise One. She was young, very young, to be assume on such a role – most Wise Women were past their moon times before they took on the mantle – but Grandfather had insisted that she was ready. He felt old and was ready to hand over the responsibility. Though still fit and healthy, thanks in no small measure to Gor-Kual's influence, he had become weary. Often these days he spoke of how he was ready to move forward into the eternal spring of the next stage of his life. It saddened Nihu deeply that it was so, for she saw clearly that it was his spirit rather than his body that was tired. Tired of life, tired of holding onto his belief in Gor-Kual, tired of waiting for something that never came. Nihu understood well that death was an inevitable and natural step for every person that ever lived, but she recognised too that it was not yet Grandfather's time. She felt helpless in the face of his melancholy.

She blinked. Her feet, as they always did, had led her to the Finger of the Gods. This stark, lonely place always brought her solace and the solitude she needed to be alone with her thoughts and feelings. Today however, this was not to be. Someone else was already there, standing at the base of the dark needle: a tall, slender, dark-skinned figure dressed in a bronze coloured robe. A sharp stab of anger coursed through her, unjustified but fierce. What was he doing here? This was her place and today she needed to be alone. Who was it? Filtering through the anger then came something else. A familiarity. A sense of déjà-vu. A knowing that she had been in this, or a very similar scene, before.

Nihu slowed her steps, cautious, suspicious of the newcomer. There had been several attacks on the village of late, attacks that fortunately the village had managed to resist without sustaining serious injury. As a result however everyone, including Nihu, had become nervous. Strangers were no longer welcome. Mentally, Nihu called for protection from her spirit guides and from the guardian spirits of the Finger of the Gods. Her steps slowed even more as she reached out to gauge the impressions she was picking up from the visitor. He seemed gentle and friendly, his energy field silhouetting him in a soft, golden glow. She could sense nothing dark or threatening about him yet still she hesitated, her inherent human fear overriding her intuitive knowing.

'Greetings, Nihu. It has been a long time since I promised you and your grandfather that I would return. I have come now to fulfil that pledge.'

The soft, deep voice was the trigger that awoke fully in Nihu the memory of who he was and of that far-off day when they had met.

'Urdh?' Of course it was. The moment she uttered the name there was no doubt remaining. 'You are here? Why? Why now? Why did you not come back before as you told us you would?'

'Because I could not. It was not meant to be so long but... circumstances... did not permit me to return earlier. Tell me Nihu, how is your Grandfather?'

Tears blinked on Nihu's lashes. 'He is well Urdh, as strong as a man half his age and twice as stubborn. But he wearies of this world. I know he will soon take his leave of us. It saddens me, for I cannot bring the joy back into his life, and without joy he is nothing but an empty shell.'

'Take me to him, Nihu. There is much of which I wish to speak with him. What I have to say may cause his situation to turn for the better. You too must join us. As his successor it is right that you also hear my words.'

So Nihu walked with him to Grandfather's hut where the three of them sat talking for many long hours, only breaking to eat and drink when the sun sank low in the sky before resuming their discussions. When at last their visitor stood up to take his leave there was a light in Grandfather's eyes that Nihu had not seen for some years. It brought peace to her heart.

As they parted at the Finger of the Gods, just as they had done on that first occasion, Urdh repeated the same promise he had made then. 'I will come very soon, and when I come I will bring my brothers and sisters with me. This time, it will be so.'

CHAPTER 8

Urdh was as good as his word. Before a week had passed, a commotion at the edge of the village compound drew Grandfather from his hut. Nihu was walking down the long slope from the ridge accompanied by six tall, thin, bronze-robed strangers. As they approached he could see that three appeared to be female, the other three male. The one at the head of the group he recognised with a leap of joy in his heart. Urdh. He had returned, bringing with him five companions as he had so long ago undertaken to do.

The strangers spoke the language of the villagers as if they had been born to it and were extremely agreeable companions. They showed a profound interest in the life of the village and its people, sharing in return stories of their own. To all intents and purposes they were no different, other than in their unusual appearance, to the inhabitants of this place. Grandfather and Nihu knew differently.

During that first, long meeting in Grandfather's hut only a few days earlier, Urdh had spoken to them of his home, a home that was not of the Earth. He had told them how he had travelled to this place from the distant stars, in a vessel shaped like an enclosed shallow dish, constructed of metals unknown in the world on which Nihu and her Grandfather lived. He had spoken of his home star, Aldebaran, with its numerous satellite planets, so different from those in Earth's own solar system. Spoken too of the origins of the human race and of how it had been seeded here by highly evolved ancient races of star people, now ascended beyond any possible contact, eons before the skulls had been created, so that the infant humans would have enough time to develop to the stage where they could assimilate and benefit from the skulls' beneficial influence and energies. And he had told them of the knowledge his people now wished to share, knowledge that would bring great benefit to the villagers in their daily lives, but also by design pique their curiosity a little so that they would be hungry to learn and understand more. Of the red skull, Gor-Kual, of her purpose and origins though, he had shared almost nothing.

This sharing of knowledge was not something that happened on that first meeting between the two races, those of the Earth and those who had travelled there from far beyond her atmosphere. That would come later. This initial encounter was purely an introduction, a getting to know one another. A building of trust. It was a trust that developed almost instantaneously, as so often happens when hearts are fully open and welcoming.

* * * * *

Later that day, as evening approached, Nihu sat with Urdh on the riverbank just below Gor-Kual's shrine. The sun had started its descent towards the horizon beyond the plateau where the Finger of the Gods stood sentinel, a sinister dark gash in the bluest of skies. As the sun dropped lower and lower, its huge crimson disc flared against a backdrop of soft pinks and oranges that merged and flowed through each other, darkening gradually into deep salmon brushed through with the briefest touches of lilac and lavender that soon became the deeper, richer hues of violet and flame. The world stood still, falling silent, as if time itself had ceased to be. A magic wand had sprinkled its enchantment over the land and captured a moment of incomparable beauty and peace, a moment that seemed a forever and yet lasted only the briefest of times before life started up once again.

The gentle lapping of the river against the bank drew Nihu from her reverie and for a reason she could not explain, she turned her head so that she was looking directly at Gor-Kual who was still set on her shrine. It seemed to Nihu that a pale glowing mist was hovering around the skull.

'Tell me about the skull.' Nihu did not know why she had made the request. She had not had any thought of asking until the words had left her mouth, for she was still not reconciled with Gor-Kual's presence. 'Where did she come from Urdh? Why did you bring her to us? You brought her as a gift, told Grandfather and I that she would speak to us, teach us, and yet since her arrival she has been silent and inert. Why has she not done as you said she would?'

Urdh looked at the young woman sitting beside him whose eyes were still fixed firmly on the red skull.

'Because it was not time,' he said simply. 'Because you were not ready for her to become part of your life, part of your purpose for walking this world. The villagers were not ready either. Your Grandfather – yes, he was more than ready, but he was the only one.'

'I *was*. I was ready,' Nihu protested, fire flashing in her eyes as they darted to meet Urdh's gaze. He shook his head.

'No Nihu, you were not. You held fear of her in your heart then and you hold fear of her in your heart still. It is that fear which stands in the way of your connection with her. It is you who is her chosen mouthpiece, her voice. She cannot speak until you accept her completely, free from all fear and resistance.' He paused, an unspoken and unknown sadness touching his face. 'I was away too long, much longer than was intended. It could not be avoided. Now that I have been able to return at last I can help you to move past that fear and take on that role.' He looked at her closely. 'Yes, Nihu. I believe you are at last ready.'

'Ready for what?' Nihu felt a wave of deep apprehension ripple through her body from her scalp to the soles of her feet.

'To speak for Gor-Kual. To utter her words as though they were your own. To be the channel for her teaching and her wisdom.'

'How shall I do that? How is it possible?' Nihu's voice held a potent combination of excitement, curiosity and apprehension.

'Just allow it.' Urdh paused. 'When I first met you Nihu, you were just a child. Your Grandfather had been chosen as Gor-Kual's keeper. We believed it would be he who would bring her words to the world. Now that you are ready to take his place I see we were mistaken. It is you who are her true guardian, and it is you who will speak for her.' He could sense the young woman's reluctance, the residue of her fear from that long ago nightmare. 'Let me show you, Nihu. Let me show you for yourself the essence of Gor-Kual, that she holds only a deep love for you all. Will you let me do that?' Hesitantly, Nihu nodded.

'Then take in your hands and sit with her here beside me.' When Nihu had done as he had asked, he positioned her hands on the skull, the left at the base facing upwards, the right at the crown facing down. 'Now close your eyes. Allow your senses to explore her energy exactly as your Grandfather taught you to do in your training with the world around you. You can do this, easily. It is a part of who you are. Just allow it to happen. Trust in it.'

Nihu sat with the red skull enfolded in her hands and allowed herself to relax, listening to her own breath, her own heartbeat. Gradually her defences, the walls she had built up against Gor-Kual, began to dissolve, were replaced by a tingling warmth that spread through her hands, up her arms, and began to flow throughout her entire body. Her heart was beating loudly, but evenly and steadily, and then the strangest sensation took it over, like her heart was growing bigger and bigger, opening wider and wider, reaching out further even than the limits of her body to embrace the world around her. Tears flowed from her closed eyelids as the most beautiful and powerful feeling overwhelmed her. It was a feeling unlike anything she had ever experienced before: warm, comforting, safe. A feeling of being welcomed back home – and it was emanating from the carved stone skull in her hands.

'It is Gor-kual's love you feel, Nihu.' Urdh's voice was low and gentle by her ear. 'Her love for you, for your people, for the whole of the human race.' How though could this feeling be just love? It was beyond words. Beyond expression. Beyond Nihu's comprehension of how love was.

'It *is* love, Nihu. The true essence of love in all its glory. Feel how powerful it is. How all encompassing. It is the same love that I, and all my star brothers and sisters across all the galaxies of the Universe, hold for you. In knowing this love, can you now let go of your fear? Are you willing to let Gor-Kual into your life?'

A heady, dreamlike combination of ecstasy, deep, soul-touching, unshakeable love, and a lightness of spirit was flowing through Nihu's body. She was being lifted, whirled gently upwards far beyond the confines of the Earth's atmosphere to where the galaxies and stars danced their eternal dance around her. It was a sensation so delicious that in that moment she never wanted it to end. A smile, as wide as the sky and as deep as the sudden joy that filled her, spread across her face. Of course she was willing, if this is what it meant.

She nodded, though she could not be sure whether her muscles had obeyed her command or not. It didn't matter, she had said yes. Immediately, floating into her mind, hovering in front of her, crystallising slowly into a clear image that was as vivid, if not more so, than if she had opened her eyes and gazed on the real thing, was Gor-Kual, the red skull.

Nihu's eyes flew open and met Urdh's coal black gaze. He smiled. 'Don't lose her, Nihu. Close your eyes. Feel her. Feel that connection between you.' At his words, a clear bell-like voice sounded in the young woman's head.

'Nihu, my precious guardian. I, Gor-Kual, skull of Aldebaran, welcome you. I have waited a long time for this moment.'

'H-h-hello.' Nihu didn't quite know how to respond. Never in all her years of spiritual apprenticeship had an object spoken to her so directly and personally. So much... well, so much like another living person talking to her.

A laugh that echoed the sweet lilting qualities of the voice rippled through her senses, not just in her mind, but travelling through her entire body in a wave of tender joyfulness. Gor-Kual was reading her thoughts. 'That is because I am not like those other energies. I know that Urdh has spoken to you a little of this.'

'Talk with her.' Urdh's voice whispered softly. 'Get to know her, and let her learn about you. It is important. Gor-Kual, and your connection to her, will be the most significant part of your life from this moment on. I leave you now. Do not rush to end this time together.' Nihu heard her companion rise and then his footsteps gradually fade as he walked away.

*   *   *   *   *

From that day, Nihu spent as much time with Gor-Kual as Grandfather had done in the early times. The skull showed her much that was not known by those humans who lived on the Earth at that time, knowledge that would remain unspoken for many tens of thousands of years into the future. She was told of humankind's origins far away in a different galaxy, of the plan that had brought those first humans to this planet so many lifetimes before, blind and unseeing, forgetting of those origins. She learned of Aldebaran, home star of the red skull, of those who had brought her to Earth, and of the worlds that orbited that star: strange worlds, magical worlds, fantastical to her eyes and ears.

Gor-Kual told Nihu how there were thirteen skulls in total, all like herself brought to Earth from distant star systems and placed around the Earth; how they had been created and why, each by a different race of highly advanced beings who had been part of the original plan to seed conscious human life on Earth. She spoke of the Master Skull, which had been forged by them as a unity. Nihu was even shown how this had been done, in dark chambers through which energy waves rippled and danced in a symphony of coloured lights as the skulls formed, seemingly from thin air, hovering above a circular bed of water clear crystal points. As Nihu watched these strange and wonderful images flickering through her mind, within her was born a powerful longing to visit these places, to experience for herself these far-off worlds and their wonders.

CHAPTER 9

I met Callum in the bar of his hotel one lunchtime about six weeks after I received that first tantalising email telling me he had uncovered something important. As I sat down across the table from him I was once more firmly caught in his spell. He seemed to look right into the depths of my soul and see my deepest, most hidden secrets. I found myself blushing. Oh for heaven's sake woman, stop acting like a star-struck teenager! Thankfully he appeared not to notice.

'So, what is this exciting discovery you've been waiting to share?' Somehow, and I don't know where from, I found the will to force my voice into some semblance of normality as his slate grey gaze locked on to my own.

Callum's eyes were shining, blazing like a fire behind the window of their lens. His passion for his subject emanated from him as a tangible force. 'I think I know where the blue skull is hidden.' His excitement was barely contained and his voice shook a little. 'I think I've found Gal-Athiel!'

I stared at him, thunderstruck. He had to be kidding, didn't he? Despite everything that had been going on - the clarity of the dreams, the so-real images, the way the ideas for the book had come to me, and a growing acceptance emerging from somewhere deep inside me that maybe there was more to this than purely imagination– I still hadn't been able to wrap my head around these skulls actually existing on this planet.

'W - what? Where?' I stammered out at last.

'That I'm not going to tell you. I want to show you. For you to be there for that part of the journey.' I must have glared my frustration and disappointment because he burst out laughing. 'I really do have to keep that to myself, Gemma, just for now.'

'So why tell me at all?'

'To keep you interested. To help you to begin to believe that all this is really real.' Those mesmerising slate eyes stared boldly into my own. The invitation was back, clear and unmistakeable. 'Because I wanted an excuse to see you again.'

His gaze sent delicious rippling shivers down my spine. What was it about this man that had such a devastating effect on me? I had known him, or at least been in his company, for what – two hours or so in total? Yet he was able to turn me to mush. With some considerable effort I pulled myself together and tried to act coolly.

'Flattery will get you nowhere, Callum.' Who was I kidding? 'I still don't know why it was so important for us to meet if that's all you can tell me.' I tried to ignore my heart dancing around in delight at his last words. Flattery, I repeated to myself firmly. He just wants to keep you on his side.

'No, that wasn't all there is.' I could feel my forehead wrinkling in puzzlement. What else did he have to tell me?

'After we met last I spent quite some time researching. Trying to narrow down possible locations. In many ways the descriptions in your book are quite detailed. Even so, it could have been anywhere within a vast track of land. I spent a lot of time poring over maps and Google Earth and goodness knows what else.

'I researched the tribes in those areas, spoke to a whole load of tribal elders, but none of them had ever heard stories of a carved blue crystal skull. Or if they had, they weren't telling. I thought I'd come to the end of the road. I was so frustrated at running up against all these dead ends that it got to the stage where I was willing to grab hold of any straw. I started sifting through random piles of old documents, journals and what have you. Anything I could lay my hands on. Anything! I knew the information had to be there somewhere and it was driving me crazy not being able to find even a hint of it.' He paused for effect. 'Incredibly, that's when I hit the jackpot!

'I was searching through a pile of old records in a small godforsaken town, well off the beaten track. Out in the back end of southern Colorado somewhere. I don't even know why I'd gone there; it was just a vague hunch. Thank god I followed it because it paid off big time. I came across a tatty old journal that had belonged to a cavalry officer back in the mid-nineteenth century. I nearly chucked it aside to be honest but something stopped me. When I flicked through it, still not really expecting to find anything of interest, one entry caught my attention. In fact, it practically leapt off the page at me. This guy was writing about a mission he and his men had been sent on. Seems it had been kept very hush hush. Reading about it, I'm not surprised. Even with the attitudes that prevailed back then it would have caused a bit of a stir.' He paused.

'Well? What did you find out?' I was eager to hear the rest of the story, even if at the same time I wasn't really expecting anything earth-shattering. Callum reached into his pocket and pulled out a crumpled sheet of A4 that had clearly been read and reread countless times.

'It was pretty unpleasant to say the least. The mission had been a full-scale raid on a native encampment. Apparently a number of tribes had come together in council to plan how they would fight the take-over of their lands. There were several hundred people gathered there, including all their womenfolk and children. The army's brief was to crush that resistance.

'It seems that they did. Completely and mercilessly. The officer who wrote the journal – a Captain James Matthews – was clearly horrified by what took place. There's one paragraph he wrote that still haunts me, word for word. I just can't get it out of my head.' Callum closed his eyes as he remembered the words. '"Even the children were not spared in this godless bloodlust. Babies were torn from their mother's arms and slaughtered like animals. Children, some barely old enough to walk, were cut down where they stood, the ground stained crimson with their innocent blood. And everywhere screaming, terror and death, a nightmare of sound that haunts my ears to this day. May God have mercy on our souls for our actions, for I will never be able to find forgiveness or peace within myself no matter how long I shall live.'" Callum's voice choked with emotion as he recited the account. I felt tears well up in my own eyes as I felt the pain and horror contained within it, and the guilt that had tormented their author.

After a few intense moments Callum continued his story, reading James Matthews' own testimony from the sheet of paper he held. 'When it was over, only a few of the native people remained standing, all of them braves who had fought so ferociously to defend their families. Amongst those few was the Great Chief of all the tribes. He was brought before the army commander where he stood tall and proud, yet despite his stoicism he could not stem the tears that flowed unashamedly down his face. We were surprised, and many of us soldiers were deeply moved, for these people never showed their emotions. This senseless and unnecessary slaughter of an entire community had been too much for even this proud leader to bear however. "Will you now surrender to us?" our commander had demanded of him.

'The Chief looked him directly in the eye with such hatred and scorn, but also with a profound pity, a pity that had shook the hard fighting man to his very core. Then the Chief had answered the colonel's demands. "We will never surrender to those who come to steal our birth-right. Like cowards you have butchered our women and children, our old and our sick. You expect us now to bow down before you?

"'This time was foretold. In years not long past our gracious Voice of the Mother warned that suffering would fall upon us, and that we would be overcome. It is clear that time has now fallen upon us. But she also told that one day, in a future many generations hence, you would return to us seeking our knowledge. When those days come upon us, and if any survive to carry that knowledge forward, then we will sit with your people and speak of what we know.'"

Callum sighed, a deep and sorrowful sigh. He looked across at me. 'The tragedy is that no-one did live to carry it forward. The commanding officer was so incensed at the Chief's refusal to give up all resistance and surrender, and even more so at his words, which he found highly insulting, that he ordered those few survivors to be taken away and hanged. Not one survived to tell their stories or preserve their knowledge...' Callum's voice tailed off as he drifted, caught up in his own thoughts. The account had obviously affected him deeply and I was unwilling to disturb him. After a couple of minutes he looked up at me. 'Now you understand why I wanted to talk to you about this face to face.'

I looked at him blankly. I knew there was something important in what he had just told me, but I was still caught up in the horror of the story he had recounted. Try as I might, it wasn't registering anywhere.

'For crying out loud, Gemma! Weren't you listening to anything I said?' Exasperation and impatience exploded from him.

'I...'

'The Voice of the Mother! The blue skull, Gemma. Gal-Athiel! Just as you wrote in your book. This is a genuine historical document, a written record from a first-hand witness – and it mentions the Voice of the Mother. Don't you see? It means it's real. It exists. Or at least, it did. Whether it still does or not...

'I followed Matthews' trail backwards. In this journal he wrote in detail about where the massacre took place, where the tribes originated. We have been able to pinpoint the most likely location to within a few miles. The terrain there fits your description incredibly closely. If the skull does still exist, that's where it's most likely to be.

I sat transfixed in my chair as the penny at last dropped and the importance of what Callum had just told me sank in. I felt weak, dizzy at the realisation. This was an outside verifiable record talking about something that up until now in all truth, and despite everything I had experienced, my logical brain still refused to see as anything other than pure fiction.

In an instant my perception flipped. Joe was right. Duncan was right. Callum was right. Cathy was right. I was not just making all this up. I had more or less succeeded in convincing myself that my dreams were simply expressions of an over-active imagination, and here they were, giving me information that was being verified. Information I had no way of knowing. I sat there struggling to take it all in.

Callum was watching me, a concerned look on his face. 'Are you alright?'

'Honestly? I'm not sure. My world has just been utterly and completely turned upside down. For the umpteenth time since this all began I'm having to let go of everything I've ever believed to be possible or real.'

He smiled sympathetically. 'I know. I've been there too. Don't worry, you'll get used to it.'

I returned his smile, a little shakily. 'I bloody well hope so. I'm not sure how many of these bombshells I can handle.'

'As many as come your way. They get to be second nature after a while and you miss them if they ease up.' His light-hearted acceptance of everything reassured me a little. 'Don't worry. I'll be here whenever you need me.' His hand reached across the table and took mine in an unmistakeable gesture of invitation. 'Come out to the States, Gemma. Come and see for yourself where we are going with this. I can show you everything I've discovered, and you can share any insights or dreams you have that may help. We can get to know each other a lot better too.'

I gently pulled my hand away; his mesmerising grey eyes stayed locked onto mine. His intensity was exciting, arousing, but it was also a little scary.

'Maybe, Callum. I'll think about it.' For what? A split second? Of course I would go. I knew that in every cell of my body. But I wasn't ready to tell him that. Not quite yet.

CHAPTER 10

By the time I arrived home, all that certainty was dissolving rapidly. In the cold light of day, distanced from Callum's passion and charisma, reason was kicking back in. It had to be coincidence. Or maybe Callum was simply putting two and two together and making five. He was so immersed in his certainty; was he able to keep an objective viewpoint, or was he allowing his obsession for the skulls to cloud his logic and his judgement? God, I was confused. On one hand it all seemed so impossible. On the other, the evidence seemed so clear and compelling.

If Callum *was* right, if he really had discovered the hiding place of one of the skulls I had written about... My brain struggled to grasp the full implications. They were almost too fantastic and improbable to contemplate. Because if the skulls actually did exist, then what about all the other stuff I'd written? Stuff that sat even more firmly in the realms of fantasy and science fiction. Was that true too? By implication, it would have to be. If I surrendered to it, I would have to accept that everything I had ever believed in was a lie. I tried to force my unwilling mind into some form of rational reasoning.

Assuming that the skulls were real – solid, physical objects – and Callum's evidence seemed to be pointing ever more strongly in that direction, then where had they come from? Had a bunch of aliens in a flying saucer really dropped out of the sky and hidden them across the prehistoric landscape of the Earth? And if I bought into that, surely I had to buy into everything else: the whole ET scenario, that they had visited here on countless occasions, walking openly among the human race. If my dreams *were* accurate portrayals of events that had occurred, then even for heaven's sake – and here I was so far out of my comfort zone that it had disappeared from view – mixing their genetic makeup with ours, living and inter-breeding with us to enhance our evolution. It was a crazy idea... Wasn't it?

Were these beings, these star visitors from across the universe, still around? Were they watching our every move? Could they even be walking amongst us, here, now, going undercover as it were? I've never really believed that humankind could possibly be the only intelligent life forms in the infinite vastness of space. Most people have a similar attitude I think. But it is a huge leap from accepting in theory that life probably exists on other planets somewhere out there in the far reaches of space to a reality that visitors from other planets are responsible for our current state of evolution, that they have been visiting us for hundreds of thousands of years, living amongst us, teaching and guiding us. No, that was impossible to swallow. And yet... For the hundredth time I wished Joe was here to share my thoughts with. He would have understood the turmoil inside me in a way I didn't feel Callum would.

Callum was so certain of everything. He believed in its truth with every part of him.

No, Callum wouldn't understand why I felt shaken to my core. How else could I feel though? If all this was real, and the evidence was becoming increasingly undeniable, then everything I had ever understood about life on Earth and where we come from, everything that throughout my whole life I had been taught was the truth, was being swept away. The firm, solid foundations of my very existence were rapidly turning to quicksand. It was not a very comfortable feeling.

*   *   *   *   *

I was soon to learn that Callum wasn't someone who would take no for an answer. Neither would he hang around waiting for me to make up my mind. Less than a week after our meeting I opened my Inbox to find an email from British Airways confirming my flight to Phoenix. What flight to Phoenix? I hadn't booked any flight. Callum, I discovered, had. Only a few minutes later his email pinged in, informing me of exactly that.

I was excited and furious at the same time, and pretty much in equal measure. Excited at the prospect of actually going to America – I hadn't had a proper holiday for several years and, now here I was being given the chance to spend a couple of weeks visiting somewhere I had always wanted to go. Furious because I hadn't had any say in it. Callum had just gone ahead and arranged everything without checking with me first.

He didn't know if it would be convenient, if I could just down tools and take off. Hadn't checked whether I had any inescapable commitments coming up, or even whether I actually wanted to go. He'd just assumed I would fall in with his request, stepped in and done it. Taken over. I felt annoyed and manipulated because, believe me, if there was one thing I'd learned in the two years since my marriage had ended, it was that I hated anyone trying to control either me or my life.

The petulant child in me wanted to cut my nose off to spite my face, to tell him sorry but I was busy and couldn't go. I knew I wouldn't though, because to my intense irritation I couldn't wait to see him again, for his beautiful eyes to look into mine in that way he had that turned my legs to jelly and my brain to mashed potato. I didn't trust him but god, he drew me like a magnet. The anger remained but settled into the background as my excitement, which refused to be quelled, took over. I was going to America. To Arizona. Maybe I would get to see the Grand Canyon? And from there to who knew where. I actually started dancing round the house, singing to myself.

I had a sudden thought, grabbed the ticket and looked again at the flight details. It was booked for the 21st September. In my initial shock it hadn't registered. I grabbed my diary. That was only a fortnight away. When was the return flight? Six weeks? The return flight wouldn't be for six weeks?

There was a lot to do in two weeks: visa, insurance, who knew what else. Where had I put my passport?

Was it even still valid? Much rummaging through boxes later, boxes I hadn't unpacked since I'd moved in a year earlier, I breathed again. I had my passport in my hands and it still had eighteen months to run. On top of all that, my book launch had been scheduled between now and then, the following Saturday to be exact. I was going to be seriously busy. Which was probably a good thing as it gave me little time to get nervous, and even less to head off on wild flights of fantasy about getting up close and personal with Callum in the heat of the desert.

GOR-KUAL: The Red Skull

Part I

THE FINGER OF THE GODS, 3

CHAPTER 11

The day after Nihu's first full encounter with Gor-Kual, Urdh and his five companions said their farewells and returned home. They were as good as their word however, and from that day on were regular visitors to the village, returning four times a year, at every equinox and every solstice. Each time they stayed for seven days, during their visit fulfilling Urdh's long ago declaration that they would teach all who wished to learn of the stars and the workings of the cosmos.

They shared their knowledge of the movements and alignments of the stars and planets, the ones that could be seen by those who gazed up at them from below and the ones that could not. They taught how these patterns affected all life and its consciousness, not just on Earth but throughout the whole galaxy and, ultimately, the entire universe, sometimes expanding it, at others contracting. Always though spiralling upwards into ever higher frequencies of vibration. They guided the people to build on their lands a great star map and a cosmic calendar of colossal proportions that for generations to come would enable them to forecast the position of the important celestial bodies and constellations, their movement, and the coming of eclipses, comets and meteor showers: those events that would influence most strongly life on Earth.

In between these visits Nihu would speak the wisdom and words of Gor-Kual. The connection between young woman and skull was now firmly forged and through this link Nihu was able to understand this information on a fundamental level. She did not know how she understood it or relayed it, for if she thought about it her mind tied itself into inextricable knots of confusion. Nevertheless, when others in the village struggled with the concepts, she always found a way to explain it so that they could grasp it clearly. Other information too was given to be shared, information of a more immediate and practical kind. Through her Gor-Kual guided the village in how to increase the fertility of their land and the yield of their crops, to create mechanical processes that would draw water from the river and sanitary systems to safely dispose of their waste, and taught them how to harness the natural energies around them to heal both themselves and others.

This knowledge was available to all who wished to learn, and many did. The small community benefitted greatly from her gifts. Gor-Kual was no longer ignored as she had once been, but despite Nihu's best efforts and the exhortations of the star visitors, the people of the village refused to have any personal contact with the red skull, happy for Nihu to carry out this task alone.

CHAPTER 12

Each visit brought new faces and new friends. Amongst them all though, one was always there. Malake. He was a poet and storyteller who would enchant endlessly those who came to listen to his songs. His skin was as black as polished jet, much darker than that of the Earth people which was itself the colour of seasoned ebony, and it shimmered in the sunlight, mirroring the bronze hues of the robes he always wore. His eyes, black as his skin, twinkled constantly like stars for his sense of humour was never far away and it reflected like lamplight within those deep wells.

At each visit he and Nihu would talk for hour after hour in an easy companionship that made time flash by in a moment. As the months passed and visit followed visit, Nihu began to feel a gnawing sadness each time the hour approached when he would have to leave once more, and the days that immediately followed his departure seemed empty and dull. She would rally then until, as the day of his next arrival drew near, a tingle of anticipation mixed with a painful anxiety would thrill though her body. Her joy at his impending return was always tempered with the unthinkable question: what if this time, he didn't come? He always did.

One evening, midway through the sixth visit, Nihu and Malake sat on the ridge above the river watching the sun set in its usual cacophony of colour. It had become a daily ritual for them, a winding down of the day's activities. As the sky darkened around them and they lay back to watch the stars emerge from their daytime hideaway, one by one pricking through the deepening blue backdrop, Nihu turned her head to look at Malake.

'Where is your world?'

'There. You see that star just rising above the horizon?' Nihu nodded. 'Follow it up to the next bright star. Do you see the cluster of stars further up and to the right?'

'The star maidens?'

'Yes. If you draw a line from that bright star to the star maidens, you'll see a large orange star about halfway along.'

'I can see it.'

'That is my home sun, Nihu. It is so far away, further than you could possibly understand. And it is beautiful, so beautiful.' His voice grew oddly husky. 'I would love to take you there sometime.'

'Could I? Could I go there with you? Is it possible?'

'I don't know. I wish that it could be so.'

The conversation continued, but something had changed. Between them had suddenly arisen a tension that had never existed before. Nihu did not understand it, did not know where it had come from or why, but she did not find it unpleasant. Though it disturbed her, it was at the same time thrilling and intoxicating. What was it? For once, she did not want to ask Malake.

Nihu shivered suddenly as the night's chill settled around them. She started to rise; Malake gave her his hand and pulled her to her feet. At his touch an electric shock raced up her arms and seemed to burst open her heart. She stumbled, and immediately his arms were around her, holding her, steadying her. What was happening? This was scary, thrilling, unnerving. A moment later, a moment that flashed by all too quickly but in which the world had stopped around her, Malake had set her back on her feet and released her. From the look on his face and the fire burning in the depths of his eyes she could see that he had felt it too.

They returned to the village in silence, neither wishing to broach the subject, neither wishing to break the spell. He left her at the doorway to her hut, in his whispered goodnight an unspoken plea and a tenderness that had never been there before. Something new had begun this evening. Something new and unexpected and wonderful, and just a little frightening. It was something that Nihu was not sure she was ready to follow to its end.

* * * * *

Later that night, as she lay on the soft blanket that was her bed, Nihu could not sleep. She was unsettled by her thoughts, even more so by her feelings, which were new and unfamiliar to her. What was this all about? No matter how much she tried to push his image away, Malake was a constant presence in her mind. When at last she did drift off all her dreams were of being held in his arms. She woke with a start, an unfamiliar sensation like a powerful heated electrical current coursing through her body. Nothing before in her life had prepared her to deal with this, whatever it was. Confused, distressed, she called on Gor-Kual for help.

'Do you not know, dearest one?' The skull's voice was gentle. 'Do you not understand what you are feeling? This is love, Nihu, the most precious gift in the universe. Do not resist. It will bring you joys unlike any other.'

*   *   *   *   *

But Nihu did resist, the turmoil in her heart and soul more than she wanted to handle. She avoided Malake completely, knowing it would only increase in his presence. She had no experience of love; it had never before touched her heart though she had seen it enter the lives of her friends and many others in the village. She did not know how to handle it, did not know whether she really wanted to. She loved her life as it was and wasn't sure she was ready for it to change. In any case, how could it ever be? He came from a different world.

CHAPTER 13

Then one day, suddenly and without warning, he was gone, the others gone too. Nihu woke up one morning to discover that Malake was no longer there, and in that discovery her heart felt like it was tearing in two. If the confusion was hard to bear while he was in the village, this pain at his absence was a hundred times worse. She learned from Gor-Kual that there had been an emergency on his home world. The mother ship and all on board had been recalled immediately to help with the crisis. More than this she did not reveal, and Nihu remained in a sorrowful ignorance. Would Malake ever return, or was he lost to her forever?

To add to her sorrow, Grandfather too soon left her, passing over into his new life in another time and another place. Nihu was grief-stricken. She had lost in the two people she loved most in the world. Her one consolation was that Grandfather's light had returned with the coming of the star people, and he had made his crossing healed and whole of spirit.

*   *   *   *   *

Slowly, over the months that followed, months that turned into a year and more, she fell back into her normal pattern of life. Although Malake was always there in her thoughts, gradually she was able to push him to the background instead of being constantly at the forefront of her mind and she could convince herself that the emotional turmoil she had felt had just been temporary and had now passed by. Until that evening when she had taken Gor-Kual to the river to bathe in its cleansing waters.

Dusk was only just touching the sky and the sultry heat of the day still hung heavily over the world. Kneeling at the water's edge, Nihu became aware that she was being watched. Slowly she rose, leaving Gor-Kual in the lapping shallows. He was standing there, on the bank beside the skull's shrine. Her heart somersaulted as his black gaze met hers, and her legs began to tremble so much she abruptly sat down again. Malake's determined look caught her breath in her throat as he stepped off the bank and came towards her. She did not resist as he pulled her into his arms, allowing no argument, and kissed her.

Holding each other as if they would never let go, they sank as one to the ground, their lips, their tongues seeking, exploring, caressing. Malake's touch was like electricity, sending delicious tingling shocks through Nihu's heated skin. Gently at first, then more and more urgently, they sought each other, hungry to know everything there was to know.

Lost to everything but her love, the world around Nihu vanished. She was swirling once more amongst the stars, as she had done with Gor-Kual on that first day. Only now Malake was with her, joined with her, part of her. As one they whirled across the galaxy in a cosmic dance of ecstasy. Stars, comets, planets spun around them in a giddying merry-go-round of light, faster and faster, in time with their own rhythm. And then she was exploding into stardust, dissolving into a shower of sparkling atoms. Expanding, expanding into the endless universe, at one with it, consuming it, as in turn it consumed her.

* * * * *

Afterwards, as they lay still entwined under the glittering black velvet of the night sky, Nihu held Malake tightly, unable to consider the possibility that he may once again have to leave her and return to his home world, maybe this time forever. She felt his lips brush her forehead. He had picked up her thoughts.

'I will never leave you, Nihu, not unless you wish it. When I had to go away from you, that last time, my heart wept endlessly through fear that I would never see you again. I also knew that if I was granted the chance to return here to you, I would never again leave your side. This I swore, my beloved, always in my heart believing despite the fears that assailed me that I would come back to you. I was certain that you loved me, even though you yourself did not know it at that time, and that this love, joined with the love I held for you, was creating a desire so powerful we could not be held apart. So it was. I am here, and you have opened your arms, your heart and your soul to me. We will always be together, if you so wish it. Nihu, you are my sun and my moon. Will we now become bound for life by this love we share?'

Her soft hand touched his cheek, his lips. 'My love, we already are,' she whispered.

She kissed him again then, and love as powerful and unstoppable as the movement of the cosmos surged through them both, radiating around them in a warm, golden haze. She snuggled closer, nestling her head further into his shoulder. With Malake's cloak wrapped tightly around them to ward off the chill of the night, they slept, waking only when the first light of the dawning sun tickled through their eyelids.

*   *   *   *   *

On the far side of the river a tall figure rose from the shadows of the rocks. The strong athletic body was taut with fury and bitter jealousy etched his stone-set face.

He had suspected as much. Nihu had been spending too much time with that star-rat for it to be any other way. He had thought, when Malake had left the last time, that it was over. He had been wrong. He had delayed too long.

Bile stung in his throat, burning and sour. He had seen it all. He had followed Nihu to this river bank, intending to speak to her, tell her of his intention. When he had seen Malake approach he had hidden, had determined to spy on them. What he hadn't expected was that Nihu would give herself to Malake this night. He spat in disgust as the memory burned through his mind, taunting and tormenting him – their two bodies intertwined, rising and falling together as they writhed in the depths of their passion; Nihu's low moans of pleasure hanging in the still night air; the final release. He had stayed and watched and listened, unable to tear himself away from the scene that was causing him so much pain.

This spectator was N'gana the hunter.

It was obscene. Malake did not belong here. He was not one of them. Was not even of this world. In N'gana's eyes, Nihu was his, not Malake's. Since they had played together as children he had decided that she would be his mate. He had never spoken of it, taking it for granted, and she had never suspected his intentions. If N'gana wanted something, he would let nothing stand in his way. Neither would he be humiliated, especially by a star-rat.

Malake would pay. Maybe not now, not this night – N'gana the hunter knew patience – but one day. He had waited for Nihu all these years; he could wait a while longer. His time would come. When it did, his revenge would be all the more satisfying.

CHAPTER 14

Malake had just said farewell to his friends who were once more leaving, this time without him. He and Nihu were sitting in their favourite spot on the bank above the river next to Gor-Kual's little home. There was something on Nihu's mind, a question that had been troubling her for some while. All at once she urgently needed an answer to it.

'Malake, my love, how can this be? You are from another world, from somewhere far from here. We are so different, you and I. I am human, born of human parents of this Earth. You are not. You come to us from...' Nihu waved her hand above her head towards the deep blue sky above them. He took her hands in his own, feeling them trembling with emotion.

'Not so different,' he told her softly. 'We are more alike than you realise. Yes, it is true that I come from a race of people who possess a far greater consciousness and mental capacity than humans have yet acquired, and that we have physically evolved a little differently in response to the conditions of our home world. But underneath it all we are the fundamentally the same. Our DNA...' He smiled at the incomprehension in Nihu's expression, rephrasing his explanation in words she would understand. 'The essence of our bodies, the building blocks that create them, is almost identical. You and I, Nihu, we both come from the same genesis.

'I am not the first to come to this world from another across the reaches of space and bond with a human. It has happened many times before and it will happen again in times to come. The children of such unions carry the strengths of both parents within them. So will humankind evolve.'

So this visitor from the stars became a part of her life, just as Gor-Kual had done so many years before. The small community quickly accepted Malake as one of their own, won over by his open-heart and kind ways. As he integrated into the human world the visits from the other star travellers grew less and less frequent until, eventually, they no longer came at all. If he ever missed their companionship or was at times homesick for his own distant world, he hid it well.

Yet often when they sat together at the end of the day, watching the endless procession of the stars through the heavens stretching out into eternity, he would speak to Nihu of his home and of his travels through the galaxies. They were stories that fired her imagination and gave birth in her to a hunger to see these wonder-filled places with her own eyes, to travel through the endless freedom of space as he had done. Sometimes, too, she would watch him as he spoke and in an unguarded moment, see in his face a wistfulness, a faraway look of sadness for a world he would never again see. It was a yearning in both of them that would never be fulfilled. So they banished it, for the most part, from their thoughts and threw themselves into their daily lives. If this longing did not go away, it was at least forgotten for long stretches of time.

*   *   *   *   *

All was not well however. Change had been stalking the land; when at last it came, it hit swiftly, brutally and without warning. The natural cycles of the Earth suddenly turned against them. Within two years, summer temperatures had risen by several degrees to levels intolerably hot for human existence. Winters, conversely, became much colder, so that snow fell and for months ice edged the river's flow. Often, the rains did not come. When they did they were so infrequent, irregular and weak that the river, their life source, once so full and abundant that even in the height of the dry season it never failed them, was reduced to a dirty trickle.

Despite the irrigation systems instigated under the guidance of Malake and Gor-Kual the crops died, for there was no water to sustain them. Livestock weakened through thirst and hunger, and the wildlife, once so abundant on the river banks, grew scarce as it migrated in search of life-giving water. Once lush and fertile fields turned into a stony, barren wasteland to rival that of the plateau that towered above them. Drought led to famine and hunger. Famine and hunger led to anger as the villagers sought an outlet for their misery. They did not have to look far to find someone who they could lay their fury on. In such situations it is always the newcomer, the stranger, the one who is different, who is blamed. So it was in this case.

The first voice amongst them was N'gana. In truth, he did not believe that either Malake or the skull were responsible for the misfortune that had befallen the community, but he saw in its suffering means to rid himself of Malake and claim Nihu for himself as he had always desired. Always quick to seize an opportunity, this was not one he would allow to slip through his fingers. If she refused him? Well, she would suffer the same fate as that unnatural mate of hers.

N'gana did not fool himself that the village would turn against her in the same way as they would Malake. They loved her dearly and would never accept any suggestion that she had caused this catastrophe. Should she refuse him, her fate would be a tragic accident, an accident that he would ensure would happen. If he could not have her, no-one would. He would not see her give herself to another again.

N'gana was too shrewd to show himself as the architect of the growing unrest against Malake. He did not need to. A subtle hint here and a quiet word there were all it took, for they fell on fertile ground. He would only step up and take the lead when this hostility had become deeply rooted.

It started as a whisper. Within a few days however, voices were speaking openly. Malake and his accursed tool Gor-Kual were to blame. No matter that life had improved immeasurably since their arrival until the events of the recent months had come to pass. They had bewitched the village, including Nihu, into trusting them, taking them in, listening to them. Nihu herself was spared the vitriol directed at her lover; she was one of them and they considered her as much a victim of this deceit as themselves. All the while, they raged, this had been the off-worlder's plan: to dupe the villagers, betray them, and eventually destroy them. The lack of logic in this was ignored, for that is what fear does when it is allowed to dominate; it annihilates all reason, love and the inner knowing of the truth.

The mutterings, the taunts, the aggressive stares soon followed Malake wherever he walked. It unnerved him, yet he would not let it show, refused to let it limit his actions, for he knew that if he gave in it would only add to the energy of enmity that surrounded him. Showing the slightest sign of weakness or fear would be the fuse that would ignite the inevitable explosion. It was coming anyway, it could not be deflected forever, but he had formulated a plan and needed to buy time for himself, Nihu and Gor-Kual.

Each time Malake left the hut Nihu's anxious eyes followed him, fearing the worst, unsure whether he would ever return to her again or whether she would discover him lying face down on the ground with a spear between his shoulder blades. She had taken Gor-Kual from her shrine by the river to keep with her, protected at all times. The red skull stayed next to them in their hut at night, and each time Nihu went out she would place her in a woven sack which she hung around her neck so that it rested in front of her heart.

CHAPTER 15

Not all in the village had allowed themselves to be caught up in this hysteria. One night, long after dusk had fallen, a low call outside their hut announced the presence of Osana. Nihu knew him well; his father had been a close and trusted friend of Grandfather. Osana was a level-headed man who knew, and remained true to, his own heart and mind.

Malake drew the grass door aside, peering to see him standing in the shadows, almost invisible against the black backdrop of night.

'Malake, I must speak with you. It is urgent. Your lives may depend on it.' Osana's hushed voice barely carried to Malake's ears. Malake ushered him quickly into the safety of the hut where, in the thick darkness, he could only just distinguish the slender silhouette of Nihu curled up at the rear.

'My friend, you are in much danger. N'gana is plotting against you and intends to act within the next day. His influence is strong. He has fed the people's fears with his words and has persuaded them that the only solution to this catastrophe we are living is to make a sacrifice of you and to destroy Gor-Kual.'

'N'gana?' Despite the premonitions that had assailed Nihu over the past weeks she had chosen to deny the truth of her knowing, unwilling to accept that her childhood friend would be capable of such actions. She felt, rather than saw, Osana turn to her.

'I do not believe you are unaware of his actions, Nihu. You are our Woman of Medicine. We know your abilities. You have perhaps chosen not to see. I come to you now to say that it is time for you to open your eyes and face what is happening. N'gana wishes you for himself and will do whatever is necessary to bring that about. If you wish to save the life of the man you love, and prevent the destruction of Gor-Kual, you can no longer hide yourself in blindness.'

'And you?' Malake's voice was soft. 'You come to warn us. Are you not afraid of the consequences if you are discovered?'

'There are a few of us, not many, maybe ten or so, who have never been deceived by N'gana's treachery. We remember all that Gor-Kual, and later you Malake, have given us. We do not and never have doubted your love, your goodness and your desire only to help us. I believe that in their hearts the others know this too. Sadly their fear has made them vulnerable to the dark words of those who have their own agenda. We have kept silent up until now so that we would not bring suspicion upon ourselves. In all conscience we can do so no longer. Malake, Nihu, please. Take the red skull and go away from here tonight.'

'Go?' Nihu was devastated. Never in her worst nightmares had she allowed herself to consider that it would come to this. 'We have nowhere to go. I have no other home than this.' She straightened her back, defiance in her voice. 'I am your Woman of Medicine, I have a responsibility here. You ask me to leave? I cannot. I will not.'

'You must do what you feel is right, Nihu. You are held in much love, you will not be held responsible should you choose to stay. But Malake must go if he is not to end his life here tomorrow. And Gor-Kual must go with him.'

'I will not leave without Nihu.' Malake's firmness stalled all argument. 'If she must stay, then I stay too and take my chances.'

'No!' The anguish in Nihu's voice pierced the night's silence. 'I will not let you die because of me. You must go, leave me. It tears my heart from my body to say this to you, for you are my life. Malake, my beloved, I could just about continue to live without you, knowing you are safe. I will not, I cannot, watch you die.'

'Nihu,' Osana said gently, 'there is something else you must know. It may make your decision easier. If you stay, N'gana will claim you for himself. Should you resist, as I know you will, he will not hesitate to kill you at the first chance he gets. His pride is such that he will severely punish such a rejection. Even if do not leave, your people may soon have to learn to live without you. Surely it is better to run and take your chances with the man you love, than to stay and die alone?'

'Run? Where?' Nihu's whole body slumped in an attitude of hopelessness. 'If they feel so strongly, and if N'gana is so determined, surely he will hunt us down wherever we are?' Another thought crossed her mind. 'And you? What about you? When in the morning they discover we have gone, they will know that someone warned us. It will not take much for them to discover your part in this. You too will pay the price.'

'We have made our own plans. We too leave at first light. We have a few supplies to take with us, not much, but all that we could gather. If you are to leave, I will return shortly with some for you.' Osana smiled in the darkness, a wry smile that could be heard in his words. 'We too have little choice. We either stay, and die a slow, lingering death from hunger. Or we leave, take our chances on finding a new place to live, somewhere that can offer us what we need to survive. In choosing that, at least if we die it will be knowing that we had tried.'

Gor-Kual stirred in Nihu's hands. The red skull, who had remained silent and slumbering for so many weeks, was waking. Nihu listened to the skull's words, allowing them to fill her mind, speaking them out loud for the others to hear.

'You are a brave man, Osana, both in coming here tonight to warn my dear guardians and in your refusal to succumb to your fate. Know this, my friend, there is a place that awaits you, a place that has been waiting for some time, although not until tonight, when you made your final choice, were you ready to hear these words.

'I am grateful that you have resisted the influence of he who seeks to instil fear, and by such means control the hearts and minds of those who allow themselves to listen to his words. Grateful that you listen only to the truth of your own heart. Go now, taking with you those who are also willing to follow their own truth, knowing all will be well.

'The changes that have come upon you are not, as some would tell, the work of angry gods and spirits who need to be appeased, or due to the malevolence of Malake or myself. But this you know already. They are instead the consequences of natural changes in the world. Sometimes these changes are slow and gentle. At other times, such as now, they fall upon it sudden and fierce. Whichever the case, they are always part of the natural order of things.

'Close your eyes now, dearest Osana. Allow your mind to clear. I will show you the road you must take to reach your new home. Hold fast to the truth of its existence, even when the way grows difficult, for it is my promise to you that you, and all who accompany you, will reach this place safely.'

Osana did as Gor-Kual asked. Immediately his mind filled with images of landmarks and trails, a detailed route map of the journey he was about to embark upon. When the images faded, he opened his eyes.

'How will I remember it all?' Anxiety had gripped him. 'There is so much.'

'You will remember. Before you leave, however, there is one more thing I ask of you. Take me with you now. Return me tonight to the place where I was found, beneath the Finger of the Gods. Bury me there so deeply and well that no-one will find me. I do not leave with Malake and Nihu. My future is not theirs. I must remain here, concealed in this place, until it is time for me to once more take my place openly in the life of humankind.'

'I...' But the red skull had fallen silent once more.

Nihu did not want to let the skull from her hands, but Gor-Kual had spoken and her wishes had to be obeyed. Reluctantly, hesitantly, the young woman reached behind for a small blanket, wrapped the skull in it and handed her to Osana. He looked at the heavy object in his hands with a mixture of awe and apprehension, knowing that in taking her he had also accepted the task she had charged him with. He was not certain he was ready to meet such a responsibility.

'What about you, Nihu? Will you go or will you stay?' He was delaying the moment when he walked out into the night carrying the skull. If he was discovered with her in his possession...

Nihu's voice was small in the darkness of the night. 'I cannot remain here if it means Malake stays with me. I will not be the cause of his death. If what you say is true, and in spite of my hopes I know it to be so, it would all be for nothing anyway. I will leave tonight with Malake, though I don't know where we will go.'

'I do.' She looked across at Malake's silhouette in astonishment. Though she could not see his face, she heard the smile in his voice. 'I have known for some time that this day was likely to come, so I made the necessary preparations. Do not worry about bringing us supplies Osana. We are grateful for your consideration but we shall not need them. Besides, you have other things to occupy you this night.'

He glanced up at where Osana was outlined against the doorway of the hut. Osana picked up on his meaning. Malake would not reveal any more in front of him. The less people who knew the details, the safer it would be all of them. No-one could reveal, either voluntarily or under duress, what he did not know.

'Farewell, my friends. I wish you all luck.'

'You too, Osana. We owe you much. We will never be able to repay your courage and friendship. Trust in what Gor-Kual has shown you. She will not fail you. Long life, my friend.'

Osana stood, gathered up the red skull, still wrapped in the blanket, and walked out through the doorway, knowing that they would never meet again.

*　　*　　*　　*　　*

When he was sure Osana was out of earshot, Malake reached across and put his arm around Nihu's shoulders, pulling her close to him. She was icy cold despite the heat of the night, and trembling. He could feel the unspoken questions she could not utter.

'My love,' he whispered, 'I have spoken much of my home during our time together. Will you come there with me now?'

Nihu's breath caught in her throat, her heart pounding as the darkness began to swirl around her. Malake's home? That meant... His home was on another world, far up amongst the stars of the night sky. It was a world that she had longed to see from the first time he had spoken of it, though she had never imagined she would ever set foot there for herself. Wordlessly she squeezed his hand in agreement, her excitement buzzing through the interior of the simple hut.

'But... how?' she was able to ask at last. 'Your people no longer visit here.'

'I sent them a call for help and asked them to come for us,' he explained simply, elaborating no further. 'They have been ready for many days, awaiting my signal to act. Now that the moment has arrived they are already on their way. They will come for us at first light tomorrow. We must be on the plateau at that time.'

CHAPTER 16

Osana left the hut still reeling from the events that had just unfolded. Vivid images of mountain passes, arid plains and standing stones chased one another other through his head, details of the route he and his fellow refuges would embark upon in the morning. In his hands was Gor-Kual – at this moment only he stood between her and the plot by N'gana and his followers to destroy her. That could not be allowed to happen. Osana could sense the power and importance of the object that had been entrusted to him, recognised that she must be kept safe regardless of anything else that may happen, even if he did not understand her true role and significance.

He stopped and listened. Not a sound broke the silence of the night. The wild birds and animals had long left this sad place in search of food and water, and the livestock were tethered a good distance away at the only spot where any grazing, poor though it was, could be found. Not a breath, not a heartbeat. He was alone in the darkness.

Osana looked up at the sky. The moon was not yet at its zenith. For now he had the night on his side, but he could not delay. It would take time and effort to bury the skull in the hard, stony ground of the plateau. Resolutely, he hoisted the skull to his shoulder, picked up a carefully worked large bone from the pile of tools at the edge of the village compound – it would serve as a useful pick – and set off on the long climb.

A long while later he at last found himself standing next to the Finger of the Gods whose tall, spindly form stood sinister against the night sky. With difficulty Osana shook the chill fingers of superstition from his bones. Worming his way as far as he could into the narrowing cleft where the black stone left the earth to thrust high into the heavens, he set to work. Laboriously, for there was little room to wield the bone pick effectively, little by little he chipped away at the rough, compacted ground. It was a hard, difficult task. His hands grew bloodied, his fingers raw as he used them to dig out the sharp, unforgiving spoil. Eventually however, he had succeeded in creating a rough hole a little over three times the depth of the skull.

Carefully he lowered Gor-Kual into her hiding place then refilled the pit, covering her completely, taking care to hide all trace that anyone had been there or had disturbed the ground. When it was done, he straightened up stiffly and tilted his head back to ease his aching neck. A shock went through his body as he viewed the night sky; the moon was already past its height and well on its way to the other horizon. The task had taken much, much longer than he had thought. He would have to return at a run. He had still to find somewhere in the meagre river trickle to wash away the dust and evidence of his night's labours, return the pick to its rightful place, get back to his own hut without being seen, gather his belongings to leave his hut again and be at the meeting point ready to depart with his fellow travellers at the appointed hour. Would he make it in time? He had to. It was the only way to avoid raising suspicions that anything untoward had taken place.

As Osana raced down the slope from the plateau he spotted, far off to his right and above him, two figures silhouetted briefly against the skyline in the moonlight. Malake and Nihu. They too seemed to be heading for the plateau summit. He could not understand why they were only now climbing the slopes. He had no time or energy to consider the question further, simply whispering a quick prayer for their safety as he ran.

To his relief, he reached his hut before the sky began to lighten and the village stirred. He gave himself a few minutes to bring his breathing and heart rate under control before he dusted himself down, picked up his meagre travelling possessions and, for all the world a man focussed solely on the challenge ahead of him, walked out into the day.

*   *   *   *   *

He had to buy them some time. The sun was only just tiptoeing above the distant hills; they would not be far enough away yet. If N'gana and his supporters discovered their absence now they would surely be caught. He thrust his raw hands beneath his clothing and turned to the crowd, addressing them in a clear, warm voice.

'My friends, today we leave this village that has been the only home we have ever known in search of another. A new home that will support and feed us as this one no longer can. There is nothing left for us here. The river is dry and the land barren. I ask you now, join us. Come with us this day.' A low murmur ran through the crowd. A few of those present were clearly angered at his words; others though appeared to be considering them.

'No!' N'gana drew himself tall. 'We have no need to leave. We will rid ourselves of he who has caused our torment, and all will return to how it was before.'

'Can you be certain of that?' Osana's words were soft, nonetheless they held a challenge. 'Can you be certain that you are right?'

N'gana squared his shoulders and stepped closer to Osana so that the older man could smell the hatred on his breath.

'I am right,' he spat. 'You are weak, Osana. A coward. You have no stomach for what must be done, so you run away with a bunch of other cowards rather than face it.'

The group waiting behind Osana stirred in anger at these insults. He signalled them to remain calm. 'As you so believe, N'gana. Your opinion means little to us. We leave today. We will not stay and die here like penned cattle. You will not stop us.'

'You will die if you leave. There is nowhere to go.'

'Maybe,' Osana's voice remained level, 'maybe not. The only certainty is that if we stay, we *will* die. This is

101

the choice we have made.' He looked out once more over the crowd of gathered villagers. 'If any of you wish to join us, my friends, you are welcome. We will wait while you gather your belongings.'

'You will stay!' N'gana had turned to the crowd in a fury. 'He speaks falsely. Do not listen to him. Malake is at the root of our misery. No longer. This morning we put an end to it. Follow me.' He turned and marched deliberately and arrogantly towards the hut where Malake and Nihu had spent their life together. Many from the crowd followed him, some with a swagger, shouting and jeering, others in silence with an air of reluctance. A sizeable number, however, did not. They had no stomach for bloodshed and were not convinced by N'gana's words of condemnation. A few of that number would later leave with Osana, the rest would remain behind. None were willing to take part in the events that they believed were about to unfold. Osana's eyes followed N'gana. He had not succeeded in buying the fugitives more than a couple of minutes. It was out of his hands now.

CHAPTER 17

'Malake! Malake! Malake!' The small crowd, with N'gana at their head, surrounded the hut, their chant sinister and ominous in the early light of day. N'gana raised his hand for silence.

'Malake!' His voice dripped contempt. 'Come out. It is time for you to pay for your treachery. You have brought evil upon us and you must be punished for your crimes.'

Silence answered him. He tried again, eager to impress those present with his authority. 'This is your last chance, Malake. Come out now of your own free will and face us like a man.' He turned to the crowd with a sneer. 'Man, ha! Demon more like. Come out, Malake, or we will come in and drag you from your lair like the rat you are.' Still silence hung heavy over the gathering. With a roar N'gana plunged through the entrance, only to pull up dead with a howl of rage as he saw the hut was empty.

'Find them!' he screamed. 'Bring them to me. He will not deny me again.'

'There.' A woman beside him pointed up at the plateau. Against the rapidly lightening sky the silhouette of two tiny figures could be seen making their way across the rim.

'Get them!' Ignoring everyone, N'gana set off at breakneck speed, soon leaving the crowd behind.

A little way away, Osana was on the point of leaving when he heard the shout. He stared up in dismay. What were Malake and Nihu doing? They were in full view, making no attempt to conceal themselves. It was suicide. Something must have gone wrong; they should have crossed the plateau and be in the valley beyond heading for the distant range of hills by now. Well, he could do nothing more to help them. Hoisting his meagre pack over his shoulder, he gave the signal to move out.

*   *   *   *   *

High upon the plateau above the village Malake drew Nihu into his arms. She was trembling. While she had dreamed for a long time of visiting his world, now that its reality was upon her she was overwhelmed with apprehension.

'Are you sure that they will accept me?' she whispered. 'I am so different to you.'

'As I am to you, my love. Yet your people accepted me.'

'To now reject you, turn against you. Hunt you. Kill you if they get the chance. What if the same thing happens to me?'

'It won't, Nihu. That I swear to you. It's not easy to explain, but my people have moved beyond the need to blame others for the things that they experience. They accept full responsibility for the events of their own lives.'

She nestled into his shoulder, reassured by his calm confidence. 'What happens now?'

'We wait. They are on their way. They will be here very soon.'

Nihu and Malake had stopped at the edge of the plateau. Its vast, empty expanse stretched out ahead of them. Far to their right, the Finger of the Gods stood its timeless sentinel, its black spear thrusting into the sky like a gigantic signpost to the stars.

'Malake!' The harsh voice echoed intrusively in the still morning air. Nihu whirled around, her heart pounding. N'gana! He was still some way away but was closing rapidly. She clutched at Malake's hand, fear gripping her. To her astonishment he was unconcerned.

'He is too late. Don't worry, Nihu. All is well.'

All is well? How could all be well? She looked around desperately, searching for an escape. There was no way out. If they ran he would soon catch them. They were stranded on the edge of an almost sheer drop with no-one to come to their aid. She was under no illusion that they would be able to withstand N'gana's superior strength. He would be upon them in just a few short minutes. Was it really all over?

Malake remained calm and unconcerned. What did he know that she didn't? He cradled her frightened and despairing face gently in his hands. 'Don't be afraid, Nihu. They are here. We are safe.' They were here? Where?

At that moment the air around them began to darken. In the sky high above, a glistening silver disc was descending towards the earth. At first just overlapping the golden orb of the sun, it grew rapidly in size, shielding more and more of its light, until the early morning turned to dusk and then darker still. No sound emanated from this object, at the edge of which rainbow flares of light danced and flickered. It hovered over the plateau, filling the sky, its shadow casting the land into darkness for many miles around.

N'gana was on his knees on the rough ground, cowering in terror at this strange, terrifying apparition that had come upon them. Nihu herself could hardly stand on shaking legs that threatened to collapse beneath her. If Malake's arms had not been holding her, she would by now also be a quivering, crumpled heap on the ground.

'They are here,' Malake breathed into her ear. 'It is time to leave.' Nihu stared up at the craft in awe, her fear dissolving as she realised that this was her future. 'Are you ready?' She nodded wordlessly.

'Then come.' Malake released her and took her hand. Looking across at her he smiled. 'Welcome to my world.'

A strange tingling filled Nihu's body. It started at her toes and travelled up to the top of her head. She felt light, a little fuzzy, like her body was no longer as solid as it usually was. She glanced down. Her feet were shimmering, hazy; it seemed that she could see through them. She looked across at Malake; he too appeared ethereal, transparent. Suddenly she was caught up in a dizzying whirl of energy that rushed through her body like a tornado, and was seized by a feeling of irrepressible exhilaration and comprehension. This was what she had been waiting for all her life.

CHAPTER 18

My lungs were on fire. I couldn't breathe. Every intake of breath was a struggle to suck in enough air. Fighting. Fighting to hold on, to draw in the oxygen my body needed to feed my heart, my lungs, my brain. To keep me conscious. A dark mist was trying to force its way down over my eyes, swirling waves of red and black, the embers of my dying fire. I couldn't battle much longer, couldn't hold on. But I had to. Had to. Because if I didn't it would engulf me and I would be lost.

Focus. Focus on what is around you. With an immense effort of will I forced open my leaden eyelids. Through the blurred lens of impending oblivion I could see a dark tunnel, its walls smooth and flowing, lit by the weak blue-white light of a fading flashlight which was flickering in its own death throes. Willing my head to turn. On either side, beyond the reach of the pale beam, there was only blackness. The impenetrable solid blackness that is only found in those deep buried places that exist far from the reach of daylight.

My mind would not respond. It refused to follow any focussed train of thought, running wilfully away on its own playlist. I was tired. So tired. Too tired to fight any more. I let my eyelids fall and surrendered to the burning agony in my chest. The red-black mist returned, but before it claimed me completely I saw the image of a young woman, blonde and pretty, standing in a neatly tended garden. She was holding two small children by the hand, and tears stained her face. At the exact moment I was swept away by that dark tide, for an instant her eyes met mine, locked onto them, in an anguished goodbye.

*   *   *   *   *

I lay in the darkness, unable to move. I was soaked in a chill sweat and shook uncontrollably from head to toe, my heart hammering a crazy drum solo against my ribs. What the hell had all that been about? I'd had a nightmare that was evident, but why? What had caused it? Even now, lying in my safe soft bed in my safe cosy bedroom, it was alive out there in the darkness that surrounded me. Real, as if I could reach out my hand and touch it. I was scared and I was definitely not happy.

Needless to say I didn't get to sleep again for the rest of the night. Every time I closed my eyes I was back in the tunnel. So I lay in the gentle reassurance of the moonlight that filtered through my window, counting the minutes and hours tick past until the birds woke to greet the new day and the sky outside began to lighten. As soon as it was decent to do so I rang Cathy. As always, she was my first port of call when anything strange, spooky or unsettling happened.

*   *   *   *   *

'Could have been a premonition.' Cathy pushed the plate of chocolate biscuits across the coffee table to me.

111

As soon as she heard my strained voice on the end of the phone she had jumped in the car and come over. We were now consuming copious cups of coffee while she considered what I had gone through.

'Premonition?' OK, now I was getting really spooked. Was this a warning as to what would happen to me if I headed off on Callum's skull hunt? Had I foreseen my own death? The thought scared the daylights out of me before I succeeded in reining myself in.

'Mmmm.' Cathy was still munching thoughtfully on her biscuit, her mind on the question, oblivious to where my thoughts were taking me. Until she caught sight of what must have been a very clear expression of impending panic on my face. 'No not for you, Gemma. It really won't be. If that was really the case, where do the woman and children come in? No, not you. For someone though…' She lapsed into silence again, thinking.

Meanwhile, my brain was tying itself in knots, firing off in all sorts of unwelcome directions and not making sense of any of them. This was not the first night that graphic dreams had disturbed my sleep – the images I was receiving almost nightly from the skulls were increasingly vivid and intense – but this was the first time it had been so real. Another incongruity also made it clear to me that the images and feelings of the previous night had come from somewhere else. The skull dreams were always set in the past, memories of ancient times now reawakened; in them I was always an observer, watching events unfold as if on a cinema screen. By contrast this time I had been part of it, had lived it with every aspect of me. I had been there, endured the pain and the fear – I was in no doubt of that. It had been me... yet at the same time it hadn't been. I couldn't make sense of it. It had had a different feel somehow, though I was at a loss to explain what it was. I just knew. Then there was that lamp... It had been a modern flashlight. I was in no doubt about that either. I could see it as clearly as if it was now lying in front of me on my coffee table, even though at the time it had just been a hazy image at the edges of my consciousness.

'I don't know, Gemma,' Cathy said at last. 'I really do feel that you had a predictive dream, though for who and when is anyone's guess.' She reached across for my hand and gave it a squeeze. 'It isn't you. That I do know. I feel it really strongly, so don't worry about it. Maybe it'll become clear at some point, maybe it won't, but as we don't know who it is, right now there isn't anything we can do.'

I knew she was right, though how I would let it go I hadn't a clue.

GOR-KUAL: The Red Skull

Part II

LEAVING ATLANTIS, 1

CHAPTER 19

Jar-Kan hesitated. He was being followed, he could sense it. By who though? Shadow Chasers? Had they grown suspicious of him? There was no reason why they should have. He had not acted in any way out of the usual. Though, by Sirius, if they had heard even the slightest whisper of what had been planned, of the actions that were being executed this very night, he would have been arrested by now whether it was legal or not. He had been careful to continue his life as normal, not changing one step of his daily routine, not acting in any way to draw attention to himself despite the fact that within the next hour his life would change forever. He took a deep, slow breath. This was not the path he had expected his life to take. How could he have expected this? What was about to happen was beyond conceivable.

Jar-Kan was a Priest of the Light, a keeper of the skulls in the Pyramid Temple of Yo'tlàn, principal city and spiritual centre of the continent of Atlantis. He had spent the last forty of his fifty two years in the peace of the temple compound and had expected to live out his many remaining years in the same way. Fate, it seemed, had decreed otherwise. While as a priest a belief in fate was not encouraged, at this point he was finding it hard to see it any other way. He was about to commit an unprecedented sacrilege, the ultimate crime, and do it with the full blessing of the temple elders and the crystals skulls that they cared for. By morning he would be a fugitive, alone and unsupported. Hunted down relentlessly by those who sought to possess the skulls for their own ends, when the act was discovered. He knew it had to be so. On his initiation into the priesthood all those years ago he had sworn to guard and protect the skulls with his life if necessary. Back then it had all been so theoretical and unreal somehow. The safety of the skulls had never been threatened; few believed it ever would be. The situation however had changed greatly over the past years. This was an oath Jar-Kan was now being called to fulfil.

He glanced around. He could see no-one, yet still the feeling of being spied upon persisted. He was wary of using his talents to seek out the identity of his watcher, knowing it would betray his identity. At that moment the last thing Jar-Kan wanted was to reveal himself as a temple priest.

There, in the shadow of a doorway. The briefest of movements caught at the corner of his eye. He would have to take a chance. Time was against him, and he could not continue on his way if he was being followed. Cautiously he opened his mind and reached out to touch the energy of his watcher. He pulled back instantly in surprise. A child? What was a child doing out alone at this hour of the night? The peaceful safe days when all could wander the streets of Atlantis without risk at any hour were far behind them. He was puzzled. Why would a child be watching him? No sooner had the thoughts touched his mind than the child stepped forward into the moonlight. His intense deep green eyes seemed to reach right into Jar-Kan's soul.

'Who are you?' Jar-Kan asked gently, not wishing to frighten the boy who could not have been more than seven years old. 'Why are you following me?'

'The sky people asked me to find you. They want me to warn you.' The boy's voice suddenly changed, resonating with a depth that came from far beyond his young years. It was no longer the child speaking, he was simply the channel for those who wanted to pass on their message. 'In the days to come you will meet one who is not as he seems.'

'Who is he? How will I know him?'

'He will come from the darkness. He will come to you offering help and friendship. Know that he seeks only to deceive. Do not be influenced by his words. Look deeper. Listen to your own heart. Feel your own truth. Keep silent. Here, more than at any other time, it will be imperative that you keep hidden your true identity and destination. He will know you are not what you claim to be, but that is all he will know. He will attempt to trick you into revealing yourself through his friendly words and cunning. He will try to kill you. Be on your guard.'

The words sounded strange coming from the infant's lips, even in the awareness that they originated elsewhere. In recognising their source however, Jar-Kan's concern for the child's wellbeing had evaporated.

Those who had brought the child to him, the star travellers who had frequently shared temple life with the priests in years not long passed, would also return him safely home.

Without another word the boy turned and walked away, leaving Jar-Kan's mind reeling. As yet he had not even begun his task and already he had been forewarned of danger. He straightened up, putting the words to the back of his mind. Now was not the time to concern himself with such things. They would come later. In this moment he had other things to do. It was time. He continued on his way, his mind slipping back to the events of earlier that day.

*   *   *   *   *

'It is time Jar-Kan, we can delay no longer. Each day the threat grows stronger. The Dark Ones grow impatient. They may make their move at any moment, and the skulls must be far gone from here when they do. That is why it must happen tonight.'

'You know that I have no hesitation in accepting my role in this Omar, still I cannot understand why Gor-Kual has chosen me to be her guardian. My connection with her is no more than that of any other of the skull guardians here. Why did she not choose the one who has been closest to her for many years?'

The two men were walking in the gardens of the pyramid temple. Its tranquil sunlit courtyards and cool pools through which fountains danced like streams of liquid diamond provided an incongruous backdrop to the heavily laden conversation. Jar-Kan's companion, Omar, was the most senior priest. He was also one of the four architects of the plan that would see the thirteen skulls dispatched to the farthest reaches of the Earth, far from the grasp of those who wished to seize them to further their own power and domination over the land.

'Ours is not to question, Jar-Kan,' the older man admonished gently. 'The skulls have each chosen their own. You know well that their wisdom is far greater than yours or mine, that their sight is not bound by the limitations of time and space as ours is. That they see all: what is, what has been, and what will be. We must trust in that, trust that their choice is correct and that there is a sound reason for each who will travel with the skulls this night. Kulu is old, no longer strong. You have seen his rapidly advancing infirmity for yourself, have tended it with your skills. His heart is still valiant but his body abandons him. Even with Gor-Kual to help and sustain him, he would not be able to withstand the rigours that lie ahead.'

The two men fell silent as they contemplated the consequences of the actions that were to be unleashed within only a few hours. They sat side by side, lost in thought, the silence broken only by the gentle splashing of the fountains and the birds chattering softly in the cool of the foliage. Eventually, Omar rose.

'I must go, my friend. There is much still to be done.'

'Are we ready, Omar?'

'We have no choice,' he replied, a cloud shadowing his eyes. 'Time has run out. The Dark Ones are ready to move and we must act before they do.' He turned to Jar-Kan, his closest friend, and embraced him warmly, a wave of deep sadness engulfing him. Omar knew well that if the plan succeeded, as it must, they would never meet again. 'Goodbye my friend. Travel safely, and may Gor-Kual keep you from harm.'

Jar-Kan's own eyes were wet as he returned the embrace. 'Goodbye, Omar. I will always treasure our friendship. Stay safe, my friend.' As he stepped back, a sudden wave of heartache swept through him, a piercing realisation that this man would soon be sacrificing his life to protect the skulls and those who carried them to safety. Omar read his thoughts and forestalled any words.

'We each do what we must do. Do not think further on this, for it will not serve you. Know only that what I do, I do for the skulls, for Atlantis, and for the future of this world. As do you.' With those final words he turned on his heels and walked away, indicating clearly that there was no more to be said.

With a heavy heart Jar-Kan left the courtyard. He was already mourning the impending sacrifice of his dearest friend, the loss of his tranquil life in the temple and of all that Atlantis had once been. The loss of everything he had ever known. At the same time there was one more thing he had to do, something he was dreading and yet which he could not, would not, avoid. A farewell visit to his parents, both now well into their seventh decade. He could not tell them he was leaving, never to return – he could tell no-one that – but neither could he walk away from Yo'tlàn without visiting them one final time and telling them he loved them. It would be difficult, he would have to keep his habitual upbeat attitude in place concealing his sorrow – they must not suspect anything was not as it always had been - but he would manage. The grief would wait.

The sun had set when he finally and reluctantly left his parents' home, lingering longer than normal with his farewells, holding them more tightly as he hugged them both. They did not seem to notice.

CHAPTER 20

The boy's words had unsettled Jar-Kan. Nevertheless, as he approached the temple complex for what would be the final time in his life, all thoughts other than what lay ahead of him that night vanished. The enormity of what he was taking on banished every other consideration from his mind. It was madness, taking the skulls from the temple, but it had to be done. They could not be allowed to fall into the hands of the Shadow Chasers, a threat that was growing day by day. Tonight, twelve priests and priestesses would enter the skull chamber, one at a time, none knowing the identity of the others, all charged with the future safekeeping of one of the sacred skulls. Each would take the skull that had chosen him or her from its resting place on its crystal plinth, replacing it with an inert duplicate, and disappear with it forever. He headed straight to his room, wishing only to lie low and gather his thoughts until the time came when he would step into the life of a fugitive.

Jar-Kan was a physician, a healer and herbalist. He often worked deep into the night testing new plant combinations or new energy techniques. No one who passed by his door would consider it unusual for his light to be still burning at such a late hour. He was a great bear of a man, standing well over six feet tall, well-built and broad-shouldered. Even now, in his mid-fifties, he was fitter than most of his companions in the temple, and carried himself with a youthful bearing that belied his years. Only the silver streaks that highlighted the temples of his full head of deep brown hair, still mostly the colour of ripe chestnuts in the autumn, and the sprinkling of grey in his neatly trimmed beard, gave it away. Vivid blue eyes, creased at the corners from years of squinting against the sunlight as he trekked his beloved countryside in search of plants for his healing lotions and potions, constantly held the good-natured twinkle of his infectious sense of humour. Laughter was never far from his lips, or a grin from his face.

Tonight however, as he waited impatiently in his study for the appointed hour, that laughter was absent, the light in his eyes muted. His mind was full with more serious considerations. He would be one of the last to leave and tension lay heavily upon him. He lay back on the soft, thickly padded couch that ran along one wall and closed his eyes, but sleep did not come. At last, after what seemed an entire interminably long night but was in fact only a couple of hours, it was time. He pulled on his cloak and grabbed the small bag that lay ready on the table. With a quick glance along the corridor to make sure no-one was around, and a final longer sorrow-filled glance at the precious books and journals that contained his life's work, Jar-Kan pulled the door closed behind him and walked forward into his new life.

*   *   *   *   *

Entering the skull chamber, Jar-Kan immediately sensed a change in its energy. Usually the atmosphere was tingling and electric even when the skulls were not active. Tonight however it felt flat and cold. Lifeless. Only three of the genuine skulls remained: Gor-Kual his own charge, the obsidian skull Gileada, and in the centre of the space, resting on a magnificent bed of clear crystal points, the Master. This was a skull of incomparable craftsmanship, created from the purest, deep purple amethyst, flawless and sparkling with clarity.

The remaining skulls were replicas, created purely to fool anyone giving a cursory glance. Some were of coloured glass, others carved from stone or crystal. Accurate replicas that they were, none carried the energy or consciousness of the original thirteen. As the true skulls had left, one by one, so their energy had left with them. How long could this remain unnoticed, Jar-Kan wondered. Not as long as the fugitive priests needed, that was certain.

He looked around, a wave of nostalgia and sadness flooding through him. This was the final time he would ever set foot in this sacred temple, his life for the last forty years and more. It was a life that had brought him much fulfilment and happiness. A life of stability and security. Now he no longer knew what the future held for him, or how long that future might be.

Everything had been thrown into unprecedented turmoil by recent events, events that had been set in motion a great many years earlier in anticipation of the rise of the Shadow Chasers' power and tyranny. Events that had so recently been brought forward as the darkness spread more rapidly than had ever been believed possible. With it had come his unexpected call to take charge of Gor-Kual's liberation and future safety.

Jar-Kan seized on these last precious moments of calm familiarity before he threw himself headlong into the waves of uncertainty and danger. His only reassurance was that Gor-Kual would be with him. Wise, strong, courageous Gor-Kual: guide, teacher and friend. With Gor-Kual at his side he would find his own strength and courage. He could do this. He would do this. He would succeed.

Jar-Kan gazed at the skull chamber, imprinting it on his memory, soaking up the last vestiges of the skulls' energy contained within it as a sponge soaks up water. It would sustain him through these next hours and days.

Twelve square crystal plinths stood around the perimeter of the circular chamber. Each held a skull, ten of them now fakes; only two genuine skulls remained as yet unclaimed. In the centre sat the massive opaque white crystal block which held the cluster of large ice-clear crystal points on which the Master skull rested. He let his eyes wander across the polished panels of pure amethyst that lined the walls, then rise to the large crystal point that hung suspended above the Master skull and acted as a focal point to gather the energy she generated.

At last, knowing he could delay no longer, Jar-Kan moved to the crystal plinth that held Gor-Kual, the red skull of Aldebaran. Created on a world far from this one from a deep brick red jasper veined with pure milky white, she had been one of his secondary charges for many years. From this moment on he, Jar-Kan, would be her sole guardian.

From under his cloak Jar-Kan drew another skull, similar in markings and colour: another facsimile, inert and cold. Compared to Gor-Kual, and even the other replica skulls, it was crude, obviously fashioned in a hurry. In addition, unlike the other duplicates, this one's markings were slightly different to the original. The lack of finesse had been unavoidable as the deadline had been suddenly brought forward by more than a year. It would suffice. It had to. Practically speaking, Jar-Kan mused gloomily, if the Shadow Chasers were in a position where they were able to scrutinise the skulls closely enough to notice the difference, all would already be lost. Quickly he placed Gor-Kual in the small bag he had brought with him, the only thing he carried, crossed to the far side of the chamber, and slipped out through a small concealed door. It was done. It was time to leave.

*   *   *   *   *

The guards were used to seeing Jar-Kan leaving the city at first light. He had done so for years, leaving at sunrise to gather his herbs and plants. They took no longer took any notice of him. Today would be like any other day; he would not act in any way out of the ordinary. His heart beating just a little harder and faster than usual, Jar-Kan passed through the gate, waving his hand in his usual cheery greeting, and set out on one of his habitual routes, striding out across the countryside towards the hills and woodland that rose in the distance. It went exactly as he had hoped. They paid him no attention, did not see that this morning the bag that he always carried to hold his harvest swung heavy from his belt and banged painfully against his thigh. They were blissfully unaware that today Jar-Kan would not be returning at sunset.

Over the course of several previous excursions he had smuggled out some essential belongings that were now hidden in an earth bank, tucked into a small hollow created by the roots of a tree. The pile was sparse, just a few of the barest essentials: some spare clothes, a blanket, money, a little food, and half a dozen basic elements from his herbal pharmacy. He had carefully sealed the items in a thick bag to guard against the attention of scavenging animals and insects before covering the hiding place with a few loose branches as camouflage, though it was unlikely that anyone would discover it. Few people ventured this far from the city these days, and this place was well away from the beaten track.

It was, as he had expected, exactly as he had left it. Taking a deep breath, Jar-Kan hoisted the bundle onto his shoulders and set out towards the north.

CHAPTER 21

Despite the gravity of his mission and his uncertain future, Jar-Kan was a happy man as he moved through the countryside of Atlantis. This was his domain, and he was filled with an unexpected peace and contentment. He was a man of the earth, someone whose family had worked the land for generations. He understood it and cherished it. Out here alone amongst its elements he was at home, more than anywhere else, more even than in the temple that sheltered him for so many years.

Jar-Kan was different to most of the other priests that he shared his life with. They revered nature certainly, gave thanks for her blessings and abundance, understood her importance and life force. Theirs was however more often than not a sterile reverence that, while recognising her importance, rarely sought a deeper acquaintance. They visited her sacred areas and energy vortices, performed their rituals and blessings, but seldom did they venture out into the midst of her wildness for the sheer joy of it. Jar-Kan, on the other hand, found a particular sensuality and his deepest fulfilment when he was lost in the intimacy of her warm earthy depths, exploring her secrets and her magic. Standing knee deep in an icy stream patiently waiting to catch a fish for his supper, gazing in wonder and curiosity at a tiny green shoot pushing its nose up through the damp spring soil, or watching a delicate flower bud unfurling before his eyes, he would lose all track of time, absorbed completely in this other world. He was happy to wander alone and joyfully lost through the delights of its changing landscape, whether in the dappled shade of a leafy woodland where a lattice of sunlight painted patchwork patterns on the soft, composty ground, or across the windswept heights of a rain battered hilltop.

The anxiety born of being out of their natural environment, which assailed most of the others who had fled Yo'tlàn that night, did not touch Jar-Kan. This was his territory; he could survive here indefinitely. He would forge his own path, navigating by the sun and the stars, avoiding as he always did the known and well-trodden routes. He did not need to carry much food or water, which at this time of year was always plentiful if you knew where to look. And he did know. Knew which roots, leaves and berries were edible, how to fish and trap small creatures for meat. Although the fare was frugal, it was always sufficient. Jar-Kan could not remember a time when he had been happier.

It could not last indefinitely, however. Within days he must rendezvous with a guide who would lead him over the high peaks. Even now, in mid-summer, these high mountain passes were cloaked in deep snow and treacherous to those ignorant of their dangers and traps.

After walking steadily for a couple of hours, Jar-Kan crested the first of the low hills that lay to the north of Yo'tlàn. He could not resist the call of his heart to stop, to look back for one final time at the distant city, its soft stone gleaming honey in the sunlight. His gaze settled on the shining golden apex of the pyramid temple, a beacon shining out into the surrounding countryside. Yo'tlàn had once been the heart of a glorious civilisation, now it was all – the temple, the city, the great continent of Atlantis itself – destined for emptiness and ruin. With the power and domination of the Shadow Chasers growing daily, its fate was irrevocably sealed. Practical and down to earth, Jar-Kan was not one for sentimentality. Nonetheless, surveying his beloved city for the final time, he felt a fist closing tightly on his heart. Nothing would ever be the same again. Nothing *could* ever be the same again, either for him, or for anyone in Atlantis.

He turned back to his path, knowing that he was not the only one with sadness in his heart this day. Eleven others – men and women, young and not so young – were also saying their last farewells to this place, leaving everyone and everything they knew behind to head out into a clouded and perilous future. Refusing to let himself be caught up in melancholy Jar-Kan hoisted his pack a little higher, turned his back on the far-off gilded rooftops, and struck out northwards once more.

* * * * *

Jar-Kan's objective was a small town nestled at the edge of the foothills of the vast mountain range that covered the central belt of the Atlantean continent. Its name is unimportant. It was just one of many anonymous small towns that meandered along the edge of these slopes. He was to make his way to the small inn that lay just off the town's main street and wait for his guide to contact him. He had been told that here he would be met by a guide, sympathetic to their aims, who would lead him across the deadly snow-bound barrier. Once on the other side, he would continue to make his way northwards to where the land met the ocean, where a small boat would be waiting to take him to the shores of that other vast continent that lay to the west. His guide would not know Jar-Kan's identity nor his mission, having being told only that he was being hunted by the Shadow Chasers for acts against their authority and was fleeing the land to avoid arrest.

Of course, once the Shadow Chasers discovered the switch in the temple, perhaps in a matter of a week or so at best and likely much sooner, all would be over. Jar-Kan had to be deep in the interior and away from main communication routes by then. He guessed he safely had four or five days, six at most, although that would be pushing his luck to the limit.

CHAPTER 22

Despite his deep love of being at one with the natural world, it was with a profound delight that Jar-Kan sank onto the soft mattress of his bed after several nights sleeping on the cold, hard ground. He luxuriated in the abundant steaming hot water piped from the hot springs that bubbled up from far underground and in the delicious meal that had been brought to his room. Jar-Kan's love for the outdoor life did not stop him appreciating comfort.

A knock at the door roused him from a deliciously dreamy state brought about by the combination of the good food and long, hot bath. In an instant Jar-Kan was alert. His guide. He opened the door a fraction, ready to counter any threat, but none came. Instead a thin, suntanned hand reached through the narrow gap and held up a chain from which dangled a small, flat, circular stone. The stone was deep mossy green in colour, etched with a delicate double spiral pattern. Jar-Kan recognised it immediately: the symbol of alliance. But he could not afford to be naïve or careless, he would not simply accept this token at face value. It could have been obtained by any number of means.

He took the proffered pendant, closing the door in his visitor's face as he turned around to look at it more closely under the light. It appeared genuine. He examined the stone carefully. All was as it should be.

This green stone was extremely rare, which is why it had been chosen. It was not something that could be picked up easily from the side of a road and shaped into a replica. Moreover, neither was it anything special to look at. An innocent glance would consider this pendant to be nothing more than a cheap trinket. Satisfied so far, Jar-Kan cracked open the door once more.

'Your name?' he demanded. 'Identify yourself.'

The man waiting outside inclined his head, understanding the necessity of these checks. 'I am Graf. You are Lumi, who I am to lead over the Peaks of the Sun.' Jar-Kan nodded in agreement. The name the man had given agreed with his own information, and he in turn had been called by the false identity he had assumed for this journey. He looked the man over, appraising him.

'I was told to give you a password, so that you could be certain that I am who I say I am,' the man continued. 'The word is "Solaris".'

It was correct. Jar-Kan continued his scrutiny of his visitor. He was slight, perhaps in the early years of his third decade, with a pleasant, friendly, open face, and suntanned from many hours spent outdoors in the fierce sun of high altitudes. Despite his slim, wiry stature he looked strong. This was obviously someone who was physically fit and used to long periods of physical exertion. Jar-Kan opened the door further and invited his visitor in.

They talked for some while of the route and the preparations that Graf had made for what would, even at this time of year when the weather was at its kindest, be a difficult, arduous and frequently perilous trek. Graf was amiable, eager to please. Too eager to please. The thought leapt unbidden into Jar-Kan's mind. And he asked questions. Too many questions. They had been cleverly phrased and insinuated into the conversation, nonetheless Jar-Kan had not been fooled. Despite the young man's apparent openness and amiability, the fugitive's suspicions were nudged awake. Suspicions that grew stronger as their conversation continued, for Gor-Kual had given him the energetic equivalent of a hard poke in the ribs. Jar-Kan could not connect with her fully – if she activated, there was a strong risk that she would be sensed and discovered. She was however clearly following the proceedings and felt it helpful to confirm her guardian's doubts. All the checks had been verified but the sharp tugging in his gut warned Jar-Kan that something was not as it seemed and that he should stay on his guard. He was frustrated that he too was unable to use his mental skills to probe further; the risk of giving himself away was equally high.

It became evident that Graf wanted to hang around, to engage him in some more conversation. Jar-Kan could not shake the feeling that he was being skilfully enticed to share more information than was safe. Wise to the ploy, without seeming to he pushed Graf politely out of the door and closed it firmly behind him. The skull guardian settled down for the night with his doubts, anxieties and thoughts of the hard journey that lay ahead of him as his uncomfortable bedfellows.

* * * * *

Jar-Kan's intuition was, as always, correct. At the far end of a patch of rough, infertile land to the east of the town a small patch of disturbed earth was the only indication of what had occurred. Beneath the shallow layer of stones and soil lay the crumpled, broken body of a young mountain guide, ally of the Light-keepers. His mutilated flesh bore witness to the crude, brutal, but effective torture inflicted upon him, a torture he had been unable to withstand, screaming out the secrets he had sworn to hold silent. Only then to be released by the razor sharp blade that had slashed his windpipe and sliced through his jugular, to leave him cold and lifeless in a pool of his own crimson blood. This was the real Graf, unable to tell of his fate, his identity taken by another who had an altogether different allegiance.

CHAPTER 23

The following morning they set out at daybreak. Graf was good company, an amenable and experienced guide whose knowledge of mountain flora and fauna was almost encyclopaedic. It was a knowledge he loved to share, and Jar-Kan was just as eager to learn about this environment to which he was a total stranger. As the day progressed Jar-Kan began to doubt his earlier suspicions. Nothing in the way Graf spoke or acted gave the slightest indication that he was anything other than he claimed to be. In the peaceful serenity of the lush green foothills the priest began to wonder if he was imagining an unreal threat. Was his uncertain and unfamiliar situation and the very real danger he was facing creating something that did not actually exist? He could almost convince himself that it was so, were it not that deep within him a spark of that initial doubt and mistrust would not be extinguished. Gor-Kual was silent. She had given her warning and would not risk revealing herself by doing so again.

Two days passed in this pleasant way. They were still low enough for the weather to be balmy, and the sun continued to shine. On the third day though something subtly began to change. They were deep into the back hills now, climbing ever higher. The air was growing thinner and noticeably cooler. Graf had become more withdrawn, talking less, his up until now permanent affability growing more forced from time to time, the questioning becoming markedly less subtle. Jar-Kan's suspicions had surged to the forefront once again, becoming firmly implanted after a couple of occasions when he had caught the guide glancing greedily at the heavy bag that still hung around Jar-Kan's waist. Graf was going to make a move. The question was, when?

Graf, however, was experienced in more than just mountain guiding. He was a skilled hunter and he was biding his time. This was his territory. He had grown up amongst these snow-covered peaks and icy, hostile landscapes, clambered as agile as a mountain goat around its naked, jagged outcrops and deep hidden crevasses from the time he was a small child. He had his orders. He would carry them out at the right moment. His eyes slipped once more to the bag that Jar-Kan carried. It must be extremely valuable because it never left his person, even when he slept. There would be a nice little unexpected bonus for him in this.

Graf and his masters, the Dark Ones, were mercifully ignorant of Jar-Kan's true identity and his reason for crossing the peaks. Nevertheless it had to be unlawful, for no sane or legitimate person would ever wish to attempt it. The route around was days longer yes, but relatively easy and comfortable, and far less perilous. Graf's orders were to eliminate anyone who tried to cross, their reasons were irrelevant. A few had tried, a handful perhaps over the past few years. None had made it, thanks to Graf's loyalty to his task and in no little part to his pleasure in carrying it out.

They were approaching the lower slopes of the main range now. He would act tonight. He had no intention of exposing himself to the dangers of the high mountains if he didn't have to. Graf may have known these peaks like the back of his hand, it only made him respect them more. He understood that even the most experienced mountain man could come to grief in a moment. Indeed, he had known many who had done so, victims of the capricious whims of the ever-changing weather which could turn from tender lover to vindictive harpy in seconds. Too many who called these mountains home had perished here, unable to escape their grip. Yes, he would strike tonight.

As he contemplated the actions he would take, the familiar bloodlust rose up in him, a hot, searing fervour that threatened to overwhelm all rational thought. His skin burned and he felt his physical arousal, hard and pulsing against his belly. An almost incontrollable urge seized him to stop and find a place where he could release this tension, let it spatter on the ground in a hot jet, but he held back, knowing that it would be all the sweeter and more intense for waiting until after he had spilled this big man's blood. It always was. In his excitement, Graf was unable to hide completely his agitation and anticipation. His mask, so carefully held in place over these past days, momentarily slipped. And Jar-Kan saw.

It was well towards dawn before Graf silently rose and looked over at the sleeping Jar-Kan. The moon was past its quarter now, a thick wedge of silver hanging in the sky, illuminating the scene only intermittently. Heavy passing clouds blocked its light for long periods, during which the assassin was almost invisible against the dark rock backdrop. His favourite blade was in his hand, a long, slim weapon whose blade was honed to razor sharpness. It would slide through flesh as easily as through a peach. He had decided to slit Jar-Kan's throat, the least risky of his options. Graf was under no illusion of the other man's superior strength. The big man slept on his back and the target area was exposed and vulnerable as his deep snores filled the air.

It would not be as easy as Graf believed however, for Jar-Kan was protected even as he slept. The red skull watched over him while he drifted in his dreams. She was the reason why Jar-Kan could rest so easily. It was his own sixth sense that woke him to see Graf crouched at his shoulder, blade already raised to strike, but before the priest had a chance to move to defend himself, his assailant was hurled backwards, staggering to keep his balance, his senses reeling. A bolt of unseen energy had delivered a punishing blow to his solar plexus. Steadying himself against the rock wall behind him he stared at Jar-Kan, his eyes travelling down to the bag that rested against his thigh. That was where the energy bolt had originated. What was in there? There was no time to wonder. Although Jar-Kan may have been a bear of a man, he was quick and agile, and already on his feet.

The younger man was no longer trying to hide his true character. His face was hard and cruel, his eyes blazing hatred. The genial mountain guide had vanished and in his place stood a pitiless killer. He was crouching, ready to attack once more, as balanced and easy on his feet as one of the mountain lions that roamed these peaks, holding his knife with an easy familiarity, a familiarity that evidenced his long record of murder. Taken back only momentarily by Gor-Kual's attack, he was confident and poised, clearly believing that he could easily vanquish his opponent, taller and heavier though Jar-Kan was.

* * * * *

As a Priest of the Light, Jar-Kan had taken a vow of non-violence upon his ordination. This did not mean that the priests would not stand up for themselves, or for others, or for what they knew was right, but such actions were always taken with a heart-centred focus of love for all. It was an approach that until very recently had always succeeded and had never required any of them to embrace violence, even in self-defence. This oath, though, was now being challenged. As intimidating as he looked, in reality Jar-Kan did not possess a violent bone in his body. He was gentle and compassionate. Would he be prepared, would he be able, to fight another man to save his own life and ensure the safety of Gor-Kual? Jar-Kan was determined that the path of a priest using violence was not going to begin with him, now, on this mountainside. In any case, in his heart he was uncertain that he would actually be able to beat his adversary in a fight. He was strong, but he had no combat skills whereas Graf clearly had many.

Jar-Kan had felt the energy surge as Gor-Kual saved him from the initial attack. He had woken a split second before she had acted, his sixth sense kicking in. In saving his life however Gor-Kual had broken her dormancy, and Graf had felt her power.

The killer did not recognise its source. How would he? He had never had any previous contact with the skulls. He did though recognise its potency. Hunger grew in him. His cruel eyes darted constantly to the bag at Jar-Kan's thigh. If what was held within still remained been a mystery to Graf, he nevertheless knew without any doubt that whatever it was, it was something of immense power. He wanted to possess those contents more than ever. Wanted to control it for himself. With that power at his command, who could he not conquer? Why, he would have the Shadow Chasers themselves kneeling at his feet.

CHAPTER 24

The two men had stopped for the night at a point where the path widened into a deep alcove in the cliff face to create a smooth, large, weather-worn cushion of bedrock sheltered from any prevailing winds. On the mountain side a natural wall of stone reached up above Jar-Kan's head perhaps another arm's length, while on the downhill side plunged a steep slope covered with stunted shrubby bushes and long wiry grass, and dotted with large rocks that had fallen from the cliffs above. After three days hard trek they were just below the snowline. Day was still some way ahead and the plummeting overnight temperature had left a rime of frost over every surface. It was not a comfortable place to be. Jar-Kan stood with his back to the wall, his escape route cut off by Graf's menacing figure. What could he do? How could he disarm and disable his far more experienced opponent without hurting him? Or without getting hurt himself? He would have to use his own form of defence weapon, one he knew only too well how to use. One that would not harm Graf. Only there was no guarantee that it would work.

'Goodbye, Lumi.' Graf's words were filled with contempt as he stood facing the priest, poised to complete his contract. 'This is where your journey ends.'

Not taking his eyes from the man in front of him, Jar-Kan reached out with his mind to make contact with his assailant's. It was the last thing Graf had expected. He shot a nervous glance at Jar-Kan, the first slight indication of fear showing in his face. Caught completely by surprise, doubt flooded in, his confidence shaken. This was not an ordinary man he was facing, this was someone trained in mind contact and telepathy. Well – Graf's attention snapped back to its purpose, restoring his arrogance – it didn't matter. So had he. He could match anyone in a mental wresting match. Or so he thought. His self-assurance didn't last long.

Graf slammed shut his own mind immediately, in doing so betraying immediately his origins and training to Jar-Kan. This killer had to be linked to the Shadow Chasers. They were the only ones other than the priesthood who were trained to such a high level of mental control. But Graf, while trained, was not adept. Jar-Kan could see it was costing him effort and concentration to keep his shields firm and in place, pulling his attention from his physical actions. So... Graf could do one or the other, but not both. This could be Jar-Kan's trump card, for he was easily able to keep his focus strong in both areas simultaneously. All he needed to do was break Graf's concentration.

*   *   *   *   *

Slowly Jar-Kan began to move. He took a steady step to his right, then another. He had no real purpose in doing so other than to divide Graf's focus. It worked. Immediately the younger man's eyes locked onto him, watching him, anticipating his next move, trying to work out where and when Jar-Kan's attack would come, sure that it would. This big man would not just stand there and allow death to claim him. He snapped his focus back to his opponent, only to find Jar-Kan's mind fully shielded and impenetrable. He could not read a flicker what was going on behind that impassive relaxed face or those steady blue eyes. Did he feel no fear?

Jar-Kan took another step. Immediately Graf's focus shattered once again, the barriers in his mind crumpling. Jar-Kan would be able to read his every move before he took it.

The priest easily sidestepped Graf's first attack. The smaller man had leapt, feinting one move as he swiftly executed another. He was quick. Rushing forward to Jar-Kan's right, at the last moment he had spun on his heels, the knife in his hand flashing up in a vicious swinging arc that, if it had landed, would have plunged into Jar-Kan's belly just beneath his lower ribs and swept upwards to pierce his heart. It was a clever, practised move, the move of a master, one that Jar-Kan had anticipated, stepping into the path of Graf's initial trajectory in an irrational and unnatural response to the attack that was coming. It worked.

Graf whirled around, incensed. That move had never failed him before; the bloodied trail of corpses in its wake bore witness to its deadly efficiency. He charged again. Again Jar-Kan avoided the hissing blade. It became a macabre dance of death, the two men circling, feinting, charging and sidestepping; a dance where Graf, no matter how skilled at his craft, could not get the upper hand. The big bear of a man predicted his every move, waiting always until the last moment before moving easily and gracefully out of harm's way.

Graf's frustration soon turned to fury, the red fire of rage dulling his senses and thought processes. In his mind now was nothing but the frenzied hunger to kill, kill, kill this man who was making such an easy mockery of his abilities. It was a fury fed by Jar-Kan's continued calmness and non-reactiveness, for he refused to actively defend himself or counter-attack, just easily, serenely taking the avoiding action he needed to take. Once or twice he had ducked to avoid a blow and Graf had been thrown over the big man's body by his own momentum. His assailant had been back on his feet in a split second, lips drawn back in an angry snarl. He was being made to look a fool, and he would not stand for it.

Graf cursed the Shadow Chasers for not arming him with one of their stun weapons. He'd like to see how this Lumi would have escaped him then, lying on the floor conscious but unable to move, watching helplessly as the blade plunged down towards him. Unable to protect himself in his last seconds from the searing agony as it skewered his heart, or maybe the ghastly whistling gurgle of escaping air and blood as it ripped through his windpipe, or... All these thoughts flew through Graf's mind in an instant as he once more whirled to face Jar-Kan, holding himself in the crouching stance of a trained killer. Fit though he was, he was panting now. Jar-Kan, on the other hand, was not even out of breath. He had been expending his energy, while Jar-Kan had barely moved.

Then he got his chance. The two men had circled around each other and were now at opposite sides to their starting positions. As Jar-Kan stepped backwards, his foot came down on a small patch of ice; a tiny rivulet of water crossed the path here and had frozen overnight. It was only a small area but he had not noticed it and as his foot went down, he slipped. The weight of Gor-Kual swinging at his thigh pulled him further off balance and for a moment the priest's attention left Graf as he fought to keep his balance and prevent himself plummeting over the edge of the path and down the slope beyond.

This was Graf's opportunity. Head down, he charged at Jar-Kan, knife held tightly in his killer's grip, ready to thrust deep into Jar-Kan's soft flesh. He would have succeeded if fortune had not still been smiling on the skull's guardian. In the midst of his own personal battle to retain his footing, Jar-Kan glimpsed a flash of movement as the moonlight caught the blade of the raised knife. Still fighting against the ice, unable to move his feet, he managed to twist his body to deflect the brunt of the blow, though not all of it. He grunted in pain as he felt the blade meet skin and slice into it a split-second before Graf barrelled into him with an impact that knocked him sideways and back onto the path.

It was the blow that ended the stalemate. In colliding with Jar-Kan, Graf had in turn found himself on the icy slide. Unable to halt his forward momentum he had pitched forward and over the edge, his yells filling the silent air as he somersaulted down the steep slope, for all the world like a puppet whose strings had been cut, arms and legs flailing uncontrollably as he was tossed mercilessly through the air. A sickening crunch echoed through the cold, still air, and then silence settled once more.

CHAPTER 25

Jar-Kan pulled himself to his knees, grasping his right arm. A crimson stain was spreading through the thick coat he was wearing. Gingerly he pulled his arm free. He had been lucky. It was a surface wound, deep enough to be sure, and it would inconvenience him certainly, but it would heal quickly and fully. Thankfully, his heavy coat had shielded him from a far worse injury. He temporarily wrapped a length of cloth torn from his shirt around his own wound to staunch the bleeding; he would tend to it properly in a little while. For now there were other things requiring his priority. Jar-Kan's healer's instincts could not be overridden; they were too much part of him. Even as he had been knocked to the ground he had been aware of what was happening, had heard Graf's cries as he tumbled down the slope.

He got to his feet and peered down into the shadows of the valley below. Where was Graf? He had to be hurt – how badly? The slope was survivable if steep but an ominous silence had settled over the area. The sky was lighter now, day was coming. Already the ledge where they had spent the previous night was being caressed by the sun's outermost rays, though they had not yet penetrated the dense gloom below.

'Graf! Graf? Can you hear me?' Jar-Kan's voice echoed in the emptiness, solitary and unheard. Silence answered him. Cautiously descending the steep, frost slippery slope at the point where Graf had gone over the edge, hampered by his injured arm and the heavy weight of Gor-Kual who still hung from his belt, he peered at every dark shadow in case it hid Graf's unconscious body, continuing to call every few steps. It was slow going, perilous, but Jar-Kan would not leave Graf here if he was still alive.

'Graf! Graf!' Still no answer. The sun's rays were creeping down the slopes towards him now. He would not give up. At last, just as he was beginning to believe he would never find the other man, his call was answered by a low groan that came from just to the right of where he stood. Steadying himself with his good arm, Jar-Kan clambered across the rough ground to where the sound came from.

The sight that met him was not pleasant. Graf was still alive, but barely. His uncontrollable fall had come to an abrupt halt when his body had crashed heavily into one of the jagged boulders that littered these slopes. Flesh and bone had been no match for the ancient rock. Graf still lay against it, twisted and ashen faced. Looking down on him, Jar-Kan felt only a powerful compassion for his erstwhile attacker, now a broken heap of flesh. He may be alive for the moment, but Jar-Kan's experienced eye told him that it would not be for much longer. The younger man's back was broken, his vertebrae crushed to dust as they slammed into the hard stone. From the blood that seeped from the lower orifices of Graf's shattered body it was clear that he had also sustained massive internal injuries. No-one, not Jar-Kan, not even Gor-Kual herself, could do anything for him.

Jar-Kan knelt beside him, taking an ice-cold hand in his own. Graf looked up at him with a profound puzzlement in his pain-darkened eyes.

'You came to look for me?' The words were a harsh whisper, hard won. 'Why? I would have killed you.' He stopped, digging deep for the strength to continue. 'Still would if I could.'

'No situation will ever be resolved for the better through the death of a human being, no matter what he holds in his heart.' Jar-Kan's words were filled with compassion for this shattered wreck of a man, so close now to death, and sorrow hung heavy on his heart. In spite of Graf's actions Jar-Kan understood from deep within his soul that a life cut short was always a cause for grief, that the life of every man, woman and child was sacred and precious. He could not feel anger or hatred, for each acts according to how they have learned to act, doing their best to survive in the only way they know how. Actions such as Graf's were brought about always through a painful amnesia of the true light of his being.

He would not leave Graf to die alone on the cold mountainside so he wrapped him in his own cloak and stayed by his side. It would not be long. He could see the younger man's life draining away into the soft earth he lay on, staining it a deep red, obscenely alive in its vibrancy under the morning sunlight. This man was no longer his enemy, a hard embittered killer; he was a frightened human being facing the greatest unknown of any life. As his final faint breath trickled from his lungs, a tear fell from Graf's darkening, no longer seeing eyes.

*   *   *   *   *

Jar-Kan straightened up painfully. The cold ground had seeped into his leg bones and muscles, stiffening them, while his wounded arm, unprotected by the cloak which he had wrapped around the mortally injured Graf, throbbed painfully under the caress of the still, chill air. He could do no more for Graf; it was time to look to himself. He collected his coat from the still warm body, wrapping it once more around his own shoulders, and then awkwardly, clumsily, started back up the steep slope to the path above. There, he tended the deep cut on his arm. First he selected the necessary healing herbs from the small collection he had brought with him and with the aid of two clean rocks pounded them to a mush. This he packed onto the cut, wincing in pain at the touch, before wrapping it in a clean strip of cloth. Laying his left hand on the bandaged wound, he sent to it a powerful surge of healing energy that was given birth in his heart and travelled up to his shoulder and down through his left arm and hand to its target. He felt the warmth pulsing as it poured into the damaged flesh, healing and renewing.

CHAPTER 26

Jar-Kan gathered together his belongings, stood up and looked around. What was he to do now? Ahead of him the mountains towered intimidatingly, their snow covered peaks almost challenging him to take them on. He would not. His mission was too important and already too dangerous for him to take on any further unnecessary risk. For the first time since leaving the Pyramid temple so many days before, Jar-Kan pulled Gor-Kual from the bag and held her in his hands. He closed his eyes and focussed on establishing their connection, lifting her so that she was level with his own face.

'Gor-Kual, ancient skull of Aldebaran, I need your wisdom and your help. Tell me now, where do I go from here? How do I protect you and take you to safety, as I have sworn to do?'

Immediately he was enfolded in a blanket of warmth that tingled like electricity. Gor-Kual was with him. 'Go back, my dear friend. Return the way you came, take the road for the coast. The next steps will reveal themselves to you. But you must hurry. Time is no longer on your side.'

So Jar-Kan turned and retraced his steps. He set himself a punishing pace, almost a run, stopping only for a couple of hours to rest during the darkest hours of the night when he could no longer see the path beneath his feet. The following day, towards noon, he rounded an outcrop to see the town laid out far below him. A warm bed and hot meal tempted him but time was running out. He could not afford to delay. Furthermore, as he looked down on the town a tightness began to take hold in his belly. It was a warning. His intuition was telling him to avoid the settlement where further danger now must lie in wait for him. It was a long detour, far from the town's outskirts, before he reached the main thoroughfare that would take him on his long road east to the ocean and the port of Dendarak. Fit and strong though he was, unaffected by his journey until now, Jar-Kan's heart sank at the prospect of so many more days' trek ahead of him. He had no choice. He began to walk.

'Ho, friend. Do you want a ride?' A goods shuttle had pulled up beside him and the driver was leaning from his window. 'I'm on my way to Dendarak, so I can drop you off anywhere on the way. It's a good long walk to anywhere from here.'

The goods shuttles regularly travelled these main arteries, bringing food from the fertile coastal plains of the east in to the less cultivated hinterlands and returning with a wealth of manufactured goods, including textiles, metal-wares and pottery. Jar-Kan hadn't heard it draw up. Like all transport in Atlantis, its motor was soundless, being solar and crystal powered. A healer and plants-man rather than an engineer, Jar-Kan had never understood the intricacies of the technology, which was highly advanced even by

Atlantean standards. It was something that at this moment he was deeply grateful for nevertheless. A journey that would have taken him a week or more on foot would now be reduced to less than a day.

The driver was friendly and talkative, which well suited the priest who let him ramble on non-stop about his family and home. It meant he was not asking questions that may have been difficult to answer. Time passed pleasantly enough in the comfortable vehicle. Now and again the skull guardian catnapped, catching up on the previous night's sleep and allowing his body to recover from its recent exertions. It seemed no time at all before they reached the outskirts of Dendarak.

'Get out before you reach the city.' Gor-Kual's words whispered through his still half dozing mind. 'Someone will be waiting to show you the way.'

*   *   *   *   *

Jar-Kan asked the driver to set him down at one of the small outlying settlements a short way from the city gates, on the pretext of having business there. The reality was that he did not have the papers that would allow him to pass through the gates, and any attempt to do so without them would inevitably result in his arrest. Dendarak was the major stronghold of the Shadow Chasers, the darkly oppressive forces that were seeking to take control of the whole of Atlantis, and were, sadly, succeeding. Their headquarters was there, along with the main garrison. It was not the town he would have chosen as his destination, but he trusted Gor-Kual implicitly. She had led him this far. Together with her allies she would lead him safely further, as long as he listened to her guidance.

CHAPTER 27

Again he was being watched. Once more he felt the sensation of eyes upon him, appraising him. He turned. Again it was a child, a little older this time, maybe ten years of age, this time a girl. Her eyes though were not the eyes of a child. In them he could see the soul of a far older being, one whose origins were not of the Earth. She was merely being used as a vessel for their words. Why an innocent, vulnerable child, and not someone older? He already knew the answer: a child has not travelled so far from that pure connection to their source, is unsullied by the distorted reality of the time and place in which she lives. She would carry with her far fewer entrenched beliefs that could stand in the way of any message that she was to share. On many occasions Jar-Kan had heard these beings speak through a priest in the temple sanctuary, had himself even served as their voice. Out here it was different. Whereas in time long gone by, when such telepathy had been as natural as breathing to every man, woman and child of Atlantis, now it was rare indeed.

The girl looked up at him, impatient to move. She was stocky, her young face prettily sprinkled with freckles, brown hair pulled back off her face in two stumpy braids. Clear blue eyes, much paler than his own, gazed up at him. In them he could see the resemblance to those of the visitors from the cosmos who had often visited the temple in Yo'tlàn. This young girl had to be a star-child, the descendant of a union between a star traveller and a human that had occurred generations ago. It made sense; they were using one of their own as a conduit.

The light beings who would speak through the child were the inhabitants of other worlds in far distant galaxies and constellations. It was they, or others like them, who had created the skulls so long ago, and their descendants and heirs were continuing the work. They knew that here, in Dendarak, in such proximity to the Shadow Chasers who would pick up any signal from her and spare no effort in hunting her down, Gor-Kual would have to remain dormant, unable to help. The star council had had to find another way to bring him the assistance he so desperately needed.

'Come. There is a ship waiting at the dockside. You must be on board when it leaves tomorrow.' The child's voice held an incongruous authority.

She led him through a maze of irrigation ditches and fields bordered with thick hedges that sheltered the crops from the often fierce ocean winds. It provided excellent cover and he followed her unquestioningly, knowing she would lead him to exactly where he needed to be. Eventually she stopped beside a deep ditch, pointing wordlessly at a conduit that was set into a bank. It was one of the main surface water drains from the city, sealed with a heavy metal grill. Jar-Kan nodded at the girl to show he had understood. He dared not speak aloud for night had fallen, any sound would carry clearly in the quiet, still air. Unexpectedly she smiled back at him, a smile that lit up her naturally serious face and transformed her back into a playful child. Without saying a word, she turned and ran off into the dark shadows of the field boundary.

*   *   *   *   *

Jar-Kan scrambled down into the ditch to survey the grill. It was circular, its diameter standing as high as his shoulder, and was firmly fixed. It would be heavy, even for him. He placed his hands on it and closed his eyes, feeling it. Yes, he would be able to move it, but it would require more than mere physical strength to do so. He focussed, shutting from his mind everything but an image of the grill sliding from its mounts as if on oiled tracks, keeping the picture fixed firmly as he leaned his weight against it, tensed his shoulders and pulled. His injured arm screamed in pain but he did not let up, keeping a firm steady pressure. He thought he felt it judder and then slip, just a fraction. He renewed his focus and kept going. Sure enough, slowly at first it began to move until with a sudden jolt it came free, almost tipping him backwards under the momentum. Taking care not to make a sound, he laid the grill carefully aside on the bank and stepped forward into the drain entrance.

Inside the conduit, it was pitch dark. He would be able to see nothing. He took a deep breath, expanding his awareness until his energy field stretched out several feet in front of him. Cautiously he nudged forwards, testing his footing at every step, feeling ahead with his hands. He made slow, steady progress. Jar-Kan gave thanks that the water, which reached above his knees, was relatively clean. This was a storm drain; more noxious waste was dealt with by a separate system. He had no idea how far he would have to go, or where he would emerge. Once more he would have to rely on his intuition to guide him.

He plodded on. It was extremely uncomfortable. The water, at first cold but tolerable, soon numbed his feet, and he stumbled frequently, occasionally falling to his knees in the frigid stream. Eventually, after what felt like an eternity, he thought he saw a slightly lighter area in the blackness of the tunnel. As he drew nearer he could see that it was coming from above where one of the surface drains emptied down into the main channel. It was too high to reach, but there had to be some way of getting up, some form of maintenance access. He groped around looking for something, anything, that would give him a way out. His fingers came into contact with what felt like giant staples fixed to the wall. He moved closer and let his hands explore them. It was a ladder of some kind, made of rough metal rungs set into the stonework. This was it, his escape route. He seized the first rung and hauled himself up.

His head was brushing the bottom of the grating but still he could see nothing of what was above. Was this a quiet side street or one of the main thoroughfares? No matter how much Jar-Kan twisted and craned his neck, his view remained negligible. Well, he would have to risk it. It was late evening. There should be very few people around. Once more he reached out with his senses. He couldn't feel anyone there. He hoped he was right. Putting his shoulders to the grating he pushed it upwards and sideways, glancing around anxiously at the harsh scraping noise it made, the sound echoing intrusively into the quiet street. There was no-one in sight. He had come up into what appeared to be a residential area where every door looked bolted and locked, every window draped and blind. He hoisted himself up, replaced the drain cover, and hobbled to the cover of a high wall. His numb feet would take a while to regain their feeling. Well, he had made it into the city. The question was, where now? He looked around with no idea of which direction to take.

A young couple approached, hurrying past, eager to return to the relative safety of their home. This was no place to linger. Shadow Chaser patrols constantly roamed these streets arresting passers-by for no reason other than a whim, or because a face didn't look right. They wielded their muscle in a show of power at every opportunity in order to intimidate and instil fear in the population for fear was their weapon of control. It was, as it always is, a highly effective one. The couple threw him a wary glance as they passed by. He must have looked pretty suspicious – he was dirty, dishevelled and sported several days beard growth. He had to get out of sight before someone reported him. Which way though? Left or right?

Right. The answer came as an energetic nudge in his solar plexus. Gor-Kual, while not awakened, was not fully dormant any longer either. She had activated herself just enough to indicate the way. In a strange game of 'hotter-colder', in which she gave Jar-Kan's solar plexus a hefty poke of confirmation at each correct choice, she led him through the city streets along a tortuous route that avoided the still busy main thoroughfares. At last Jar-Kan found himself at the edge of a wide paved area beyond which the moonlight glittered on the tiny waves of the ocean's edge. Directly in front of him a ship rested at her moorings, her slender masts piercing the starry night sky, black shadows against deep midnight blue.

How on earth was he to gain passage on that ship? If it was legitimate they would not simply let him walk on board without a pile of authorised paperwork. If carrying out illegal business it would be equally impossible unless he had a large bagful of gold with which to buy his passage. In both cases, if he was discovered as a stowaway, even if he was able to somehow slip on board unseen, he would like as not be simply thrown overboard regardless of which it was.

CHAPTER 28

Jar-Kan waited and watched. He had complete faith that something would happen soon to show him his next move. He would not have been brought this far only to fail now.

There. Someone had come out of a small building a little further down the dock and darted quickly towards the ship, scurrying up the gangplank to disappear in the dark shadows of the deck. Then another, followed by two more. In all, he saw well over a dozen people board the ship in ones and twos: men, women, the occasional child. All hurrying, clearly not wishing to be seen. Finally he understood. These people were a human cargo, Atlanteans trying to escape the harsh regime the Dark Ones were slowly inflicting on the land. Yes, this was to be his escape route even if he still didn't have the remotest idea of how he would talk his way on board. That he would somehow succeed, however, he no longer doubted.

Jar-Kan left the shelter of the doorway where he had been hiding, running across the moonlight-dappled dock. He paused against the back wall of the small building and peered around the corner. Right there, two paces away, a door was wedged open inviting him in. Jar-Kan slipped inside. At the other side of the room a lone figure was huddled by a second door, the one that faced the ship and from which the passengers had exited. He hadn't heard Jar-Kan enter but sensed there was someone behind him and turned to see who the newcomer was. As a shaft of moonlight from the open door hit the second man's face Jar-Kan stepped back in alarm and dismay, coupled with not a little disbelief and, he could not deny it, distaste. Of all the people in the whole of Atlantis that it could have been, this was the one he least expected to find here, and the one he would have least chosen to come face to face with: Kua'tzal.

Jar-Kan had never hated anyone in his life, but if he had, it would have been this man crouched in the open doorway in front of him. Kua'tzal, a priest like himself, but in Jar-Kan's eyes a collaborator with the Dark Ones. Kua'tzal didn't even try to hide his admiration for the Shadow Chasers and all they stood for, never spoke against them, and served as the temple's representative in negotiations with them. Jar-Kan could never understand why Omar had never censured him and would not hear anything said against him. Now he was here in this small hut on the outskirts of Dendarak, clearly waiting to board the ship and leave Atlantis. Why?

The thought flicked into his mind. Surely not. It couldn't be. Jar-Kan could barely entertain the idea. Why else though would he be here hiding like a fugitive? Could Kua'tzal really have been entrusted with the safe passage of one of the thirteen skulls? Or – another idea crossed his mind – was he just trying to save his own skin, having somehow caught wind of what was going on at the temple? Whatever the reason, Jar-Kan's own presence was clearly just as unwelcome; a look of equal dismay had settled over Kua'tzal's aquiline features.

'Kua'tzal?' Jar-Kan stifled the word as Kua'tzal placed a finger to his lips. Someone was coming. The weather-beaten face of one of the ship's crew crooked around the doorway, flashing surprise as he took in Jar-Kan's bear-like figure standing behind Kua'tzal. 'Who are you? What are you doing here?' Suspicion hung icily on his words.

'Lumi,' Jar-Kan replied, re-assuming his earlier alias. 'I seek passage.'

'You aren't on the list.' The sailor looked him up and down, and Jar-Kan felt his mind probing his own. This was no run of the mill mariner. The man had been trained in similar techniques to the priests. The sailor's eyes ran over Jar-Kan's travel-worn clothes, sizing him up. 'OK,' he nodded after a brief pause. 'You feel safe enough. But we'll be watching you closely. One wrong move and you'll be keeping company with the fishes. Come on.' He was clearly impatient for them to be moving, his eyes constantly darting from them to the perimeter of the dock area as if expecting unwelcome visitors at any moment.

'Why the haste? I thought we weren't leaving until tomorrow morning?' Kua'tzal was clearly concerned at the change of plans.

The crewman shook him off impatiently. 'You haven't heard then?' He was hustling them across to the dockside as he spoke. 'Word has it that the Dark Ones have taken control of the pyramid temple in Yo'tlàn and arrested everyone inside. If that's true, they'll be locking down every port in Atlantis. We can't take the risk of delaying our departure and getting trapped here. We're leaving on tonight's tide. Which is any moment now.'

Indeed, even as Jar-Kan and Kua'tzal ran up the gangplank it was being pulled up behind them. The deck was a flurry of unnaturally silent activity as ropes were stowed, moorings slipped, and sails prepared. Slowly, silently, with the aid of her crystal powered engines, the ship moved away from the dock. The journey into the unknown had begun.

CHAPTER 29

'You lucky devil. I wish I could come with you.' Cathy wrapped me in a huge hug. 'I'll miss you. Have fun.' She chuckled. 'Especially with that Callum guy.' Yes, I'd told her all about him and how he turned my legs to jelly, and I hadn't heard the end of it since. Her face turned serious. 'Stay safe, Gemma. It's a big country.'

She had driven me to the bus station where the Heathrow coach was waiting. My bags had been stowed and it was ready to leave. I hugged her back. 'I'll be fine, Cathy. Callum's meeting me at the airport so I'm not going to be let loose in America on my own. I'll keep you posted.'

'You'd better.'

'Hurry up, I haven't got all day.' The driver was getting impatient waiting for me. Planting a quick kiss on Cathy's cheek I turned and clambered up the steps, finding an empty seat next to the window. Outside, Cathy waved furiously as the coach pulled away.

I leaned back in my seat and let the butterflies come, butterflies the size of seagulls. In spite of my bravado with Cathy, I hadn't flown for years – it had been a miracle that my passport was still in date – had never at all flown on my own before. Now here I was on a coach to the airport, heading out to who knew what adventures. It was exciting, but oh so scary at the same time. All I knew of America I had learned from films and the television, and I knew the picture they portrayed would be as far from reality as Sherlock Holmes or Midsomer Murders were from real life in England.

I breathed deeply in a not altogether successful attempt to relax. The last few weeks had been a bit manic and overwhelming, the preparations for this trip coinciding with the admittedly low-key launch of my book. On top of that, I was being pulled in two different directions with regard to the skulls. On one hand was Callum, with all his fire and enthusiasm, pushing me to focus on his search for the blue skull, Gal-Athiel. Which was, after all, what this trip was about. On the other, a third skull, Gor-Kual, had entered my nightly dreams over the past couple of months and I had been kept busy recording her messages. Sitting in the coach, watching the English countryside pass by, I wasn't sure what I was heading into next, but if past experience was anything to go by, it wouldn't be dull.

For the hundredth time since leaving home I checked my handbag: flight tickets, insurance, some dollar bills, driving licence (there was absolutely *no way* I was going to drive anywhere despite what Callum thought, but he had insisted I bring it anyway). Passport... Where was my passport? It had to be there. Panic flared and then died away as the small maroon document emerged from the deepest recesses of my bag. Passport. It was all there.

* * * * *

Five and a half hours later, the British Airways 747 taxied out onto the runway at London's Heathrow airport, picked up speed and rose up into the skies above England. I was on my way to America...

CHAPTER 30

I arrived at the Sky Harbour airport in Phoenix knackered, grumpy and grubby. It had been a l-o-n-g flight. I don't do travelling well, I find it impossible to sleep on planes, so this was about as much as my inexperienced inner adventurer wanted to deal with at the moment. All I wanted was a shower and sleep.

Fortunately, getting through the American immigration and customs was a lot easier and faster than I had feared, having heard all manner of horror stories from well-meaning friends and acquaintances over the previous week or so. Less than an hour after landing I was dragging my case through the doors to the arrivals lounge. I scanned the vast concourse; Callum had promised he'd be here to meet me. This late in the evening the airport was quiet and I wouldn't have been able to miss his lanky six feet two if he'd been hovering somewhere. There was no sign of him. My heart sank. This was exactly what I did *not* need or want right at this moment.

Now what? Callum had obviously been delayed but how long would he be? Should I wait or... I knew he had arranged for us to stay somewhere near the airport overnight before we headed off to who knew where in the morning. Unfortunately for me, he hadn't given me the name of the hotel and I hadn't thought to ask. And even though I had his cell phone number, my own dinosaur of a phone wasn't tuned in to work in the USA. Stop Gemma. Think. I walked across to a kiosk, bought myself a large coffee and returned to sit on one of the hard metal mesh seats and consider my position. I was so tired that my brain was struggling to string two coherent thoughts together.

OK, time to take stock: it was late, and I was exhausted. Callum wasn't here. The question was, how long to wait for him before I took a cab and found my own accommodation for the night. He had no way of getting hold of me, although I suppose he could have relayed a message through customer assistance and its loudspeakers. And I had no way of getting hold of... Of course, the public phones. I *could* get hold of him. Why hadn't I thought of that? Except they all needed a phone card and I didn't have one and didn't have a clue where to get one... Grown up and mature and capable as I like to think I am, all I wanted to do in that moment was curl up and cry.

'Gemma!' I whirled around at his voice, relief flooding through every cell of my ready-to-drop body. I had never been so pleased to see anyone as I was to see Callum at that moment. He swept me up into his arms in a great big bear hug which to him probably meant nothing but nonetheless, weary as I was, set my heart racing.

'Callum. I thought you'd forgotten me.'

'I could never forget you, Gemma.' His eyes locked into mine as if looking deep into my soul, but there was something not quite real about it. He was just flirting with me again. I didn't want to have to deal with that right now so I pulled my gaze away.

'You're late!' I sounded peevish and I didn't care. He looked at me again, this time noticing just how tired I was. His voice changed. 'I'm sorry. I was held up. A phone call. Come on. Let's get you to the hotel before you fall asleep on your feet.'

He picked up my case and led me out to his car, a tatty station wagon that had seen much better days, where he threw the case unceremoniously in the back. With a squeal of something mechanical that sounded far from healthy he dovetailed the station wagon into the neon lit stream of traffic that flowed almost constantly to and from the airport, and put his foot to the floor.

* * * * *

I woke late the next morning to the sun streaming in my window. Just like at home I hadn't bothered pulling the curtains, preferring to see the sky and the stars. It took me a second or so to remember where I was, and when I did I lay for a minute or two luxuriating in the comfort of the massive king sized bed, dreaming of the adventures that might lie ahead. Excitement started to bubble up inside me. OK, I admit it. I headed into Indiana Jones territory a bit, allowing myself to get carried away with my imaginings. So what? The reality was that I was about to head out into the desert on a treasure hunt for a mythical sacred power object in the company of a charismatic renegade archaeologist and his maverick crew. If that wasn't Indiana Jones-y, I don't know what would be.

If I'm honest, a big part of me still thought Callum was chasing smoke trails. Despite the notebook and the Scandinavian find, the possibility of us finding something tangible was a notion I still couldn't take on board. It was just too implausible. The phone ringing pulled me from my thoughts. It was Callum.

'Morning, sleeping beauty. Ready for our adventure?'

'Morning, Callum. Absolutely. Once I've had some breakfast that is, I'm ravenous.' I'd been so tired the previous night I'd turned down Callum's offer of dinner and fallen straight into bed.

'See you downstairs for breakfast then in ten minutes?'

'Make it twenty.' Neither had I showered before collapsing into a deep and dreamless sleep.

Twenty minutes later, further revived by the pummelling hot jets of the power shower and a clean set of clothes, I met Callum in the breakfast lounge. Over some really good coffee, and equally good pancakes and maple syrup – I was beginning to love this country – Callum filled me in on the plans. At least I thought he had. I later came to realise that he left out certain important details that he thought might put me off. Sitting there in the motel on the verge of an adventure, sharing breakfast with Callum, listening to him speak about the adventure ahead, still part of my mind was away with the fairies, dreaming about how lovely it would be to do this more often, perhaps in a more intimate way. For goodness sake woman, I scolded myself, give it a rest.

As we walked out of the cool air-conditioned comfort of the hotel a wall of heat hit me. I think I might have gasped at the shock. It was like walking into an oven. Callum had let me sleep late so by the time we left it was heading towards eleven o'clock in the morning. The dashboard read-out put the outside temperature at 92°f (which I eventually worked out to be the mid-30s centigrade, phew!), and it was only going to get hotter. I was, both literally and figuratively, a half a world away from the damp, chilly late English summer I had left behind.

We were heading north out of Phoenix towards Page and Lake Powell, where we would meet up with the other members of his team and finalise the plans. Callum refused point blank to discuss them with me any further during the drive, telling me it was only fair that everyone should be in on it together. I was disappointed but he would not be persuaded, so we talked instead about the notebook he had found. He had left it in Page with the rest of his gear, and promised to show it to me as soon as we arrived at the motel, a promise I would not let him back out of. We had at least a good four or five hours drive ahead of us and after a couple of hours our conversation petered out into a comfortable silence.

I was fascinated by the constantly changing landscape around me. North of Phoenix the flat desert plains stretched away into the distance, dotted all over with the upright arms of tall saguaro cacti standing sentinel. They looked for all the world like a set from one of the old cowboy films that I used to watch with my dad on a Saturday afternoon when I was little. The sky was an improbably blue blue, its colour intensified by the station wagon's tinted windows. Beyond the cactus plains, way off in the distance, rose up a purple-tinged mountain range through which the interstate highway switch-backed up to Flagstaff before it entered a vista of dry scrubby desert plain once more. The station wagon's dodgy air-conditioning system kept the interior only a few degrees cooler than outside; it was very warm. Together with the steady hum of the engine it was lulling me into a pleasant state of drowsiness. Though half-closed eyelids I watched Callum's hands moving on the wheel. They were strong, sun-tanned. Capable was the word that came to me. His fingers were long and sinewy, the hands of a craftsman. I watched them caress the wheel, wondering if they would ever caress me in the same way...

'Not far now, Gemma.'

I came to with a start, heat flooding my face as his words brought me back from a far from innocent reverie. Had he noticed? Thankfully, it appeared not. Careful Gemma, I warned myself, you're going to have to keep a close watch on those wayward thoughts if you aren't going to get caught out. I sat up straighter in my seat and looked properly out of the windows. We were still crossing what seemed to be empty desert. Would I ever get used to these vast expanses of wilderness?

CHAPTER 31

The motel in Page was smaller and less luxurious than the one in Phoenix but I liked it. It had character. The bedrooms were quirky and the lounge was decorated with all sorts of local knick-knacks and memorabilia.

The other members of the team were out when we arrived so after another quick shower – the drive had been extremely hot and dusty – I met up with Callum in the lounge. As I walked in my heart did a quick double beat, not for a change at the sight of Callum, but because of what he was holding in his hand. It was small, dog-eared notebook, bound in worn blue leather. Neither of us spoke as he handed it to me; I sank into one of the huge, squishy armchairs to read it. An hour later I surfaced, tears streaming down my face, eyes red and swollen. Reading it direct in James Matthews' own handwriting was even more emotionally powerful than when Callum had quoted it to me on that previous occasion.

'Did this sort of thing happen often?'

'Too often.' Callum replied, his face set. 'Some are well-documented, like Sand Creek, or Wounded Knee. A great many more went unreported. That's not to say it was all one way. The native Americans did their fair share of slaughter but they were usually fighting for survival, for their lives and land and way of life, not just out of greed and a hunger for domination.'

Callum was clearly fired up about the subject and I was all set to ask him more when a cheerful hello interrupted us. The two other team members, who Callum introduced as Frankie and Davey, had returned.

'Well? Did we get the permit?' Frankie was almost dancing with expectation.

'Yes, though not until yesterday evening. I was beginning to wonder if we ever would.'

Callum turned to me. 'That's why I was late picking you up. We were waiting on official authorisation to head into the wilderness lands. The call came just as I was leaving the hotel to come and meet you. Honestly Gemma, you have no idea of the hoops I have had to jump through to get this expedition off the ground. Hey, no matter. We're all systems go.'

'Yes!' Frankie punched the air in delight and did a little dance. I liked her immediately. She was natural, open, and totally herself.

'So when do we go?' Davey was quiet and reserved, a complete contrast to the extrovert Frankie. Nevertheless, he couldn't keep the excitement from his voice.

'We head out first thing tomorrow morning. There is one condition. Well, to be honest there's a whole pile of conditions, but one will affect us all most directly. We're going to be heading into a sensitive environment, both ecologically and culturally. This might not be a reservation, even so we are invading ancient tribal lands that the local population still consider sacred. In order to keep everyone happy we can't take motorised vehicles in. We'll have to go in on horseback. They also want us to be accompanied by a local guide, so I've asked Ches Whitecloud if he'll come with us.'

'Horses?' Did that mean what I thought it did? I looked at Callum, horror struck. 'Horses? You never said anything about horses.' Callum saw the look on my face and banged the heel of his hand against his forehead in frustration at himself.

'Oh hell! I never thought to ask. Please… don't tell me you don't ride, Gemma.' I could only shake my head. No words would come out. The only riding I'd ever done was a few beach donkey rides during childhood holidays. Sitting here now, that seemed a million years ago. Callum considered it for a moment then shrugged his shoulders 'Never mind, you'll soon pick it up.' That was it? That was his answer to the situation? I wasn't happy and I said so in no uncertain terms.

Frankie glared at him and leaned across to squeeze my hand. 'Don't worry, Gemma. We'll make sure you get a really quiet, well-behaved horse. It's not difficult. Really. You just have to sit and let it carry you.' She winced. 'Although your butt may think differently after a day in the saddle.'

Great! But there really wasn't much I could do about it. Either I climbed up on a horse and got on with it, or I stayed behind. After travelling almost half way across the world to get here, staying behind was most definitely *not* an option.

While I was mentally gearing myself up for the next day's challenge the conversation moved on. Callum had spread a large map out on the floor between the chairs and Davey was already on his knees studying it closely.

'Gemma, come look where we're going.'

I shook my head. I wasn't sulking from the horse business. It was simply that, oddly, I didn't want to know. I was eager to go with them but was filled with a strong, inexplicable reluctance to learn any of the details. Callum shrugged again and turned back to the map.

While the others were discussing the details, most of which were going right over my head, I took the chance to study Frankie and Davey more closely. Frankie I had already warmed to. She had an infectious, friendly energy about her that was irresistible. She was also gorgeous: young, maybe in her late twenties, with a figure I could have ever only dreamed of even if I had been twenty years younger. Her jade green eyes continually twinkled with laughter and she wore her deep brown hair up in a high ponytail that showed off her model features perfectly. Yes, I liked her a lot even if, heading rapidly towards middle age as I was, I couldn't help feeling a pang of envy at her looks.

I took to Davey straight away too. He was small and slightly built with that nondescript appearance that doesn't create a second glance. Personality-wise he was the polar opposite to Frankie. He had a quiet, studious air and carried with him a calm serenity that I found soothing and reassuring. I was glad he was in the group. I had the feeling that he would be a welcome calming influence during the days ahead. In the conversation that was going on around me he was the perfect foil to Frankie's exuberance.

Davey was the second-in-command archaeologist in the group after Callum. Frankie, she would tell me later, was not only an archaeologist, she was also the group's metaphysical researcher (she called herself a 'truth seeker'.) What is more, I would learn that Frankie possessed an encyclopaedic knowledge of all things mystical, mythical and mysterious. I got the feeling the three of them together formed a great combination. I couldn't help wondering, with all their expertise, what on earth I was doing here with them.

'There's one other thing. Gemma, you should hear this too.' Callum's words broke through my drifting reverie. He sounded irritated for some reason. 'We have a new team member.' He held up his hand to stave off the inevitable questions. 'No, I'm not happy about it either but we haven't got any say in the matter. The people that are funding this project are insisting he comes along, otherwise it isn't going to happen. Before you ask, I don't know anything about him except his name, Jack Milner, and that he's also an archaeologist. He'll be meeting up with us at the ranch tomorrow.'

He stood up and stretched. 'OK. I suggest we hit the sack. We'll be leaving here at five thirty in the morning to pick up the horses at noon, and we have some long days ahead of us.'

Needless to say, irrespective of the early start I didn't sleep much that night.

CHAPTER 32

When we set off the next morning I was overjoyed to discover I would be accompanying Frankie in her almost new Mitsubishi Warrior, not least because it was quiet and comfortable and the air-conditioning worked perfectly. It would also give me the chance to get to know her better, something I was really eager to do. Davey and Callum were following on behind in Callum's considerably less luxurious station wagon.

Frankie was great company and we quickly cemented our new friendship. She knew the area well and was a mine of information. 'I did my doctorate in this region,' she explained, 'a study of the ancient and vanished civilisations that once lived here.' As we drove past empty settlements – ghost towns I suppose you'd call them – and long deserted ruined stone buildings perched vertiginously on the edge of the cliff tops or even in the cliff sides themselves, inaccessible to all but the most agile of mountain goats, Frankie gave me a history lesson.

'The history of this whole area is fascinating.' I could hear the passion in her voice. 'The people who once lived here – no-one really knows who they were or where they came from. We don't know where they went either, only that at some point they abandoned their homes and settlements and apparently vanished into thin air.' She smiled across at me. The topic was obviously dear to her heart and she was enjoying sharing her knowledge of it. 'From what we can discover they were a pretty sophisticated society of farmers, hunters and traders, but we don't know much. They didn't leave us many clues, just odd bits of pottery and a few other bits and pieces. What amazes me is that they didn't just live in these inhospitable places, they seem to have thrived here.'

As we drove Frankie continued her story, telling me how many of these ancient peoples built their homes high up in the cliffs or on the top of inaccessible peaks. At one point the road wound through a series of canyons and she pointed out ruins to me as we passed, slowing the Mitsubishi so I could get a better idea of what she was talking about. From what I could see, these people must have spent their lives clambering up and down impossible pathways on sheer cliff faces. Frankie was a master storyteller with a wonderful way of making it all come alive and time flew by.

Soon we were travelling across the flat, dry desert plateau once again. I had no idea which direction we were heading in and didn't feel the need to ask. I simply watched the ever-changing landscape unfold in front of us. I was awestruck, as I had been the previous day, by the endless empty expanses of nothingness. Back in the UK everything is, really, pretty much on top of everything else. Out here, the vast tracts of dry scrubby desert seem to go on forever, only dotted here and there with a few tiny run down settlements or the occasional ramshackle homestead.

As Frankie drove I grilled her about Callum, for whom she obviously had a great deal of respect and admiration. I thought I was being subtle. It soon became evident I was being about as subtle as a brick. She slowed the car and turned to look at me, her usually humour-filled eyes serious.

'Callum is a charming, charismatic man, Gemma, and he's clearly caught you in his spell. Take it from me, it's not a good place to be. I know you probably won't take a blind bit of notice at what I'm telling you but I'm going to say it anyway. Don't go there. Don't let him reel you in any further. Callum is a great guy. I think the world of him. But when it comes to relationships? Seriously, he sucks! He just doesn't get them.' She frowned. 'I know what he's like. I've worked with him for six years and I've seen it happen too many times before. He doesn't do it on purpose, but there is always someone new who comes along and catches his eye and he can't say no. It's never him that gets hurt though.'

My face must have given me away because she sighed and turned her attention back to the road. 'OK, but don't say I didn't warn you.'

We drove on in silence for a while, my thoughts too uncomfortable for me to want to talk. I wasn't cross at Frankie, I was cross at myself. Because although I didn't want to admit it, I knew she was right. I had felt it from the beginning, that sense that he would be dangerous to know, that to get involved with him would be playing with fire. The certainty that if I did, I would get burned. The sensible route to self-preservation would be to build the barriers up between us and to keep him at arms' length, both physically and emotionally. What really irritated me was that I knew it wouldn't happen. I was too far gone. The right word, the right touch from him and any resolve I had built up would melt away as quickly as snow under this torrid desert sun.

I had no doubt that it would happen. Callum may have been busy since he picked me up at the airport, his mind filled with the impending expedition, but the glances he continually threw in my direction left me in no doubt as to his intentions. It irritated me that I wanted him too, badly. Keeping him at bay, resisting his approaches as well as my own desires would be exhausting. Sooner or later, I would give in.

GOR-KUAL: The Red Skull

Part II

LEAVING ATLANTIS, 2

CHAPTER 33

They had travelled far together, that small group of Atlanteans who had boarded the ship so many nights ago in Dendarak. Just a few moments earlier they had been put ashore in a small rocky bay that was heavy with seaweed and pounded by the ocean breakers, and they now stood huddled and uncertain under a grey, cloud-tossed sky as the wind blasted the breath from their lungs and carried it away along the shore. They were alone in a new world, unfamiliar to any of them, on the very edge of a continent that would one day, far in the future, be called Europe. They did not know if this place was inhabited, and if it was whether those who lived there were friendly or hostile. Did not know what obstacles to their path the terrain would present to them, or what other potentially mortal challenges they would face. Did not know their destination. In truth, they did not have one.

It did not matter. All who had stepped down onto that desolate wind-torn shore were prepared. What lay ahead could not, they believed, be any worse than the slow suffocation of the life-breath of Atlantis at the hands of the Dark Ones. They watched in silence as the ship sailed away, their eyes tracking her sleek lines as she ploughed through the leaden waters until she shrank to a tiny dot in a massive sea. There was no rush. There was nowhere they had to be.

Each man and woman who stood on that beach and watched their lifeline disappear was filled with anxiety at what the future would hold. Yet not one of them would have chosen differently. When finally the ship vanished over the horizon, as one they turned and began their long trek into the unknown. In that moment none but the two refugee priests were aware that accompanying them they had two of the greatest gifts and allies they could have wished for – the sacred skulls: Gor-Kual, in the care of Jar-Kan, and Maat-su, whom Kua'tzal carried with him.

Two days later that situation changed. To Kuat'zal's surprise and reluctance, Maat-su requested that he reveal her presence to the group though she did not give him her reasons. His apprehension was warranted. Initial open-mouthed disbelief was quickly followed by deep anger, born of a very real fear that the Dark Ones would follow them and hunt them down in their hunger to acquire the skull for themselves. It was only when Maat-su herself spoke to the group, her soft voice filling their minds, that they quietened and were reassured. She would lead them to a new home, she promised them, a place of safe refuge, of plentiful water and fertile soil where they would thrive and grow. It would be a place of powerful, beneficial energies, where they would build a society that would encompass all the blessings of Atlantis. And so she did. But that is Maat-su's story, to be recounted at another time and in another place.

By contrast, Gor-Kual's presence was not to be revealed; she had made that clear to Jar-Kan even before they had made landfall. His journey, his destiny, was to be different to that of the others. While together now with the larger group, who would remain a tightly bonded unit under the guidance of the skull Maat-su, at some point in the future their paths would separate and Jar-Kan would once again forge his own trail. That though was still far ahead of him. For now he had companionship, people to walk with, and talk with, and laugh with. Friends with whom he could share the challenges of this new life.

*   *   *   *   *

Over the course of the ocean voyage – nineteen long days with little to do but gaze at the horizon, get to know their travelling companions and contemplate the unknown and likely perilous road ahead – the two men forged a firm friendship. For hours each day they sat and talked, perched at the bow of the ship as it ploughed through the ocean to its distant destination.

Jar-Kan's suspicions of his fellow priest were soon put to rest as Kuat'zal shared with him the reasons behind his actions. Kuat'zal had explained how he had been asked to assume the role he had played, how he had met the request with reluctance but had in the end agreed to it because he had recognised its importance. His task had been to get close to the Shadow Chasers, earn their trust by convincing them his sympathies lay in their cause. It had been a plan condoned, if not actually orchestrated, by the senior priests of Yo'tlàn. No wonder Omar would not censure the rebel. Kuat'zal had been acting with his blessing.

Jar-Kan could scarcely imagine what this courageous act had cost his new friend, who had been ostracised and cold-shouldered by virtually every other priest and priestess in the temple, including himself. He felt a wave of guilt surge through him – he had judged this man without knowing the facts, and he had judged wrongly. It must have been a difficult and draining life to live, never able to let his mask slip or a hint of the truth escape.

Over the years it had taken its toll, that was evident in Kuat'zal's hunched posture and tense, lined face, old before its time. As the days passed however, and he was able to at last share his long held private burden, the real Kuat'zal began to emerge from behind the carefully constructed alter ego. The smiling, gentle man who little by little appeared was a far cry from the hard-faced, taciturn Kuat'zal who had previously stalked the corridors of the Pyramid Temple.

When they could not be overheard, the two men reminisced about the temple and the quiet, peaceful life they had left behind. Kuat'zal would speak of the Dark Ones and the threat that they posed. Much of what he shared was privileged information known to only very few, information acquired during his meetings with the Shadow Chasers. They would discuss in whispers how the Shadow Chasers' devastating ambitions would affect their beloved homeland, and speculate on the fury those same Shadow Chasers would have unleashed now that they would have discovered they had been thwarted in their plans to seize the power of the skulls for themselves. For fury there would have been. It was unlikely that anyone in the temple at that moment, whether priest or innocent visitor, would have been spared.

Jar-Kan and Kuat'zal could not have anticipated the extent of that fury, which far surpassed anything that anyone could have been foreseen. The Shadow Chasers had not only taken away everyone unlucky enough to have been in the temple at the time but had also destroyed the skull chamber itself, smashing to shards the crystal plinth and cluster that had held the Master skull when they found her missing. It was an act of vandalism whose deep-rooted ramifications were not immediately evident. Only much later would they show the full extent of their devastating consequences.

Eight days into their sea crossing Jar-Kan and his companions would experience for themselves a forerunner to those future cataclysmic events.

*   *   *   *   *

It was a beautiful afternoon with clear blue skies and not a breath of wind. The sea was like glass, barely a ripple breaking its surface. The ship had resorted to engine power to make headway, her sails useless in the calm conditions. The crystal powered engines ran silently; no noise other than the swish of the bow through the sea intruded into the idyllic scene. Passengers and crew alike were enjoying the opportunity to relax as the ship moved swiftly through the clear waters.

It came upon them with little warning. The first indication that anything was wrong was the frightened, incredulous shout from the look-out on the bridge who was pointing back over the stern towards the horizon, the direction from which they had come. Her sharp eyes had spotted something unusual and terrifying.

The inexperienced passengers could see nothing. The crew however recognised the danger immediately and leapt into action, ordering the passengers below with instructions to rope themselves to anything that was firmly fixed to the hull and bulkheads. They paid no attention, standing gazing out over the sea, seeing no danger.

Until it was there, suddenly, unmissably, looming up in front of them, an immense wall of water hurtling towards the ship, dwarfing it in its shadow. The giant swell was still some distance away but even now it was huge, and closing rapidly. As one mind the Atlanteans ran then, seeking refuge below, hurrying to do as the crew had ordered only seconds before.

The wave, a smooth flowing mountain almost a hundred feet high, was racing silently and menacingly towards the ship, towering ever higher above them, dwarfing them in its shadow. Although it wasn't breaking it looked as if at any moment it would topple over and crush everything beneath. The captain and his crew roped themselves to the bridge from where they battled to turn the ship head on into the sea surge. If they hit it any other way the ship would capsize and sink to the dark ocean depths, carrying everyone on board with her. They only had one chance, and by Sirius it was a remote one, but it was their only one. If they could ride this wave...

Jar-Kan was the last passenger to leave the deck. As he turned to slam the hatch shut behind him he saw the sky turn a dark, dense, menacing green. The sea had risen up in front of him to fill it. He darted into the cabin, grabbed a sheet from his bed and, wrapping it around himself several times, secured it firmly to the metal stays of his bunk.

When the wave came, it hit them with all the violence and uproar of an apocalypse. The ship floundered and tossed in the onslaught, its decks flooded. At one point she disappeared completely, lost under the crest, and those on the bridge, who found themselves submerged in the cold watery tomb, believed it was all over. Moments later she burst through the other side of the wave. She was being shaken like a child's rattle in a tantrum. Inside, even firmly secured fixtures came crashing down, loosened by the battering.

Then, in a moment, the ship settled and the world around them fell suddenly and eerily still, the only sound that of a child crying. It did not last. Before anyone could make a move to unfasten themselves, the nightmare began again. The bow of the ship reared up until it seemed like it must topple back over on itself, only to crash forward and down the other side of the swell like a seabird diving for fish.

Three times in all the sturdy ship survived the ocean's assault, testament to the skill and dedication both of those who built her and of those who stood that day in the face of hell and guided her through it. When it was over, those on board crept out barely able to believe that they were still alive. The ship's superstructure was badly damaged but repairable. Miraculously those on board had come through the ordeal more or less unscathed; cuts, bruises and a couple of minor fractures were the only legacy of what had occurred.

Terrifying though it was for those caught up in it, this was only a glimpse of the events that were to befall Atlantis in the months and years ahead. It was a fate no-one could have predicted.

$*$ $*$ $*$ $*$ $*$

They had come a long way and would travel the same again many times over before they reached their promised land. The travellers did not overreach themselves, keeping to an easy pace. There was as much time as they wanted and there was little point in exhausting themselves when it was not necessary, for while the skulls may have known the ultimate destination, the humans still did not. It was possible that they could be travelling their entire lifetime, and they were determined to enjoy the journey.

Day followed day followed day as they walked. The long light hours of mid-summer that had met them when they had arrived in this place were rapidly growing shorter. Mornings often greeted them with a cool mist that smelled of damp leaves. The equinox was approaching. Sometimes they stopped and rested for several days, making camp in a pleasant spot, always knowing they would be going on. Their journey's end would be far from this gentle land of woodlands, rivers and abundant supplies of fruit, roots and game. Where this understanding came from, they did not question, simply accepting it, for all trusted in Maat-su implicitly.

This was more than a journey to a destination, this was their life, at least for now, and they were making the best of every moment of it. Jar-Kan especially drank it all in with the hunger of a scholar: the unfamiliar plants and creatures he encountered, the new and unfamiliar energies that ran through the earth below his feet here, so different from those he had studied in Atlantis. Also, in a strange yet exhilarating way, the freedom from the restrictions of his life in the temple, restrictions he had willingly embraced but that nonetheless at times frustrated him. He was happy and at peace as he accompanied his friends, so often forgetting about the future. Autumn turned to winter, winter to the first signs of spring. Still they went on. But it would not last forever.

CHAPTER 34

Jar-Kan was alone again in this land, or maybe it was a continent, that was in many ways still so strange and unknown to him. He was in the most beautiful of landscapes, surrounded by gentle wooded valleys in the crook of which crystal clear streams chuckled and gurgled over their stony beds. A soft, reassuring scent of damp earth and newly leafed vegetation surrounded him as he walked, and from time to time the rich perfume of some unrecognised flowering shrub embraced his senses. It was spring here and the world around him felt fresh, vibrant and new. In spite of his anxiety he felt fresh and alive himself.

The others were heading east. The previous night Gor-Kual had indicated strongly that from here on his route was to the south. Was it wise to separate? Jar-Kan didn't think so. It didn't feel wise. But Gor-Kual had been very clear, as had Maat-su for her group; it was time for each to follow his own destiny. Both he and Kua'tzal had known this day would come, had to come, so it was that, despite the misgivings of all and their sadness at parting after so much time together, they had only two hours ago gone their separate ways.

Jar-Kan took a final glance over his left shoulder. His former travelling companions, all of them by now dear friends, were just disappearing over the crest of a distant hill. As he watched, one of them – he couldn't see who from this far away – threw an arm in the air and waved a final farewell. He fought down a growing wave of apprehension that threatened for a moment to engulf him. He really was alone now. No, he quickly corrected himself, he had his knowledge of the natural world, and more importantly he had Gor-Kual. A man could have no better travelling companion.

*　　*　　*　　*　　*

That night Jar-Kan made camp on the bank of a small stream that meandered across the middle of a wide grassy valley, a rare open space in this heavily wooded landscape. Gor-Kual was tucked safely in his pack and the night was warm and scented. He began to feel a little more relaxed, allowing himself to enjoy the pleasures of his situation. Wrapping himself in his blanket, he fell into a deep sleep.

His eyes flew open. Something was prowling around within feet of where he lay. Not a human. He could smell an overpowering odour of animal, the unmistakeable reek of a carnivore. He lay unmoving, reaching out with his senses to try and pick up more information. It was big. It was hungry. But it was also confused. This thing on the floor - was it her next meal, or wasn't it? If it was a meal, and it certainly smelled like a meal, why didn't it move? Her prey always ran when it picked up her scent. That way she knew her food was fresh.

Could Jar-Kan communicate with the creature? It would be a risk. If it misfired, as it could if the contact scared it, he would be filling her belly for the next few days.

'It is no threat. Do nothing.' Gor-Kual's words whispered in his mind.

Jar-Kan remained motionless, scarcely daring to breathe as the beast sniffed and snuffled around, occasionally snatching at his clothes with her teeth as if seeking to goad him into movement. In the face of an overwhelming desire to run, the priest somehow succeeded in holding his courage.

Jar-Kan let out his breath in a slow, silent whistle. The beast had at last moved off. His stillness had confused her. To his great fortune she had been a pure hunter rather than a scavenger, and had left what had appeared to it to be another animal's kill. It had been a close thing though, a warning that in the seemingly benign land he was moving through danger still lurked and could come upon him at any time. From now on he would be on his guard, would set up an energetic safety barrier around himself before he slept. Why though had Gor-Kual not warned him? It was a question to which no answer was forthcoming.

*   *   *   *   *

As the days passed, days he lost count of – and really there was no point in counting, it would serve no purpose – the landscape around him changed. He was climbing gradually higher; he could sense it in the thinner air and cooler temperatures. The verdant wooded valleys slipped into high rolling hills, thick with forest, which in turn gave way to open meadows and grasslands as he left the treeline behind. Although food and water was harder to find here he always had enough, thanks to his knowledge of the natural world and the intuitive powers that led him to what he needed. In the rare occasions these failed to bring results, Gor-Kual was always there to guide him.

In spite of the apparent idyll Jar-Kan was nevertheless unable to rid himself of the sensation that something was wrong. In all his days and months of travelling alone he never came across another person and he began to wonder why. Throughout the first part of their journey through this land his group had regularly encountered first small villages. Later they had frequently crossed the path of small bands of nomads or individual travellers. Since they had parted company he had seen no-one. On a couple of occasions he had come across a pile of sun bleached human bones – a man or woman, overtaken by sudden death as they journeyed – but not a living soul. What was going on? Why was this land deserted? The question began to burn in his mind but no answer came, and Gor-Kual did not enlighten him.

CHAPTER 35

There it was again, a strange, high-pitched whimpering cry. What animal made that kind of sound? It had to be in pain, the distress in the cry was unmistakeable. Yet... The more he listened, the more Jar-Kan heard the human in the cry: pitifully, hopelessly human – confused, bewildered, frightened, and a whole lot more. And young! Suddenly the understanding flowed through him. This was a child's cry, a young child at that.

He had heard the sound some while before and in its faintness had at first dismissed it. As it had continued, unceasing, so his curiosity had been awakened and he had turned to the direction from which it came, his feet leading him almost unconsciously to seek its source. With his new understanding his steps were now filled with an urgency that had not been there seconds before, becoming faster and faster until he broke into a run, only stopping briefly from time to time to get his bearings on the cry.

It was a few moments before Jar-Kan realised that he had gone too far. The sound, which up until a few paces previously had been ahead of him, now came from just behind him. He had missed it. Slowly he retraced his route, peering behind every rock and bush. There, behind that bank. He followed it round.

The underside of the bank had fallen away leaving a niche, like an earthen cave. In its shadows, staring up at him with wide, blue eyes sat a child, barely more than a babe in arms really, her face grubby and tearstained and smeared with the contents of her nose. She was naked, as most children he had met had been, and filthy from top to toe. He looked at her with surprise and horror. This infant could barely be walking. What was she doing alone out here in the middle of this wilderness? A moment later he saw it, further back under the bank: a leg, an adult leg – a woman's leg – cold, grey, unmoving.

He stepped closer and allowed his eyes to accustom to the gloom of the shadowy recess. A young woman, or rather what was left of a young woman, lay there, life long deserted. He felt the contents of his stomach rise as he stared down at her bloated corpse. She would have once been beautiful, he could tell that even now, but the ravages of whatever illness had claimed her, together with the decay of death, had turned her body into an obscene parody of its former self. A tunic of ragged, badly cured animal skin continued to spare her modesty. Her limbs, grey and swollen in death, were covered in mottled bruises of yellowing purple, fingers grotesquely clawed in her final spasms, her staring vacant eyes ringed dark. He swallowed hard and turned away. He could do nothing for her.

And the child? What of the child? Was she already incubating the disease that had killed her mother? He looked down at the infant. She was gazing up at him, her tears drying, her wide baby eyes trusting. He could not leave her. He would not leave her, even if he was risking his own life in taking her with him. Jar-Kan knelt and opened his arms to her. She tottered to her feet, arms out reaching to him, asking with her gesture that he take her in his own. He did so, holding her tightly and reassuringly, and as she snuggled down trustingly against his chest, seeking the comfort and security of his closeness, his heart melted at her innocence and vulnerability. In that moment he fell completely and irretrievably in love with his tiny charge. He was committed, and whatever would come of it, would come.

*   *   *   *   *

Over the lower slopes of the hillside in front of him were scattered around a dozen crudely built huts. They looked to be constructed of a rough framework of wooden poles – branches and the stems of young saplings mostly – covered in layer of mud that had probably been collected from the bed of the river he had just waded across. There was no sign of life.

In Jar-Kan's arms the child, whom he had named Nuala, slept soundly, nestled in as if she wanted to become a part of him. Her breath tickled his chest. Two days had passed since he had chanced upon her; to his relief there was still no sign of the fever in her. Jar-Kan was beginning to allow himself to hope.

'Ho!' he called in greeting as he drew nearer. Only silence answered him. He was uneasy. Something wasn't right. Was he walking into a trap? The next breath of the breeze told him otherwise. It carried the sweet, sickly odour of death, of rotting bodies and decaying flesh. Instinct told him to turn away, to leave without going further. Something stronger pulled him on. He needed to know.

The child still slept in peaceful oblivion, though even in slumber she buried her face deeper into his cloak, seeking to block out the stench.

The first body lay just inside the circle of huts, lying where it had fallen, too weak to find shelter before death claimed it. Then another, then another: men, women, children, elders and infants. He counted twenty in all lying in the open, each bearing the dark purplish yellow mottling on the flesh that remained. Carrion birds wheeled overhead and from within some of the huts, deep growls warned him of scavengers doing their work. Jar-Kan was sickened to his stomach. Why had he not just passed right on by? What had compelled him to enter the village itself? He did not know, but it was time to leave. Was this then the reason why he had not seen another living soul in months until he had stumbled upon Nuala two days previously? A plague that hid like a poison beneath the surface of this beautiful land?

It was not a place to linger. He had seen enough. He had seen too much, his churning stomach was making that clear. Why had he felt so compelled to enter this village? As he hurried out of the village Jar-Kan increased his pace even more. The sooner he was well away from this accursed spot, the better.

CHAPTER 36

Jar-Kan's heart was racing. No. Please, no. He looked down at Nuala as he cradled her in his arms, rocking her gently in an attempt to comfort her. She had become restless the previous evening and throughout the night had grown more and more feverish. Jar-Kan had used all the skill he possessed but it had made no difference. Now, in the first light of a new day, his worst fears had come to pass. A bruise-like mottling had appeared on Nuala's tiny leg and was spreading, darkening, as each hour passed.

Please, no. Jar-Kan loved the child as his own though she had been with him only a few days. He could hardly bear the feeling of hopelessness that filled him as he cradled her tiny, fever wracked body. This had always been the probable outcome, the thought had been with him constantly since that first day, but he had refused to allow himself to dwell on it. Now that the reality was upon him it felt like his heart was being ripped apart.

'Gor-Kual,' he pleaded. 'Help her. Make her well again.'

'I cannot.' He could hear the compassion in the red skull's words. 'I cannot.' She would say no more.

Jar-Kan sat all day nursing the child, praying, hoping, pleading with he knew not who that she live.

Holding her tightly when she shivered so fiercely that it seemed her bones must shatter, cooling her with a rag dipped in water when fever turned her skin to fire, soothing her when she whimpered in her pain and distress. All the while, her blue eyes, huge in that pale little face, gazed up at him in total trust, a trust that tore him apart as he looked back down at her, knowing that he could not meet it, knowing that he could not save her.

And then, in a moment, so quickly that he hardly saw it happen, she was gone, the light in those baby eyes extinguished as if someone had simply blown out a candle flame. Emptiness took its place. A heavy, hurting, heart-wrenching emptiness that ripped Jar-Kan's soul from his body. The trembling stilled. The whimpers stilled. And through his tunic, Jar-Kan felt the moment the tiny, weak, fluttering heartbeat also stilled. Time stopped then as the tears came and Jar-Kan wept. Wept for this child who would never now grow up, would never live a life. Wept for the love that had so recently exploded within his heart only to be stolen from him too soon. Wept too for his own deep loneliness and sense of mortality.

He did not know how long he sat there cradling the tiny, lifeless body of the soul that had so deeply touched his own, but as he finally set the last stone on top of the small mound that covered Nuala's corpse he raised his head to see the sun starting to sink in the sky. In that moment he understood clearly that it would not be long before his own body joined that of Nuala, her mother and those other villagers on the open grasslands of these high plains. In his grief the voice of Gor-Kual whispered to him. 'Be at peace, my dearest friend. Be at peace.'

*   *   *   *   *

Jar-Kan shivered violently despite the warmth of the mid-summer sun that hung like a golden disc in the clear blue sky above him. At the same time sweat poured from his skin soaking his clothes, and his shivering intensified. This was it then, the fate he had known would sooner or later claim him. He clenched his teeth against the tremors and they rattled in his skull as he forced his unresponsive legs to move. He would not get much further, he could not, but as long as he was able to place one foot in front of the other he would not stop. His destination could be just around the next bend in the river, or just over the crest of the next hill. If he stopped before he could physically go no further he could fail within yards of success.

He did not know where he was heading, having long ago been assured that he would recognise it when he arrived. Poor comfort now when that arrival looked far from certain. Yet still Gor-Kual was at his side, guiding him ever onwards. When the sickness had come upon him five days earlier he had known its inevitable outcome. As had she.

'My dearest friend,' she had whispered, 'you condemned yourself the moment you sought out that cry. And yet what else could you have done? I will help you as much as I can, give you as all the strength that is within my power to give, but even I cannot change what will be.'

She had been as good as her word, filling him with her strength and the courage to go on when others would have curled up and waited resignedly for death. He should not by rights have made it to his feet that morning, yet somehow he had hauled himself upright and staggered on. His arms and legs were now covered in the tell-tale purple-yellow mottling, his face puffy, his eyes bloodshot. Only Gor-Kual was keeping him alive, and even she could not stave off death indefinitely.

As the day progressed, Jar-Kan's progress slowed even more. He was barely moving forward, shuffling on deadened feet only inches with every step. He constantly stumbled, shredding his palms and knees on the rough ground until they were a bloodied mass of raw flesh.

He fell once more. Sprawled on the ground, in desperation he fumbled in his pack and drew out Gor-Kual. His eyes locked onto her, unfocussed, wavering, pleading. 'Please,' he begged, his voice no more than a harsh whisper, 'no more.'

She took pity on him then. No sooner had the words issued from his cracked, blistered lips than she withdrew her energy from him and he slumped forwards to the ground, his last breath rasping from his lungs as his body shuddered in its final spasm.

As Jar-Kan's fingers relaxed in death, Gor-Kual rolled from his grasp and tumbled down the slope he had so painfully just crawled up. There she lay, exposed and vulnerable on the open grasslands, gazing up at the sky as she reached out across the emptiness of space in a call for help to those distant worlds from where she had come, so long ago. On this world, Jar-Kan's no longer seeing eyes still remained fixed upon her as if watching over her, even in death.

And so they lay, the skull and her guardian, one waiting for rescue, the other now far beyond its help.

*   *   *   *   *

The two strangers who walked over the grassy hillside towards where Jar-Kan lay came unnoticed by anyone. There was no-one left to notice. All who had once lived and thrived in this land were now dead, victims of the same disease that had claimed the priest. Not one remained.

They approached Jar-Kan's body with sadness in their hearts, a sadness that was reflected in their huge, dark eyes. They were odd looking people and, had there been anyone to observe them, they would have been seen as something other than human, which indeed they were. These were Arcturians, one male, one female, originating from far across the galaxy, come here to rescue Gor-Kual. They were humanoid in form but the differences were clear. These star travellers were small, the size of perhaps a ten year old child, with pale ivory skin and large, dark eyes. No hair grew on their slender bodies, which were clothed in a snugly fitting tunic and trousers of a soft, metallic fabric whose subtle hues changed colour with every movement. Around them glowed a golden haze that emphasised their silhouette. This was a defensive light shield, set in place to protect them from the virulent virus that had already claimed so many helpless lives.

Above them that night in the star-crowded sky, twin silver moons blazed down on the Earth below. One was her own satellite, magnificent and beautiful in her fullness, shining down on the night-darkened world as she had done since her beginning. The other was the silvery grey disc of the craft that had brought the Arcturians here and remained, hovering silently far above the world's surface, patiently awaiting their return.

This was the rescue mission, sent to retrieve Gor-Kual before she fell into the hands of those who could not know her power and who, in their not knowing, could wreak destruction. She had been taken from Atlantis to prevent such an event being created deliberately. It could not now be allowed to happen through ignorance.

CHAPTER 37

It was just before noon when we arrived at the ranch. We had been travelling steadily for over five hours and I had acclimatised to the deceptively cool artificial environment of the Mitsubishi. Stepping stiffly out into the blistering heat of the day pretty much took my breath away. I rummaged for my sunglasses as the white hot sun burned at my eyes.

The landscape here was as inhospitable as any I had seen since I arrived, and yet at the same time it was starkly and captivatingly beautiful. This was the first time I had really been out in it, properly felt its grandeur and intensity at first hand rather than from the sheltering, distancing cover of a car or hotel room. I fell in love with it on the spot, even though it felt as alien to me as the surface of the moon. I wandered across the dusty yard to where the scrubland started.

'Don't go off the track,' Davey warned. 'There may be a rattler or scorpion hiding in the shade.'

I took a very large and very rapid leap backwards. Rattlesnakes and scorpions? The thought hadn't even entered my mind when I had said I'd come. It was a decision I wondered if I would regret. I can cope with wild animals, even snakes don't really freak me out, but scorpions, bugs and other creepy-crawlies are another matter. Scorpions, ugh!

'Uh, is there anything else you think I should know about, Davey?' I was picking my way gingerly back up the track, my eyes darting from side to side as if I expected a bug a foot high to leap out at me at any second.

'Well, there are tarantulas, but they probably wouldn't kill you...' He paused to think. 'There is a remote possibility that we may come across some killer bees.'

'Oh, come on.' He was winding me up now, wasn't he? He wasn't.

'No reports of killer bees north of Phoenix I'm relieved to say.' Callum had ambled across from the pile of equipment that he had just unloaded. 'And all those other beasties will be a hundred times more scared of you than you are of them.' I wasn't so sure about that. 'In any case, you're unlikely to see any of them, except maybe at dusk. Unless you stand on one, of course.'

Great. But it was too late to do anything about it now. I was here, and there was no going back. Oh Gemma, what have you got yourself into?

*　　*　　*　　*　　*

The horses were standing quietly in the yard under the care of our guide, Ches Whitecloud, a cheerful looking Native American. Later that day as we rode he would tell me how he was born of the Navajo nation, a people who roamed these former hunting grounds long before any white settler set foot on the east coast of this vast continent. I warmed to Ches. It would have been impossible not to. His face wore a permanent grin and his eyes glimmered endlessly with good-natured mischief.

We were loaded up and ready to go but we could not leave yet. The final member of the team, the mysterious stranger in our midst, had not arrived. Callum did not look best pleased. I, on the other hand, was quite happy to delay the moment when I had to clamber on to one of these animals. I was leaning against the wooden wall of a barn in a small patch of shade eyeing them nervously when Davey joined me.

'If it's any consolation Gemma, I'm not much of one for riding either. Darned creatures don't have any brakes. Give me a motorcycle any day.' He was probably just trying to make me feel better but it made me smile. I appreciated the gesture and I told him so. 'No, I mean it.' He glanced nervously across to where Callum was pacing impatiently. 'Don't let on to the others though, I'd never hear the end of it.'

'Five minutes. If he's not here in five minutes we're leaving without him. Mount up, Gemma. Davey.' No, Callum was really not happy.

'This one is yours, Gemma.' Ches was gesturing towards a small black and white horse. I looked at the animal apprehensively. It seemed innocuous enough.

'His name is Billy,' Ches informed me as I walked up to it, 'hand picked him myself for you. He's strong, gentle and as reliable as an oak tree. Just how you want your men to be,' he added with a wink. 'He'll behave. He's used to novice riders so he won't get spooked at anything and take off with you.' I sincerely hoped Ches was right.

I looked around nervously. Davey's horse stood equally quietly. Callum's mount on the other hand had sensed the impending departure and was getting a bit skittish, pawing the ground and tossing its head.

Davey grinned a slightly forced grin at me. Maybe he had been telling me the truth after all. 'We'll trundle along together at the back and let the others wait for us,' he winked. I kinked my head in the direction of Callum's horse and raised an eyebrow.

'Well, that's Callum for you,' he answered. 'He relishes nothing better than a challenge. Likes to prove he can bend any creature to his will.'

A little shiver ran down my spine. Did the same apply to me? Was I just another challenge? There was no time to think on it further.

'Come on, Gemma.' Callum's voice was impatient. 'Get up on your horse.' OK, OK. But how?

Davey again came to the rescue. He bent and cupped his hands by my knee. 'Put your foot in my hands, grab the saddle pommel – that bit that sticks up at the front – push up with your leg and swing your other leg over.' Just like that? Well, nothing ventured…

To my amazement it worked and I found myself seated on Billy's back. For the second time I felt a flush of warm gratitude towards Davey for his kindness. Callum had been nowhere, had not come over to give me a hand despite knowing my inexperience. Irrationally perhaps I felt irritated by his lack of sympathy. I looked around carefully, not wanting to upset my somewhat precarious balance. Davey and Callum were also in the saddle, as was Ches, who was holding the lead reins of the three pack horses. There was no sign of Frankie or of the new guy, Jack Whateverhisnamewas.

Right on cue, Frankie trotted into sight around the corner of a stable block, seated upon one if the most beautiful creatures I think I have ever seen. It was a huge, powerfully built stallion whose coat gleamed like polished mahogany and it carried itself like a king among horses. Frankie saw me staring and grinned. 'Gemma, meet Maestro, the one and only love of my life. I couldn't leave him out of this adventure, could I?' She glanced around. 'Mr Mystery not here yet?' She didn't sound at all sorry. Like the others, she was unhappy at having an outsider muscling in on the party. I was touched that they hadn't felt the same way about me.

'No, looks like he's missed the boat. Shame. Let's move out.' Even as Callum was speaking however, the sound of an engine muffled his words and a car pulled into the yard. The driver, who I took to be Jack, leapt out with profuse apologies for being late. Without dismounting, Ches took Jack's rucksack from him and fastened it to the back of one of the pack horses.

'Mount up, we're just moving out.' No greeting from Callum, just a few brusque words. He was making it clear to Jack where he stood, right from the outset. Jack in turn didn't rise to Callum's overt hostility. With surprising athleticism he vaulted straight up into the saddle – believe me, it was pretty impressive to see – grabbed the reins and wheeled his horse around to follow us out into the wilderness of the desert. I had a feeling that if it came to it, it would be an interesting match between the two of them, and it would be anyone's guess who would come out on top.

CHAPTER 38

It was a long and uncomfortable day for me, and for Davey too. He hadn't been joking when he said he was a reluctant rider. We ambled along at the rear of our equine caravan watching the others enviously. Frankie rode with an effortless grace, but then again, so Davey informed me, she had practically been born in the saddle. It was a joy to watch her. Jack looked to be competent enough, riding easily if not spectacularly. As for Callum, well, he rode exactly as I would expect Callum to ride, with a natural ease and grace, in a showy cowboy style, both reins in one hand, wheeling his horse with the pressure of his thighs and a light flick of his wrist.

Whereas I felt wobbly and unstable, and was worried about what would happen if Billy decided to gallop off. I certainly wouldn't have stayed on long. I felt like a large sack of potatoes being trundled along on a wobbly cart, with all the sense of balance of those potatoes. I was in no doubt that any landing on the hard ground would be just as heavy as that same sack's would be. Furthermore, it was hellishly hot. We had set out at noon in the heat of the day and ridden for hours under the scorching sun. In spite of the wide-brimmed hat I wore, I was suffering. The standard English summer weather had not prepared me for this.

By the time we stopped for the night I was so saddle sore I could barely move. Sitting, walking, even just standing still, were all equally painful. I could not bring myself to remotely entertain the idea of getting back on that four legged instrument of torture the following morning. The others watched me sympathetically, all except Davey, and that was only because he was suffering almost as much as I was. I was wincing for the umpteenth time when Ches approached, a small green bottle in his hand. He held it out to me. 'Try this Gemma. It's an old remedy of my people and will work wonders. Unfortunately it does stink a bit but it's worth putting up with it.'

I took the bottle from him, unscrewed the cap and sniffed cautiously. Bloody hell, he wasn't joking, the fumes had brought tears to my eyes. 'What's in it?' I asked dubiously.

'You don't want to know.' I got the feeling Ches was only half joking, but to be honest I was in such excruciating discomfort that I think I would have tried anything. Bottle in hand I headed for the tent I was sharing with Frankie. As I turned to zip up the door, I saw Davey hobbling off towards his tent holding an identical bottle. He saw me and waved it.

'Ches's magic potion!' he called. Oh, I hoped so.

In the privacy of the tent I stripped off and poured some of the contents into my hand. It glooped out in a thick greenish-brown sludge. Was I really going to rub this over my thighs and backside? I moved, and squeaked in pain. Too right I was.

Ten minutes later Frankie poked her head through the doorway, and pulled it out again just as quickly with a gasped 'Christ almighty!' A few seconds later she peeped through again. 'Ches?' I nodded. 'God that stuff stinks!' She came in and sank onto her camp bed. 'It'll be worth it in though. You'll be back to normal in the morning.'

I doubted that very much but I didn't argue, I was too tired. I'd discovered that riding is hard work, a lot harder than I'd ever imagined, even at our easy pace. I just had time to mumble 'G'night Frankie' before my eyes closed and I was gone.

Frankie deserved an award for staying in that tent all night without a murmur of complaint. It smelled rank. Sharing a tent with Davey, Jack had not been so tolerant. He had taken one breath of the stench, picked up his bedding and headed out to sleep in the open air.

*   *   *   *   *

To my amazement and utter disbelief the following morning all my aches and pains were gone, as if they had never been. Davey was right as rain too. I returned the almost empty bottle to Ches with gratitude. 'You are a magician, Ches. Where did you learn how to make this stuff?'

He smiled, his eyes lighting up as he remembered. 'My father was medicine man for my people, as was his before him and his before him. He taught me much.' And that was all he would tell me.

We set out early, but even at seven in the morning the thermometer was already climbing. Today we would ride until late morning, then find some shade where we would rest up until mid-afternoon, so avoiding the hottest part of the day. The previous day, leaving just before noon when the sun was at its highest had not been a great idea,even if it had been unavoidable. The heat had taken its toll on all of us and we had not made the progress Callum would have liked. It was a situation he did not intend repeated.

Now that my muscles and the chafing had eased, thank you Ches, I was actually starting to enjoy myself. Billy was as steady and tolerant of my clumsy signals as I had been promised and I was slowly finding my seat. I felt more stable and balanced, less like I would slide off onto the ground at any step. Gradually I relaxed and was able to take in at the harsh beauty of the desert landscape we were traversing.

All around us tiny lizards basked in the hot sunshine and once a snake slithered out of our path as we approached. High over our heads, in a cloudless sky of a deep cornflower blue – I had never imagined a sky could be that colour - eagles and other birds of prey circled, drifting on the powerful thermal currents rising from the overheated ground. I was astonished at the amount of wildlife we encountered as we moved through this inhospitable land. Strangely horned deer appeared on the horizon and vanished again just as quickly while small mammals – rabbits, squirrels, mice – darted here and there, racing for safety as we approached. And the chipmunks – dozens of them – tiny, cute and oh so speedy. They had no fear, it seemed, and carried on as if we were not there.

The landscape was changing as the hours passed by. When we had set out the previous day it had been flat plain-land, punctuated by the table tops of the mesas that in places rose a hundred feet and more above ground level. Today we were entering a different world, a world of sheer-walled canyons and craggy cliffs. In place of the ubiquitous mesas standing proud and tall, here the land dropped away, no longer carved by the wind and rain, but instead by the steady inexorable erosion of the rivers and streams that more often than not still gurgled through their depths so far below, their course invariably marked by a ribbon of aspen trees, pale golden in their autumn dress. The climate was changing too. We were climbing higher and the temperatures were blessedly a few degrees cooler. It was still hot, but much more bearable.

CHAPTER 39

That second night we made camp on the flat plateau of a canyon top. By the time the tents were pitched and the equipment unloaded, the day was drawing to a close. I wandered over nearer the rim. Not too close, I think I've mentioned before that my head for heights is not good. I was facing east, the sun setting at my back, blazing the red rocks in front of me in the flame of its rays. It was quite possibly the most breathtakingly beautiful spectacle I had ever witnessed. As I watched, everything began to move and change as the shadows cast by the dying day crept across the land, while in the slowly darkening sky above me one by one the stars were coming out. I sensed rather than heard someone behind me and turned to see Callum standing there. He was watching me rather than the natural light-show unfolding just in front of his eyes.

'Beautiful isn't it?' he asked, his eyes never leaving my face. I nodded, words eluding me, my heart beating just a little faster. He had the look of a man who had waited too long for his prey and would wait no longer. I wasn't sure I was ready to be that prey, not yet. Would I be able to resist him? Deep down, did I really want to? My heart stepped up its tempo as he moved towards me.

We were some distance from the camp and out of view of the others. Callum was standing right in front of me now, looking down into my eyes. The look in his scared me a little, but excited me too. This was not a man who would take no for an answer when there was something he wanted, though I didn't for one minute believe he would force himself on me against my will. Instead he would wear down any resistance, little by little. I had no doubt of the efficacy of his powers of persuasion. I may not have felt ready to take the next step in this, but I was more than ready to be persuaded.

A rumble like muted distant thunder broke into my awareness. It was enough to shatter the spell. The drumbeat grew louder, echoing up from deep in the earth. I turned to look down over the rim and in that moment, a herd of horses charged into view around a bend from the head of the canyon, the sound of their hooves condensed and amplified by the high stone walls and narrow channel of the gorge. They were snorting and whinnying in the sheer exuberance of running wild and free.

I felt totally in tune with them. Since I started this journey into the unknown over two years ago, I had been seized by a sense of freedom the like of which I have never experienced before. I stared down at the herd as it passed by almost directly below me, the sense of joy in my heart so overwhelming I let out a loud Whoop. I heard another echo beside me. Frankie had heard the rumbling too and had run to witness it. I turned and grinned at her in delight. Thirty or forty horses hurtled past in a maelstrom of colour, their manes and tails tossing, lifting a cloud of dust that hung behind them in the still evening air.

'Are they wild?'

Frankie had a look of sheer rapture on her face as she watched them pass. 'Not exactly.' She turned to look at me, her face glowing. 'They'll belong to someone, but they're allowed to run free. So they are owned, but wild, yes, in that they remain unbroken and untamed.' She linked her arm in mine. 'Are you coming back? Ches will have supper on the plates by now.' She stopped, glancing at Callum, looking a little embarrassed as a thought crossed her mind. 'Did I gatecrash something?'

The moment though was well and truly gone, had dissolved the moment the horses announced their arrival. Callum shook his head. 'No, we were just watching the sunset.' He didn't seem disappointed or put out at the interruption, and as Frankie and I walked past him I understood why when he gave me a broad, blatant wink. This wouldn't stop here. I had a tingle in my belly and a warm fire chasing round my veins as I returned to the campground. My common sense might have been resisting Callum's advances, but nothing else in me was.

*   *   *   *   *

We had packed up camp and were on our way well before daybreak the following morning. Callum was hoping to reach our destination by noon, which would give us several hours to begin our exploration of the area. I found it a strange almost otherworldly experience, riding across these empty lands in the chill eerie half-light that precedes the dawn. The overpowering sense of being totally alone in the world was something I had never experienced before. It was humbling and elating in the same breath.

Sunrise, when it came, rivalled the previous evening's sunset in its splendour. The sky turned from a misty cream to a riot of gold, salmons, oranges and deep pink. Playing the previous evening's film in reverse the shadows rolled back as the sun rose above the horizon and climbed ever higher in the sky, flooding the world around us with light.

We had been riding for two or three hours when the landscape changed again, the canyon lands softening gradually into a low range of hills. The excitement building within the group was obvious. We had to be near our goal. We crested a low pass and there right in front of us, the hills vanished, replaced by a wide empty plain. Callum drew his horse to a halt.

'OK, this is it. We're here. We'll find somewhere to set up camp, then split up into three groups and spread out to search for any possible caves. I'll go with Gemma…' I ignored Frankie's knowing wink at me. 'Frankie, you go with Ches. Which leaves Davey with Jack.'

A short while later the tents were pitched and the equipment unloaded from the pack horses, which were watered and left tethered in the shade of a large pine at the edge of the camp ground. Callum and I were to head north, Frankie and Ches would go to the south, while Jack and Davey headed back into the hills to search there. Too impatient to get the search underway to worry about the midday heat Callum decided to set out immediately. I was grateful we were a little higher and the temperature a couple of degrees cooler, nevertheless it would still be a hot, uncomfortable experience. He issued each pair of riders with a short wave radio.

'Keep your eyes peeled for anything that even remotely matches Gemma's description. Shout out loud if you find something.' I couldn't believe what I was hearing. Was Callum really basing this whole needle in a haystack search on what I'd written in my novel?

'It's all we have to go on, Gemma.' He'd read my thoughts. 'There are a wealth of old Indian legends about star treasure being buried somewhere in these hills, and there were a few other clues I found that helped me to see we were heading on the right track. But the exact location? Well that's anyone's guess. These hills are riddled with caves. Searching them blind would take us months. Your description, long shot though it is, is all we have to go on.'

To say I was dubious was an understatement, yet as I stared at the hills that rose up in front of me I experienced an odd sense of familiarity, as if I had seen them before somewhere.

*   *   *   *   *

We set off in our allocated directions. The hills jutted out into the plain in a series of rocky tongues and we quickly lost sight of the other groups. Callum was so fired up that he urged his horse into a fast trot, which was not good news for me. I was still not very stable and comfortable in the saddle. After three days, I had just about mastered walking; trotting remained more of a challenge. It had to happen. My balance loosened as Billy's foot slipped on a stone and suddenly I found myself pitching forward over his neck. I hit the ground hard, to lie gasping for breath where the wind had been knocked out of my lungs. Callum leapt off his horse and ran over to me looking worried.

'Gemma?' I just about managed to wave my hand, unable to talk. 'Are you OK?' OK? What a stupid question. I had just fallen off a horse and I couldn't breathe, let alone speak. I felt his hands gently feeling my shoulders and shrugged him off.

'Yes, I'm OK,' I managed to gasp out, 'just winded. Oooh...' I had sat up and felt the beginnings of a world class bruise on my hip. 'And a bit bruised.' I finished, grimacing. Luckily for me I had fallen off in the base of a dry, sandy gulch where the soft sand of the dry river bed had cushioned me from any serious injury.

'Come on, sit down for a minute.' Callum helped me struggle to my feet and over to the shade of a straggling tree. 'You were lucky. A broken collar bone out here would be no laughing matter.' He gently touched my cheek. 'I'm sorry Gemma. I forgot you weren't a rider. I should have kept to a walk.' He was getting closer. Any second now he would kiss me... I still wasn't sure, and lifted my eyes from where his held them captive.

I froze, my eyes locked onto the hillside behind him.

'Gemma? What's wrong?' I could hear the frustration in his voice but my attention was elsewhere. There it was. The cave. The image I had seen in that dream of so many months ago returned as clear as a photograph and superimposed itself on the hillside in front of me. There was the dark, low opening, two thirds of the way up. The two images matched exactly, merging into one another in front of my disbelieving eyes. It all fitted, even down to the rocky outcrop on which the eagle had perched to guide the skull guardian Takuanaka to the right spot.

'Gemma? What is it?' Callum's voice was sharper now, trying to get some response from me. Still the words wouldn't come. Instead I lifted my hand and pointed, trembling. He followed my gaze and my outstretched finger then turned back to me, his face alight with excitement. 'That's it?' His voice was shaking. I nodded, unable to speak. 'You're certain?' Again, I just nodded. The words simply refused to form in my head.

This time he did kiss me, taking me completely by surprise as he scooped his hand round my neck and pulled me to him, kissing me hard and full on the lips. For the second time in a quarter of an hour I lost my breath completely, but before I had time to respond, he was gone.

'We'll finish this later,' he promised, his hand already on the shortwave radio, calling the others. 'You really are one incredible woman, Gemma.'

CHAPTER 40

Less than an hour and a half later we were all, with the exception of Ches, standing in the entrance to the low-ceilinged cave. This was not part of Ches' role and he had no interest in joining us. This area was sacred to his people and he feared disturbing its guardian spirits. He had told us that he would go out into the hills later, under the moon, to speak with these spirits in ceremony and ask for them to bless us and our search. Everyone else it appeared, Jack included, was buzzing with excitement.

I, on the other hand, was not. Exploring tight, dark, narrow underground spaces held little appeal for me. Also, to be honest, a small part of me was still stubbornly trying to find a way to deny what was going on, even in the face of everything that had happened. Isn't it strange how we find any possible reason not to accept things that are outside of our belief system, even when we have experienced them directly. It was crazy but true; that little part of me still wanted to believe I was making all this up.

I tried to wimp out. I would have much preferred to stay back at the camp with Ches. Callum though was having none of it. 'We need you, Gemma. You know about this. Good god, you even recognised the cave entrance. We need you here if we are to have any chance at all of finding this thing.'

With a lot of persuasion I managed to negotiate a compromise. If the route got really difficult and I started to feel too claustrophobic, Callum would bring me back to the entrance and they would carry on exploring without me.

*   *   *   *   *

It was a peculiar feeling, standing in that low, wide opening. I was overwhelmed with a sense of déjà-vu, a feeling that I knew this place, even though I had never set foot within two thousand miles of here until a few days before. We moved to the back of the cave, squeezed through the narrow vertical cleft just as Takuanaka had done centuries before... and there was the chamber with the two openings.

'We go left,' Callum stated. 'It's what Takuanaka did. Gemma, if you have any sense of which direction we should take from here on, let us know.'

Once past the first chamber however, the powerful sense of recognition I had vanished completely. Of the images that I had experienced while writing the book I remembered this far and no further.

Now that we were properly in this underground world, Davey, who was a qualified caver, assumed leadership of the group. He took time and care in fixing a guide line to an anchor bolt he had jammed in to a small crack in the rock at about waist height just inside the entrance. Safety was the priority and, while Callum was openly impatient to proceed, he accepted the necessity of the delay. The line would be unreeled as we walked and we would follow it back. It was literally our lifeline, essential if we were not to get lost. THAT was a thought I banished from my head every (too frequent) time it popped up.

The further we penetrated underground, the less natural this whole place seemed to be. But if it was man-made, who could have accomplished such a monumental feat? How? And why? The others were as fascinated and bewildered by it as I was. It was immense, a subterranean maze of Minoan complexity and scale. Every few feet, side tunnels branched off the main thoroughfare, or the main route forked. A few brief exploratory excursions showed clearly that the side tunnels had countless other tunnels exiting from them too. This whole area was a honeycomb. It was not reassuring to know that so little was holding up everything that sat above it.

Even if I was not exactly at my happiest, thanks to the relatively easy progress I found myself less uncomfortable than I thought I'd be. Time ceased to mean anything as on and on we walked, by common consent keeping to the main artery. The further we went, the more I could feel everyone's spirits sinking as we registered the scale of the gargantuan task that lay ahead of us. Looking for a needle in a haystack was nothing compared to the search we were embarking upon. After what seemed a very long time we came out into a small chamber where the tunnel branched into three. There was no obvious main path, nothing gave us a clue, and I had no information to offer, so we just went left.

Three hours later we were back in the main entrance cave after exploring dead end after dead end. I was exhausted, nowhere near as fit as any of the others, and had been no help whatsoever. I had had no insights, no bursts of recognition, nothing. Then again, to be honest I had never expected to. The initial buzz of excitement had muted. We all recognised that this was only the first stab at what could prove to be a very long, drawn out search, a search that held no promise at all that we would achieve the longed for result at the end of it.

*   *   *   *   *

It was late. I was sitting alone staring into the flames of the campfire in a not altogether successful attempt to take in everything that had happened: Callum's discovery of the journal; my arrival first in America, and then here only a few hours ago; finding the cave entrance and it looking exactly as I had seen it before in my mind. Mostly though the overwhelming and highly disconcerting sense of familiarity I had felt. Davey and Frankie had gone off to pore over maps and old documents, professional heads in place. Jack had turned in early for the night. Ches and Callum, well, they were who knew where. I was relishing these quiet few minutes.

'Gemma.' Callum's low voice at my shoulder pulled me from my mental wanderings. I turned to look at him and he held out his hand. 'Come on.' Under his other arm he was carrying a thick blanket.

My heart began to beat just a bit faster. This was it then. He had come to finish what had been started earlier in the day, as he had promised he would. He pulled me to my feet and led me out into the dark desert night. While we walked I looked up at the sky, as I had done every night since we set out on this trip, not yet tired of its breath-taking beauty. I had never seen so many stars; they filled the sky. Through it all flowed the misty twinkling swathe of the Milky Way, like the wake of some gigantic interstellar ship. I started to speak but Callum put his finger to his lips and smiled again. I understood. Any words would break the spell of this magical cosmic moment.

We walked for perhaps half a mile or so. It was clear that Callum knew exactly where he was heading, had planned this all meticulously, already scouting out the perfect spot. I wondered when he had found the time to do it.

He halted as we rounded a large outcrop of rock that stood like an island off the main range of hills. They, and the campfire, were behind us. In front of us the flat desert stretched away endlessly, merging invisibly into the twinkling infinity of the night. I found myself trembling with an equal measure of nervousness and anticipation. I still wasn't sure I was ready for this. My experience with men was limited, to say the least.

241

OK, I'd been married to Dan for twenty five years, so in that respect I wasn't inexperienced, but as he had been my first and only lover, in every other way I was.

Callum let the blanket fall to the ground, pulled me into his arms and kissed me. Gently at first then more and more hungrily, his tongue seeking mine, his lips hard and demanding. My anxiety forgotten, I responded fiercely. Heat flooded through me. Every nerve, every cell was awake and aroused. Nothing mattered any more except these moments and this man.

He broke away, leaving me gasping and shaking. His face betrayed how much he was enjoying the effect he was having on me. Believe me, it wasn't one-sided. I was keenly aware of the effect I was having on him too, could feel him hard and pulsing against my stomach, could hear his breath coming faster and his heartbeat quickening. He spread out the blanket and drew me down beside him. Through it I could feel the heat of the sand, still warm from the sun. With impatient fingers he pulled at my shirt buttons, my underwear, until I was lying naked and vulnerable under the starlight. I reached out for him just as eagerly, stripping off his shirt, his jeans.

Somewhere far in the distant recesses of my mind I could hear common sense and self-preservation screaming 'No'. It was the only part of me that was and it soon fell silent. This was a battle it was never going to win.

Callum's lips, his fingers, setting me on fire. My own, embracing him, devouring him. Never in all my years with Dan had I been taken over by such passion and desire. My inhibitions melted away under Callum's touch. Nothing was forbidden as we explored every inch of each other. I had never felt so vibrant and alive. Had never before been so hungry for the touch of a man. It was as if I had been engulfed by the raw, primal essence of this untamed land. We were not making love, this was very different to that experience. It was as if something outside of us, something far greater than anything I had ever imagined existed, was moving through us – a powerful fusion of the two great forces of nature. When at last he moved in me, my world exploded into a million glittering fragments of almost unbearable intensity that hung suspended in momentary eternity, before falling with the gentleness of snowflakes to wake me.

GOR-KUAL: The Red Skull

Part III

MITHRAS

CHAPTER 41

"It was in the fourteenth year of the reign of King Mithras that our people were visited by those who descended from the skies. They came to us in vast silver vessels that hovered over the rooftops of the city like shining discs, silent as the night and three in total, the beings within them numbered in their thousands. One by one they appeared amongst us, materialising from the very air. One moment nothing, the next a horde of glowing, silver-haired beings stood amongst us, outnumbering us by many to one.

They were taller than we, a head at least and many much more, though we ourselves were not of small stature. They bore themselves with such a gentle, kindly air that despite their multitude not one of us felt threatened by their presence, yet we sensed their power and their dominion over us should they choose to express it. Sensed that any show of enmity or aggression would be gently but firmly quashed.

I sank to my knees before these angels, for angels they must have been though they bore no wings. No earthly creature ever looked thus, nor permeated such an air of goodness and love. Those around me had bowed down likewise, as did those who now left their homes and approached to see what was happening.

'Do not kneel before us as though we were your masters. We come to you as friends and as equals.' The words rang clearly in my head, though I was certain not one had opened his mouth to speak. All around my fellow men and women were as dazed as I. All had heard these words clearly, no matter how far they stood

from these strangers. None made to rise from his knees despite the words. Surely the presence of these radiant angel beings demanded our respect and submission.

We say to you again, beloved ones, do not kneel before us. We come seeking your friendship and not your servility.' With these words the shining people stepped forward, each stretching out a hand to one of us, taking ours and raising us to our feet. Still our eyes were cast down upon the ground, not daring to look up and meet their own. Some, despite the gentle words, feared punishment for impertinence, others that to merely look into the faces of these giants would result in them being turned to stone. For myself, and I am certain many others, I feared what I would discover there hidden within, a discovery that would turn my life upside down forever.

'You fear us, when there is nothing to fear.' The words and tone were that of a father reassuring his frightened child. 'Your world today is full of fear. Soon you will understand that there is no reason to hold onto it. That all is well and always will be, if you allow it. Soon you will come to know us as friends.

'I would ask now that you lead me and my delegation to your king. We wish to hold conference with him.' Involuntarily, before I could think to stop myself, my eyes flew to his face. No-one asked to speak with the king. It was forbidden. The king summoned people to his presence; they did not request to approach him. In that instant the being who towered over me locked his eyes onto mine and I knew that the king would accept their request and welcome them to his palace. For in the depths of those eyes, whose colour even now I cannot recall, I saw a power beyond anything imaginable. A power that could, if it chose, bend men's will to its own, cause mountains to crumble and rivers to change

their course. I did not understand it or how it could be, but I saw it and knew it was so.

'Will you take us?' That unfathomable gaze was reaching into mine. I knew he was addressing me. 'Will you take us to your king?'

'M-m-me?' I was a mere weaver. I would not be permitted to enter even the outer courtyard of the palace, never mind its inner sanctuary. 'I-I-I cannot. I mean I would not be permitted. I have no influence, I am nobody. If I tried... My life...' I tailed off, not wanting to consider the possible consequences. Our king was a good, just man but he expected the law to be strictly followed.

'You will be safe, we guarantee it.' It was as if the tall man (I call him a man now, though to me then he was still an angel) was reading my mind. For a reason I could not explain I believed him. Maybe it was that piercing gaze, or maybe it was what I saw behind it. Maybe it was his almost tangible air of confidence and invincibility, or the light that seemed to emanate from him in a shimmering cloak. I didn't know. Strangely, it didn't matter. I believed him, I trusted him, and that was enough.

I found myself nodding my assent, even as inside my head was screaming at me. 'Are you mad? You have never even been within hailing distance of the palace walls. How on earth do you think you are going to bring these beings before the king?'

He smiled, pleased. 'That is good. The rest of us will remain here amongst you. I ask nothing of you other than that you take them into your hearts and your homes, for they carry only goodwill to you. Do not fear us. We are simply curious and wish to learn more about your lives. We will not be a burden on either your time or your tables.'

248

From the market place, where these beings had first appeared before me, I led the small delegation of two men and three women (I call them men and women, though they were not like any men or women I had ever seen before) through the narrow streets, past market stalls, animal pens and homes where minutes before people had been conducting their everyday lives as in their usual, unhurried way. Then the angel beings had appeared and as of that instant, normal daily life had come to a standstill.

Groups of men, women and children stood clustered together in every street, staring at the newcomers in a combination of confusion, fear and curiosity. Who were they? Where had they come from? What were the huge silver discs that hung in the sky above the city casting a vast, immeasurable shadow over the ground below? And how did they stay there without crashing to the earth? Surely this must be a powerful form of sorcery.

The strangers simply smiled and waited. Waited for us to grow used to their calm, unthreatening presence, for our curiosity to grow stronger than our fear, as they knew it would. And it did. One by one, their insatiable appetite of curiosity too strong to resist, it was the little ones, the children, who led the way, tiptoeing closer: wide-eyed, timorous, prepared to run away at any unexpected movement. As the children edged nearer, anxious parents and grandparents looking on, not trying to stop the children but as yet not daring to approach themselves, the angels knelt, slowly, carefully, so as not to frighten the little pioneers, and opened their arms to them. Enfolded them in a warm embrace of love and security, so comforting that the children laughed and squealed in delight. If these were sorcerers, they were sorcerers of the most benevolent kind.

All this I registered as I led the small party of emissaries through the tangled maze of streets towards the palace. As I drew ever nearer so my anxiety grew. I still had no thought of how I would succeed in gaining access to the palace, or an audience for those I was taking there.

'Do not concern yourself, my friend. All is well.' I turned to see their leader smiling at me. They were indeed his words I was hearing though I still did not understand how it could be, for his lips never moved and no audible sound came from his mouth.

* * * * *

I did not know it then, could not have known, that this was not the first time the angel people had walked amongst us, though it had been many, many generations since their last visit. I soon came to learn that it would not be the last. For this time, however, and in ignorance of all of that was to come, I led them that day to the gates of the palace. Two hard-faced guards, as strong and invincible as living statues of bronze, barred our way.

'Who dares approach the palace without invitation?' one growled menacingly as our party halted before them.

'I bring visitors from far-off lands who wish to speak with the king.' Somehow, despite the trembling in my legs and the rapid thumping of my heart beat, I succeeded in keeping my voice steady and to feign some semblance of confidence.

'You dare to bring them when the king has not requested their presence?' The thunderous roar of the guard's voice and the fury held within it hit me like a hurricane, almost knocking me backwards off my feet.

Those I had brought here stood calm and unruffled in the face of the storm; the one who I took to be the leader now stepped forward. 'I asked this man to bring me here. He is simply offering the kindness of guiding a stranger in these lands to this palace. Do not target your anger towards him. He does not merit its fury. If you are to place blame anywhere, place it with my companions and me.'

The guards looked at him open-mouthed. Yet again he had not uttered a sound as these words flowed from him and all heard them.

'I am Oolan, leader of my people. We have travelled far to come to you today.' As he spoke, one of the huge silver craft drifted silently to hover directly overhead, far above the palace wall. 'Please send word to your king that we wish to speak with him on a matter of utmost urgency. He will wish to see us.'

Maybe it was his calm, assured tone - though I believe it was more the sight of this fantastical improbable object that sat like a huge second sun in the skies above them – but the guards called immediately for a third to bear Oolan's message to King Mithras. Within minutes the soldier had returned with word that the king would receive his visitors and had commanded that they be taken to him immediately.

Oolan turned to me. 'We thank you for bringing us here, my brother. You can come no further. Return now to your home and your family who will be wondering where you are. Speak with those of us who are amongst you and know they are your friends, as am I. Farewell. Be in peace.'

With those final words he and his companions turned and walked through the gates of the palace to their audience with the king. Why had they come? Where had they come from? What would happen now? I would never find the answers to my questions.

*   *   *   *   *

The angel beings did not stay long, only a day on that occasion, though they returned from time to time. Always there were two strange and inexplicable consequences of their visits.

The first was that after they left us no-one remembered that they had been here... until they came back, at which point every previous visit was recalled in total clarity and they were greeted as the old and dear friends they had indeed become. It was as if all memory of them was switched off at the moment they departed, to be reactivated only on their return. Perhaps this strange situation explains why no stories of those visits, which our angel friends have told us were so frequent in times long gone by, have ever been told. That is why I am writing this down now, for today they walk amongst us once more, and now is the only time when I am able to recall what has gone before. When they leave us on the tomorrow, these thoughts too will leave me once more. From this time on though, my writings will remain to bear witness that they had ever been here, even though my memory will not.

The second is the effect their presence has on the people of this land. It is as if their peace and serenity is contagious, spreading like a virus to each of us, one to another. It is something that has grown stronger with each visit. Anger amongst us is now rare, violence even rarer. Men, women, children alike, we all smile more, laugh more, are more considerate and compassionate towards each other. I cannot explain it, for it is beyond my comprehension, but it is happening, and I can only put it down to the presence of our angel beings."

CHAPTER 42

Inside the palace the five silently followed the guard through the sumptuous, cool, light-filled corridors and chambers. The palace was vast and ancient, built by the current king's ancestors centuries before. After many minutes' walk their guide stopped, indicating a huge doorway that was sealed by a pair of massive, ornately carved wooden doors.

'The King's chamber,' he announced, bowing. 'He awaits your arrival.' With those words, he bowed again and returned the way they had come.

Without hesitation the visitors pushed on the heavy doors, which swung effortlessly open. Beyond was an enormous room, lavishly decorated with rich silks and satins in a riot of jewel-bright colours. Drapes, tapestries and rugs covered the walls and floors, gold flickered everywhere in the muted sunlight that filtered through shaded windows, and the heady scent of incense perfumed the air. At the farthest end, on a shallow raised dais, a tall, regal figure reclined on a low, ruby satin couch. This was King Mithras. They stepped inside, closing the doors behind them, crossing the expanse of exquisite marble floor. As they did so King Mithras rose and went to greet them. It was an action unheard of before in his reign.

'Greetings, King Mithras. I am Oolan.'

'Greetings, my friend. Yes, I know who you are. You are welcome here. Your visit has long been expected.' The king indicated the dais where large, comfortable cushions had been set on the floor in front of the couch. 'Come. Sit and tell me why you visit us now. For though your visit may have been foretold, the day was not, nor the reason. Tell me, why have you come at this time?'

'King Mithras, we are here because we have foreseen a danger that threatens the safety of Gor-Kual. We admit readily that we do not know when this will reveal itself, or from what quarter, but now this threat has been born, it will grow. We felt it essential to warn you of this as soon as we became aware of it so that you may act in good time to ensure her continued safety.'

'She is safe. She sleeps as she has slept since she first came to us, so that none may trace her. Like every one of my ancestors before me I have sworn to protect her with my kingdom and my life. No my friends, in this I believe you to be wrong. She is in no danger. I am the only one who knows of her existence. As no-one else knows she exists, no-one can seek to harm her or steal her away.'

'Nonetheless your Majesty...' The discussion, often fervent and assertive though never descending into what could be described as an actual argument, continued for hours. King Mithras would not be convinced that any threat to Gor-Kual could possibly exist or ever would. His guests remained equally adamant that it did and that over time it would intensify. That one day, on an unknown date in the future, an attempt would be made to take her from him. The meeting ended without resolution. The king was obstinate and proud, certain that he possessed the might to resist any potential, and currently theoretical, attack. The visitors for their part were too uncertain of the timescale and any other clear details to be able to convince him, or push too hard for decisive action.

King Mithras accompanied his visitors to the door of his chamber. 'Do not worry, Oolan. If the threat does come, Gor-Kual will protect us. Please, let us part speaking of more pleasant things. My star friends, it has been a long time, too long, since you last graced this kingdom with your visits. Many kings and queens have ruled here in those years. Now that you have made contact with us once more, it would bring great joy to my people, and to me, if you would return often.'

Oolan nodded his assent. His concern however was still evident. He would not take his leave without some final words of warning. 'We take much pleasure in your invitation and will gladly visit you and your people from time to time.' He held the king's gaze. 'I hope that in future meetings we may succeed in convincing you of the threat we foresee. Gor-Kual sleeps now as she must, for all your sakes. But know that once she is woken, those who seek to possess her will come to claim her. She will not be able to protect you from their wrath. Hear our words, your majesty. You must stay alert, and Gor-Kual must remain sleeping.' With those parting words, Oolan and his companions turned and left.

*   *   *   *   *

Gor-Kual. A lifelike skull carved from flawless jasper of the richest, deepest brick red, programmed with all the knowledge and wisdom that the race who created her possessed, imbued with their essence and energy. A sacred skull, one of only thirteen ever created to possess an independent consciousness, one of pure love and service to humankind. She was a living, conscious being, though few who merely looked on her would see her as such. To most, she would appear simply an inanimate object, a carved ornament of questionable attraction.

She was ancient, as ancient as the first child-like humans who wandered this world, in whose awakening and their spiritual evolution she had been brought here to assist. She had seen much, experienced much since her creation, from the distant world where she was birthed through the desires of highly evolved and benevolent beings to her first sensations of this planet, from the earliest civilisations of Africa to the paradise-turned-hell of Atlantis. For now though she was sleeping, as she had been sleeping for so many years, her energy a mere flicker of its waking power, her consciousness dormant.

After her guardian had fled with the red skull from Atlantis to keep her from the clutches of the Shadow Chasers, the Dark Ones who sought the power of the skulls for themselves, they had eventually reached the shores of an ancient and wild Europe, from where they had travelled south. Here the guardian had fallen ill, prey to diseases unknown on his own continent and without immunity to their ravages, he had died. Even Gor-Kual's potent healing powers had been unable to save his life. When the priest had stumbled and fallen for the last time on the gentle slopes of a grassy hillside, she had been left vulnerable, visible, lying on the open ground for any passing wanderer to chance upon.

Action had to be taken. Gor-Kual could not just be left where she lay. The danger of her falling into the wrong hands, either through accident or design, was too great. Even as she rested beneath the gentle rays of the sun there were those seeking her out for their own dark purposes, for the Shadow Chasers, after they had discovered the deception at the Temple, had sworn to retrieve each and every one of the missing skulls. Powerful and conscious though Gor-Kual was, without the physical protection of a human guardian she was vulnerable, especially against those such as the Dark Ones who were able to shield against the influence of that power. A mission had been launched by the descendants and allies of those who had created the red skull so many tens of thousands of years before, a mission to retrieve her and take her to safety.

The rescue party could not however, simply take Gor-Kual home and bide their time until the moment came for the red skull to join her brothers and sisters openly in the world once more. In order for the energetic circuit that had been created on the Earth to be maintained, from the moment the project had been instigated, so long before, the skulls had to remain within the influence of the planet's energy field.

The star travellers had searched for and eventually located a family of honour, power and leadership, in whose future lineage they could discern the same strengths and qualities carrying forward through the generations. They had brought Gor-Kual to this family, entrusting her to their protection, warning them that if they activated the skull, woke her from her dormant state, those who sought to acquire her would know and be drawn to her as to a beacon. She must be allowed to lie sleeping until the day, far in the future, when all thirteen of the skulls would be once more reunited in the service of humankind. A day when all the people of the Earth would learn of their existence and their purpose.

So it was that Gor-Kual had been brought to Mithras' own ancestors countless generations before by angel beings such as those who had so recently returned. King Mithras knew, though no-one else living did, that these people came from a distant star system, far from the life-giving light of our own sun. That they had brought the sacred red skull here to his forefathers for safe-keeping to prevent her falling into the hands of those who sought to abuse her power. Those long dead kings had sworn a blood oath that they would protect her, would never activate her power or share their knowledge of her or her origins. It was an oath that had been upheld throughout the ages, sworn in turn by Mithras himself when he had attained kingship of this land.

She had remained hidden and protected. At some time several centuries earlier, during the construction of the present palace, she had been sealed in a chamber deep within its bowels. There she slept still. King Mithras had never set eyes on her, never touched her, yet he knew where she was concealed, knew how to access her hiding place. Knew how to wake her from her sleep.

CHAPTER 43

"The palace and its small kingdom in which we lived were set alongside the banks of a mighty river. It was a verdant oasis in a landscape of sun-parched sand and rock. The land was lush and fertile, irrigated and enriched by the flood waters that came to us each spring and left their gift on the fields. It was a place of beauty, the red sandstone walls of the palace surrounded by emerald gardens of fragrant shrubs and flowers, silhouetted against the golden sands of the surrounding desert and the shimmering deep blue sky overhead. Food and water was abundant, and our king, Mithras, while strict about the law, was a just and kindly man who cared greatly about his people and ruled wisely and well. We were, in the main, happy, healthy and content.

The angel beings came amongst us from time to time to speak with the king and offer us their friendship. They were gentle and wise, though never shared with us information on their home country, which must have been many months travel from our own. Nor did they speak of the purpose of their visits. That was for King Mithras alone to know. This happy situation continued for many years, until the time when all began to change, dark days fell upon us, and the angel beings no longer came.

It was not noticeable at first. Perhaps one or two remarks that the flood waters each year were lower than the year before, that they drained away more quickly. Observations, comments, that was all. The river had always been there, had always been reliable and sustaining. No-one doubted that it always would be. This was just a temporary fluctuation, nothing more. No-one really paid any great attention or felt the need to worry – until the year the flood waters did not come at all.

That must have been around the fortieth year of King Mithras' reign. He was growing old by then, well into his sixth decade, as I was myself. It marked the beginning of the end of our happy, easy days. From that year on the flood waters abandoned us. The soil grew poor, no longer renewed by the river's annual goodness in the way it had always been, and our crops grew weaker and sparser. We carried water from the river to the fields to irrigate as best we could. It was not enough.

Soon the unfamiliar shadow of hunger touched us all and did not leave. The river itself, always so mighty and constant, began to fall, its waters shrinking almost before our eyes. And they shrank quickly. Within two years it was a mere trickle running through the base of the vast, dry channel that once it had filled. Where it had gone, why it had gone, we did not know. In truth, we did not care. Our only concern was that it no longer flowed, was no longer there to meet our needs. We realised too late how much we had taken its life-sustaining presence for granted in this otherwise barren and arid world in which we lived.

Famine took its toll as, year after year, crops failed and livestock perished. Disease took hold and our once vibrant population was decimated as the waters sank ever further beneath the sands of the desert until only a few small islands of water remained. It was said that even our king was not immune to this torture, suffering as his people suffered. Rumours spread that he grew weak, his former strength deserting him as his muscles wasted and his heart began to fail. He had to act, to find a *solution before we were extinguished altogether. His advisors, his seers and oracles, his magicians, none it seemed could offer it to him."*

∗　　∗　　∗　　∗　　∗

It was as Mithras lay restless one night, waiting in vain for sleep to take him and offer some respite from the troubled thoughts that incessantly plagued his waking hours, that the solution came to him. A solution that was unthinkable. A solution that would break every taboo that had ever been set upon it. There had to be another way... There wasn't. Even the angel beings had deserted him in those desperate days.

Gor-Kual. The red skull. She could help. She was powerful enough.

For days Mithras lived in torment, torn between the desperate plight of his beloved people and the sacred, inviolable oath he had taken on the day of his coronation. It was an oath that had passed from father to son, mother to daughter, king to king and queen to queen since the beginning. Mithras himself had taken it silently, privately, as was the tradition, the day he had assumed his crown. It was the betrayal of this oath that Mithras was considering. Daily, the situation was worsening until he could no longer bear the suffering around him. He no longer had a choice. Fate had intervened and was bringing the angel beings' prophecy to pass.

* * * * *

His breath ragged, his heart fluttering, his legs no longer able to support him, King Mithras sank gratefully onto the cushions of his bed. He was weak, too weak, ravaged by the same suffering that touched his people. In his hands he held a heavy woven bag. Gor-Kual. He had unsealed the chamber where she had lain undisturbed for so many centuries and brought her to his chamber, and the effort had exhausted him. Moreover, a deep fear was growing in him. What he was about to do would break a vow that had been kept for well over thirty generations.

With trembling hands Mithras reached into the bag and drew out Gor-Kual, who flashed blood red in the flickering candlelight. He had not been able to see her clearly in the darkness of the palace foundations but here, now, she glowed with an ominous air. A cold finger of ice traced down the king's spine. What the true consequences of these actions would be only time would tell. The stark warning of the star visitors echoed through his thoughts, as clearly as if they were standing before him. For a moment, he hesitated.

No, he would not be dissuaded. This was the only way to save what was left of his people. As King, it was his duty to do no less.

He raised the skull up in front of him, level with his own face. She was heavy. His frail, wasted arm muscles soon began to ache and tremble with the effort of holding her. Refusing to give in to his discomfort he persisted, gazing into her vacant eye sockets. With the knowledge that had been handed down to him from his father, knowledge he never believed he would ever be called upon to use, he stilled his thoughts and stretched his mind out towards the red skull.

'Gor-Kual, I call upon you now. We have guarded and protected you over many lifetimes. We have done as we promised we would. Gor-Kual, my people are suffering and I cannot help them. I ask you, help us now in return.'

The skull seemed to quiver and pulse, coming alive in his hands. 'Greetings King Mithras, my guardian. What is it that troubles you so that you awaken me to seek my help?'

'My people are dying, Gor-Kual. We have no water, no crops, no food. Your power is great. You have the power to help us. Blessed Skull of Aldebaran, I ask you now, help us. Let the rain come and the river flow through our land again, to grow our crops and feed my people so that they may be strong and healthy once more.'

'The power within me is no greater than the power you hold within yourself, my protector. It is simply that you do not know that you possess it. However, I sense that the situation is grave, and that there is no time at present for you to discover this power for yourself or learn how to use it. Yes, I will help you willingly. Know though that in awakening me, you bring great danger upon yourself and your people. Many, many years have passed since I first came to you, yet those who sought me then seek me still. Be on your guard, King Mithras. Be alert for this danger, for it will come.'

An iron-tight fist of foreboding gripped the king's belly. He forced it down. What was done was done. What would be would be. He would face the consequences if they came. No, sadly, fearfully, he corrected himself, when they came. He was in no doubt that he had just set in motion a series of events that would not be stopped.

* * * * *

Late in the following day, dense clouds gathered in the sky above the kingdom and for the first time in living memory rain fell upon the land. Soon after, a deafening, thunderous roar reached the ears of the desperate population. Moments later a churning, foaming wall of water hurtled down the almost dry river bed, quickly filling it to its former level.

The people laughed. The people cried, knowing nothing of what had taken place within the palace, only that their prayers had been answered. It took only a few days for the healthy fresh green tips of new crops to push through the soil, a sight that brought joy to their hearts. Within weeks there was food on the tables once more. It was not much in those early days, but it was more than they had seen in a very long time. Slowly they regained their health, their strength and their spirits.

* * * * *

King Mithras, while relieved that the suffering of his people had eased, continued to suffer his own torment. Gor-Kual's words and his own guilt haunted him day and night. What further as yet unknown nightmare would his actions bring upon them all? He slept little, and in the brief times that he did, was tortured by his dreams. Far from regaining his strength as his people were, the king's health continued to deteriorate.

The king had taken Gor-Kual back to her hiding place in the depths of the palace foundations for, even in his knowing of the inevitability of what was to come to pass, he clung to the desperate hope that in returning her to this place she would once more sleep. That his action had gone unnoticed by those who hunted her. In his heart he knew that it was too late. The deed had been done, and there was no going back. Gor-Kual had been awakened. The warning of the angel beings, spoken on their first visit to him so many years ago, played over and over in his mind. How long would it be before their prophecy came to pass?

CHAPTER 44

Mithras' fears were justified. From that first moment when he had forged his connection with her, Gor-Kual's energy had been activated and her frequency beamed out into the world.

Far away on the other side of the continent that vibration had been detected, and a search put in place to discover its source and retrieve the skull. The Priests of the Light were not the only ones to have left the shores of Atlantis before it sank forever beneath the waves. Many of the Dark Ones had also left, many of them in a blatant act of pure self-preservation. A few though had held another agenda, prepared to go to any lengths to hunt down the skulls and their guardians and gain the skulls' power for themselves.

The man who was now preparing to set out in pursuit of Gor-Kual was Drakuno, a descendant of one of these original skull hunters. Through the ages since that long ago time, the all-consuming hunger and fire to possess one of these sacred and powerful objects had been passed down through his family. It remained undiminished, constantly fed and strengthened by dreams of power, wealth and domination. Drakuno was already powerful, ruler of a vast kingdom, possessor of unimaginable wealth and commander of a mighty army.

Yet even this was not enough – Gor-Kual still eluded him.

Many times over the thousands of years since the temple priests had fled Atlantis, his family had believed themselves to be close to their goal, only to have their ambitions crushed. Stories abounded of false leads, blind alleys, bizarre accidents and mysterious unexplained deaths that had cursed their every attempt to set hands on the red skull.

Several generations previously the fervour had dimmed, dampened by the toll of so much failure. His great great grandfathers and uncles had channelled their hunger for power into conquering and subjugating neighbouring kingdoms before reaching further afield. As a consequence Drakuno now ruled a vast empire and was able to mobilise every resource he needed for his offensive. The fire had been reborn in him, had burned fiercely through his veins for as long as he could remember, fuelled further by the tales of past failures. He was ambitious, merciless and ruthless, focussed unerringly on his objective. This time, he would allow nothing to stand between him and the red skull.

Why it should be Gor-Kual in particular when there were another twelve skulls that were hidden around the world for the finding Drakuno did not know. The whys and wherefores had been erased by the passage of time. He knew only that it was with her alone that his connection lay. That no matter what happened with the other skulls, he would know only when she had been awakened. He was in no doubt that this event would occur within his life-time, that he would track her and seize her for himself, for it had been foretold. He, Drakuno, treasured son of the Dark Ones, would finally fulfil the task appointed to that long dead Shadow Chaser and stand supreme.

*   *   *   *

That desperate night, at the exact moment that Mithras had spoken to Gor-Kual, Drakuno too had been woken from his sleep, roused by the powerful pulses of her reactivated energy field reverberating out into the night. Though more than a thousand miles away, he had felt them as strongly as if she had been in his chamber with him. His time had arrived. Immediately he had ordered his army to prepare for a lengthy campaign, for he did not at that moment know where Gor-Kual was or how fierce the battle would be before he could claim her. And claim her he would, of that he was certain. Within a month all was ready and Drakuno led his army of ten thousand well-trained and battle-hardened men out on their long march.

*   *   *   *   *

'My King, word has reached me that an army marches on us from the East. It is not known who leads it but if reports are true, and I have no reason to doubt their accuracy, we are vastly outnumbered. We will not be able to resist them.' Toomka, Mithras' chief advisor, could not keep the anxiety from his voice.

'You know this to be correct?'

269

'I believe it to be so, my King. Our sources are completely reliable.' Mithras knew from experience to trust Toomka's information implicitly. It had never failed them before. The king's gut tightened. It had begun. So many months had passed since he had woken Gor-Kual to ask for her help. Life had returned to a semblance of normality though many scars of the dry times remained etched on the hearts and in the memories of those who had survived them. He had begun to hope that, despite the dire warnings of the star beings and his own fearful forebodings, nothing would happen. The dark clouds of despair that had begun to evaporate once more settled heavily around him. He pulled his mind back to the moment.

'Where? Who? How many? How long until they reach us?' he demanded.

'I do not know who, my King, though it is said their leader wears a darkness around him like armour. They march from the east and will be upon us within two days, perhaps less.'

'Why were we not alerted earlier?' Two days? Mithras' heart sank further. What hope was left?

'Your majesty, no-one in their path has survived to tell the tale. It was pure luck that one was able to escape their latest massacre.' Toomka looked directly at the king, something he rarely dared do. 'King Mithras, they outnumber us by perhaps a hundred to one, if not more. We could not withstand their attack. The only hope we have is to surrender.'

'Toomke my friend,' the king's voice was heavy with sadness, 'if this is who I believe it to be, we will none of us survive their onslaught no matter whether we fight or we surrender. They will wipe us from the surface of the Earth as though we were no more than cockroaches. Leave me now. There is something important I must do before they reach our walls. Ask Kha-lim to come to me in two hours.' The advisor bowed. 'Tell the people to gather what food they can, then bring them all within the palace walls. If they are to stand any chance at all, it will be here.'

When Toomke had left the room, Mithras allowed his head to fall in despair and sorrow. This was the beginning of the end and he recognised it clearly. After a moment, the old king straightened, defiance in his posture, refusing to accept defeat until the final moment when he would come face to face with the man who would lay waste to his kingdom. He squared his frail shoulders, drawing up the courage and determination that still glowed within him, blowing on their embers until they burst into flame. There was work to be done.

As quickly as his protesting, aged body would permit, King Mithras hurried down to the foundations of the palace walls to fetch Gor-Kual. Whatever happened now to himself and his people, he would honour his pledge to protect her and keep her from the clutches of those who came to take her. As he held her once more in his hands a wave of power flowed from her into every cell of his body, bringing strength and resolve.

CHAPTER 45

Exactly two hours later Kha-lim, the king's eldest and favourite son, entered Mithras' chamber. He found his father seated on a couch, the red skull in his hands, staring into a far-off place.

'Father?' Mithras started as Kha-lim's voice broke through his reverie. 'You wanted to see me?' Kha-lim was staring in curiosity at Gor-Kual. Until that moment, he had been unaware of her existence. Her purpose and importance was unknown to him.

'Sit down, Kha-lim. There is much I must tell you and little time left in which to do so.' There was so much tension and sorrow in the old man's voice that Kha-lim did as he was bid without uttering a word. His father was suffering more than he had ever seen him suffer before, even at the height of the dark days. He was in no doubt that what he was about to hear was of the utmost seriousness. He waited.

For the next hour Mithras spoke to his son, telling him of Gor-Kual and their long-lasting guardianship of her, of the oath and his breaking of it, and of the peril that now faced them. 'They must not be allowed to possess her,' he finished. 'She must be taken away from here and hidden. I cannot do this, my son, I am too frail. In any case my place is here with my people. If they are to die because of my actions and my betrayal, then I must die alongside them.

'I am old, Kha-lim. In a few short months you would have taken my place as king and ruler of this kingdom. At that time you would have learned the secret of Gor-Kual for yourself. I would have spoken to you of her before, should have spoken to you of her before, but my betrayal of her weighed too heavily in my heart. My son, I entrust her to you now. Take her to a place of safety, hide her where none will ever find her. There is no time for delay. You must leave now.'

'No, father. I cannot.' Kha-lim stood defiantly. 'My place is here, fighting at your side.'

'I am no longer important. Kha-lim, my beloved son, you must understand – Gor-Kual is your only priority. Do not argue. I am your father and your king, and I command that you obey me.' His voice softened as he gazed on the face of his so dearly loved son. 'Please, do as I ask of you. This must be. I cannot say enough how important it is that she be kept safe. You are the only one who can do it.'

Kha-lim opened his mouth to argue further but the urgency and desperation on his father's face stilled his protests. Reluctantly, he agreed. 'Very well, father. I will do as you ask. As soon as she is safely hidden, I will return to you.'

Mithras embraced his son tightly, knowing they would never meet again. By the time Kha-lim returned, it would be too late. The enemy forces were already at their door. But he kept his silence.

Kha-lim picked up Gor-Kual, stowed her in the bag that lay beside his father on the couch, and with a final sorrow-filled farewell glance at Mithras turned and walked out of the chamber. Five minutes later he galloped through the palace gates and disappeared into the blackness of the desert night.

With a heavy sigh King Mithras sank back down on to the couch. It would not be long now.

*   *   *   *   *

Kha-lim had set out into the desert with no thought of where he would go, his only intention to find a safe hiding place for the skull and return to the palace as quickly as possible. Before he had travelled more than a dozen miles however a clear image entered his mind. The Caves of Khamun. They were a veritable labyrinth. No-one who did not know the confused interconnecting twists and turns of the dark passageways would find the skull there. Anyone entering the tunnels through idle curiosity would more than likely spend their remaining days wandering lost within them. Kha-lim however did know them, had spent so much time there in past times, bewitched and enthralled by their other-worldly beauty and complexity. When still a boy, he would take a bundle of supplies, slip out of the palace and camp out for days at a time in their silence and solitude, exploring and mapping their tangled arteries in his head. What is more, they were close, a day's ride at most. He would be able to hide Gor-Kual beyond anyone's reach and return to fight – and die if necessary – by his father's side.

He drew his horse to a halt and paused to take his bearings. Digging his spurs into the flanks of his mount, he wheeled around and set off in the direction of the caves. It was a decision that would cost him his life.

*   *   *   *   *

Kha-lim had been riding hard for over three hours across the hard, stony floor of the desert. The eastern sky was growing perceptibly lighter as dawn approached. His goal, the Caves of Khamun, were still several hours away but he should reach them before the sun touched its peak. He could then rest over the hottest part of the day and would be back at the palace sometime just after midnight.

In the desert here, sand had long given way to a rough, sun-baked ground that was littered with stones. It was hard on his horse's feet but he could make better time. Low outcrops of rock jutted randomly from the ground while, here and there, a larger, jagged bluff towered above him, the remnants of an ancient, long-eroded mountain range.

It was as he rounded one of these bluffs that an arrow struck him squarely on his left breast. He toppled from the saddle, dead before he hit the floor, never seeing his assailants. Death had struck silently and swiftly at the hands of the scouting party that had spotted his approach, the advance guard of Drakuno's army. Kha-lim had not been recognised or singled out. The invaders were methodically and cold-bloodedly slaughtering everyone who crossed their path. It was sheer luck on their part, and misfortune on Kha-lim's, that he rode straight into their midst. It was only as the invaders approached his corpse searching for spoils that one of them seized his horse and spotted the heavy bag hanging from its saddle. Not daring to keep its unusual contents to themselves through fear of Drakuno's brutal retribution, one of them mounted the horse and returned at breakneck speed to where Drakuno was camped with the main body of his army.

CHAPTER 46

Drakuno strode through the main hall of the palace, his arrogance tangible. As he reached the dais where once, so many long years before, King Mithras had sat in council with the star people, his lip curled in a scornful sneer. There, forced to his knees, his hands wrenched painfully behind his back by the soldiers who held him, was Mithras, stripped naked, yet one more humiliation forced upon him by his conqueror. Old, frail, unable to defend himself, he had been quickly and easily overpowered, his life only spared on Drakuno's express orders. Yet the king remained defiant and proud, believing Gor-Kual and Kha-lim to be safe and far from Drakuno's reach.

When however, with an exaggerated flourish Drakuno brought the red skull into Mithras' view, the old man finally crumpled, every last vestige of fight drained from him. Horror, despair, grief washed the colour from his face. If Drakuno had the skull, then he, Mithras, had failed – and his beloved son Kha-lim must be dead. He would never have relinquished it any other way. Tears filled his eyes and trickled down his ashen cheeks. He, Mithras, king and protector, had betrayed his people, his friends from the stars, his ancestors, his oath, and himself. And he had betrayed Gor-Kual.

Oblivious to Mithras' pain, uncaring, Drakuno slid his word from its scabbard. Devoid of any emotion he ran it through the old man as if he had been nothing more than a rat. Mithras slumped to the floor, his crimson blood staining the pristine golden marble.

'Clear up this mess,' Drakuno ordered coldly. As if he were doing no more than haul away a sack of stones, a guard seized an ankle and dragged the king away, his naked lifeless body smearing blood behind it. It was the ultimate indignity for a once great ruler.

Alone for the first time since Gor-Kual had come into his hands, Drakuno breathed deeply and smiled a dark, satisfied smile. This is what he had been waiting for. This was what his family had been waiting for over the thousands of years that had passed since his long-dead forefather had left Atlantis on the trail of the red skull. His time had come.

Drakuno lifted Gor-Kual until she was level with his own face, staring into and beyond the empty eye sockets into the depths of her skull. As he felt her power surge through him he sighed with an almost orgasmic pleasure. This was how it was meant to be. With Gor-Kual beside him he would be invincible. He glanced at the stained floor, drying brown in the heat of the day. That pathetic old man. He had had no idea of what he possessed. If Mithras had used her as he himself intended to use her...

Suddenly the ground shook violently beneath his feet. Small shards of stone, loosened from the ceiling, smashed to the floor around him. Drakuno clutched the red skull to his chest, stood perfectly still and waited. It was a slight earth tremor, nothing more. It would soon pass. Sure enough, the shaking stopped. Letting out his breath he lifted her once more, allowing himself to be drawn into her depths. He, Drakuno, had succeeded where none before him had, not his ancestors, nor any other Shadow Chaser of Atlantis. He had captured one of the original sacred skulls, and he would use her power to increase his own.

He stumbled as the tremors began again, much more violently than before. Walls, floor, roof – all shook and cracked at their intensity and ferocity, which seemed to have no end. This time, larger chunks of stone dislodged from the ceiling and crashed down inches from where he stood. This was no minor quake. The whole building was coming down. He had to get out.

Grasping Gor-Kual under his arm Drakuno sprinted for the doorway. Just as he reached it a heavy, white marble table toppled to the ground, knocking him over and pinning his legs beneath it. A crushing agony overwhelmed him and he dropped Gor-Kual, who rolled away from him, just out of reach. Fighting the excruciating pain in his shattered legs, paying no heed to the masonry that was still raining down, oblivious to everything but his frenzied need to reach the skull, to retrieve her, Drakuno stretched as far as his trapped body would go. There... He had her... Just under his fingertips. Ashen pale, clenching his jaw at the effort and at the torment in his lower body, his fingers crept infinitesimally forward, hooking at last into her eye sockets. He inched her back towards him, drawing her closer, every movement punishing him, until his hand at last closed over the crown of the red skull. In that instant a flat stone the size of a shield dropped, crushing his own skull. The quake stopped as suddenly as it had begun and an eerie silence settled over the palace.

No-one came to find Drakuno. All entrances to the chamber were blocked by tons of fallen masonry that would take days to clear. His soldiers never had the time.

That night a sandstorm, the like of which had never been experienced before, buried the palace and the city around it to its rooftops, entombing forever all those who remained within, erasing almost all trace of the thriving kingdom that had once existed there.

CHAPTER 47

I don't know what disturbed me. I woke up with a start and lay for a few moments in the half-light confused by my unusual surroundings before my mind caught up and reminded me where I was. When it did, a warm shiver of excitement thrilled through me. I was in a tent in the middle of a desert somewhere in the south west of the United States (though exactly where, I had absolutely no idea). Me!

And last night... I flushed at the memory.

Across from me Frankie was snoring gently, just her nose and the top of her head peeking out from her sleeping bag. Outside, the horses, which were tethered just behind the tents, seemed restless, rustling their hooves and whinnying nervously. Was that what had woken me? Had they been disturbed by coyotes maybe, or a mountain lion? We hadn't seen any but Ches had pointed out their calls to me several times as we sat around the campfire on the previous two nights. To the not quite well-hidden enough amusement of the others – thanks guys! – I found it more than a little unnerving. I was so out of my depth in this stunning but arid wilderness, which was most definitely NOT the safe, cosy, tamed English countryside I was used to. At home I only had to worry about knocking over the odd jaywalking badger or rabbit, or stepping on a hedgehog in the dark. Which was on a bit of a different scale to rattlesnakes, tarantulas (which, thank god, I hadn't yet seen any of) and large, hungry carnivores. Ches had taken pains to reassure me that they wouldn't approach humans. I really hoped he was telling me the truth. Maybe they wouldn't be so backward in having a sniff around the horses though.

I scrambled stiffly out of the tent to see that the sun was only just pushing the top arc of its sphere over the horizon. It had to be early still. Despite myself I glanced across to Callum's tent, feeling as I did so the heat rising in my face at the memory of the previous evening. What had I been thinking of?

I had surprised myself, and him as well I think, at the hunger and abandoned wildness I had shown as I gave in at last to his magnetic pull. This morning I was feeling extremely self-conscious at the thought of coming face to face with him. I had shown him a part of me that no one before had ever seen and probably never even knew existed, a part of me even I had only suspected may lie buried deep beneath the surface of my reserved English exterior. But this wild, primeval landscape had woken something wild and primeval in me . Now that it had been let out, I wasn't sure I would be able to shut it away again completely.

Thankfully there was no sign of movement from Callum's tent. Trying pretty ineffectively to put my heated thoughts from my mind, I wandered over to the horses. After my initial nervousness, I had discovered a great deal of affection for these creatures, and especially for my own gentle, patient, tolerant Billy. They had quietened down, whatever had disturbed them now gone, and I was met with soft muzzles and low snickers of greeting.

The beauty and stillness of the just awakening desert morning was bewitching. I forgot to move, forgot almost to breathe. I simply stood there and let its spell wash over me. The rising sun cast ever shifting shadows over the hills and valleys so that from one moment to the next nothing looked the same. On the horizon, the sky, soft pale blue washed with creamy pink creamy pink, slowly deepened in colour as degree by tiny degree the sun climbed higher in the sky. Small mammals darted here and there, getting their business finished before the heat of the day drove them into the relative cool of their underground burrows. I was entranced, would have willingly remained locked in that moment forever. I had fallen in love at first sight with this land, so alien to the damp green countryside of my English home. It was a love that had only grown deeper over the last three days.

I was so wrapped up in it all that I didn't notice immediately. Slowly however, it sank into my awareness that one of the horses was missing. We had brought nine: one each for the riders and three as pack-horses to carry the equipment. I counted three times just to make sure. Eight. One was missing. I ran through them. Billy was there, and Frankie's big stallion... Jack's. It was Jack's horse that had gone. Maybe he had just wandered off but I didn't think so. Ches was in charge of caring for the horses and did so diligently. Riding alongside him that first afternoon he had shared with me how he had grown up with them, could ride before he could walk. Clearly he loved them with a passion. I had seen how painstaking he was in his care of these beautiful beasts. This had not happened because of any error on his part. I had to let him know.

Thoughtfully I wandered back to the small huddle of tents. The camp was still silent and sleeping. Where was Ches? I couldn't find him anywhere. I was still feeling shy – no, let's be honest, not shy, highly embarrassed - about facing Callum so, making up my mind, I walked over to Jack's tent.

'Jack.' I called softly. 'Jack.' No reply. I tried again. 'Jack, I'm sorry to disturb you but your horse has gone.'

'Uh?' The sleepy voice that finally answered was Davey's. He was sharing the tent with Jack.

'Sorry Davey, It's just that Jack's horse is missing and I can't find Ches, so I thought I should let him know.'

'Jack?' I heard the tone of Davey's voice change. He was suddenly wide awake. 'Gemma, he isn't here.' A pause before he continued. 'Hasn't been for a while by the look of it. His bed is cold. You'd better let Callum know.'

Well, I had to get it over with sooner or later. I hurried across to Callum's tent, still finding myself hesitating as I got to the entrance, those memories once more coming to the fore and turning my face crimson. Swallowing, I called his name. 'Callum?'

His voice was as sleepy as Davey's had been, but his carried in it a subtle nuance that I chose to ignore. 'Gemma.' Evidently Callum too had been thinking about the previous evening. Great, just what I wanted. I reddened even more, grateful no-one was around to witness it. To cover my complete lack of composure, I put a brusque, no-nonsense tone in my voice. 'Callum, Jack's gone. So has his horse.'

In an instant Callum was out of his sleeping bag – like the rest of us he'd slept in his clothes to ward off the chill of the desert night - pushing past me, heading towards the pile of equipment we had readied for exploring deeper into the caves.

'Fuck!' The expletive exploded into the still, morning air. 'He's taken a load of the ropes, tapes and a couple of lamps with him.' He whirled around, his whole body taut with anger. 'I knew I was right not to trust him. The bastard is trying to put one over on us. He's gone after the skull on his own.' For a long moment no-one spoke.

'What do we do now?' The question was unnecessary and we all knew the answer would be before I had even finished it. Callum was a man driven when it came to the crystal skulls.

'We go after him.' His face was set, angrier and more determined than I had ever imagined he could be. 'That skull is ours to find. I have spent my whole life working for this and I am not going to let some jumped up little Johnny-come-lately take it away from me.'

* * * * *

Ches returned around half an hour later to find us all booted and ready to head up to the caves.

'Where have you been?' Callum was short almost to the point of rudeness to the amiable guide but Ches paid no notice.

'Speaking with the spirits, as I have done every day since I was ten years old. Asking for their blessing on this intrusion into their sacred world. You know this my friend, so why do you ask me now?'

'Jack's gone.' Callum's dark mood wasn't letting up. 'Did you see him?'

'No. How long ago did he leave?'

'We don't know, but I'll bet my last penny that he's gone back to look for the skull. We're heading up after him now. Stay here and keep an eye on the camp. If he does by any chance come back here, keep hold of him.'

Ches looked across at Callum, an odd expression on his face. 'He will not return.' His words sent unpleasant chills through my body and I wanted him to explain what he meant. Instead he turned and walked across to where the horses stood, looking sad. He would not tell us more.

Within half an hour we were standing outside the cave entrance, loaded with lamps and ropes. We were all subdued, unwilling to believe that Jack had double-crossed us. Even Frankie's ever-present sparkle was muted. All except Callum. He was even more fired up than ever, resolved to come out on top of this battle. As for me? I was caught in the grip of a dark cloud of foreboding, unable to shake off an unpleasant feeling that we were about to go somewhere we had no right to be. At that moment I would have quite happily given up on the whole business and caught the first plane home. But I couldn't, so it was time to fix my stiff upper lip firmly in place and get on with it.

I stepped from the glare of the already baking morning sunlight into the shadows beyond the entrance. Immediately I felt the soft heaviness of an unseen blanket drape itself over me, and my anxiety eased. In some unfathomable way I understood that this was the presence of Gal-Athiel, the blue skull that Callum had come here to find. I had no time to question further. The rocky chamber vanished briefly before my eyes and words, thoughts, filled my mind. *Today they will find the chamber. It is no longer necessary to keep its location from them. I am safe.*

The cave reappeared, shimmering back into my reality, the words echoing in my mind. Would that really be the case? Would we succeed in finding the cave and the skull today? Or was I being told something else entirely? Callum's impatient voice interrupted my musing.

'Right, let's go. We can't afford to waste any more time hanging around.'

GOR-KUAL: The Red Skull

Part IV

GAL-ATHIEL, THE FINAL CHAPTER

CHAPTER 48

In the mid-hours of the night Jack crept out of the tent he shared with Davey and slipped across the deserted campground. His only concern was Ches. The native American guide had the eyes of a hawk and the ears of a bat. He slept, by choice, in the open air, and the slightest movement could wake him. To Jack's good fortune Ches was nowhere around. An hour earlier he had risen and headed for a hilltop an hour's walk away. This land was sacred to his people and he needed to make peace with its spirits for their intrusion.

Relieved, Jack gathered together the ropes, lines and lamps he would need then, burdened by his load but making as little sound as was humanly possible, he untethered his horse and led it away, back up the slope to the cave entrance. His feet were as agile as a mountain goat, the result of his years of training and discipline, and he moved silently through the night with only the light of the stars and the quarter moon to show him the trail.

When they found the cave earlier in the day Jack had been watching Gemma as closely as Callum had. He too had seen the expression of recognition cross her face as she walked into the first entrance chamber. This was the place they had been searching for alright. The blue skull was hidden somewhere in this labyrinth. It was his job to find it before anyone else.

As the group had moved through these first sections of passageways the previous day, Jack committed the route to memory. It wasn't necessary, the guide line they had set up was still firmly fixed in place, but Jack was taking no chances. He followed it to its end, to the point where a junction split the main tunnel into three. This had been the focal point for their initial exploration. Callum had chosen the left hand tunnel, simply because they had to start somewhere, only for it to lead, after a long, exhausting two hour scramble, to a dead end. They would return in the morning to investigate the other openings. The thought spurred Jack on. He did not have the luxury of time on his side.

Straight on or right? Right. Why he chose right he didn't know, and actually he didn't see it mattered. He had no idea where any of them would lead anyway. He fastened the end of the new reel of guide line he carried to the existing bolt and set off, paying it out behind him as he went.

Deeper and deeper into the underground maze he descended, his powerful flashlight throwing its dazzling beam over the roof and walls while the light from his head torch danced along the floor ahead of him. Jack was a practical man, not prone to flights of fancy or an overactive imagination, nonetheless he felt unnerved at being in this place alone where it seemed that something or someone was watching him from behind the impenetrable blackness of every tunnel entrance. It was very different exploring these caves on his own than it had been earlier in the company of the others.

On both sides the eerie dark mouths of countless side shafts leered at him malevolently. Despite being an experienced caver, far more experienced than he had allowed the others to believe, Jack had to fight down the growing anxiety that he would get lost and end up wandering through this maze with no hope of escape until his strength at last gave out. In truth, it was no unfounded fear but a very real danger should he make a careless move. No-one knew he was down here. There would be precious little chance of a rescue party coming to look for him.

Time lost all meaning as he followed tunnel after tunnel, losing count of the number of times he had to retrace his steps. The first reel of line had come to its end; he tied the second firmly to it. Even when not retracing his route it felt like he was continually twisting back on himself in the tangle of passageways, having to make a decision at every fork or side tunnel. Early on he had taken the decision to stick always to what appeared to be the main passageway, though after numerous false turns when what seemed to be the main artery petered out to nothing, it soon became clear that the size of the tunnel meant nothing. Still, with nothing else to go on it was as good a way of picking a route as any other.

It must have been several miles later when Jack stopped and peered into the dark void ahead.

Something was different, though he couldn't for the life of him figure out what it was. On a flash of inspiration he switched off both the powerful lamp he was carrying and his head torch. Immediately, heavy, suffocating blackness wrapped itself around him like a shroud, clogging his lungs. He fought back the panic. It was just his imagination at work. Nothing had changed other than the light being extinguished. Nevertheless he felt cold fingers of fear tracing down his spine, as if someone was walking softly over his grave.

What was it that had caused him to stop and shut himself in to this perpetual subterranean night? Jack was disorientated, blind, only able to tell up from down because of gravity. His heartbeat was regular as a clock ticking, sounding unnaturally loud in the silence. Nothing else intruded. As his eyes accustomed themselves to the darkness, however, something totally unexpected appeared ahead of him. He could see something, and he shouldn't have been able to. Could his eyes be lying? No, it was real. An almost imperceptibly paler area, just visible as a faint glow of sickly luminescence. But it couldn't be, not this far down. Surely his mind, his eyes, were playing tricks... weren't they?

The penny dropped and his jaw fell open. Could it be? Fleeting sentences from Gemma's book, which he had only hastily scanned, flickered around the edges of his thoughts. Had he really stumbled, by luck rather than judgement, on the very thing he had been searching for? He swiftly flicked on his lamp again, its sudden blast of fierce light painful to his eyes as it instantly flooded the passageway. Jack hurried forward as fast as the tortuous uneven tunnel would allow.

As he drew nearer to the unearthly glimmer, Jack switched off his lights once more and allowed himself to be guided by its beckoning. He reached the doorway and paused, his eyes sweeping the interior, still getting used to the extremely low light levels. He took a couple of cautious steps forward gazing up at the spectral glow emanating from the rock of the ceiling. Stopped suddenly as his foot made contact with something that rustled as he nudged it. He glanced down and jerked back in surprise. He had nearly stepped on a body that lay curled up in the middle of the space. More sentences, distant whispers, but too ethereal, drifting tantalisingly away even as he reached out to grasp them.

Peering more closely, Jack realised that the corpse was lying in the centre of a rough circle of small stones, its quarters marked with the same pebbles: a rudimentary medicine wheel. Had this been a place of ritual? It was certainly a sacred place, or this man who lay by his feet would not have spent the time or energy to create it. Sacred enough, important enough, to die for. Jack knelt by the body, for the moment his deep fascination for all things indigenous washing from his mind the true purpose of his coming here. He flicked on the lamp to get a clearer look. Without touching the corpse, which he found to be in excellent condition, mummified naturally but so effectively by the atmosphere in this strange place, he examined it carefully. Although he possessed an almost encyclopaedic knowledge of the tribes who once lived in these areas, of their variations in costume and personal decoration, he found himself unable to identify its origins.

Eventually, frustrated that his lifelong studies had failed him, Jack lifted his head and looked around, remembering his mission. His eyes followed the torch light as it scanned the walls of the room. Despite himself, despite knowing what he had been told would be here, he jumped as they swept across the skull, his usually unruffled-able poise draining away. It was a deep sea green and it was watching him, he would swear it, its eyes flashing in the torch beam as if they were alive.

A former marine, Jack was not prone to bouts of fantasy, nonetheless he couldn't shake off the impression that the skull was warning him off. An icy wave washed over him, a wave of primordial, instinctive fear that he should have paid heed to but didn't. Logic had kicked in, overriding his gut. This was an inanimate object which could pose no more danger to him that any other piece of stone. It was rare that Jack paid no attention to his instincts, they had saved his life on countless occasions, but this was so far from logic that he could not accept their warning. What is more he was under orders to recover the skull before Callum and his group found it (and if he didn't, to acquire it regardless) and take it back to his paymasters. He was being rewarded handsomely for his trouble.

He stared at the skull for a few long moments more. In his heart of hearts he had not believed the skull had really existed, had felt that he was being sent on a wild goose chase. It was too absurd, something that rated alongside their other crackpot schemes like the remote viewing, telepathic communication and psychokinetic projects. And yet here he was, staring it down in a small cave deep below a range of hills in the middle of nowhereland, south-west USA.

'Well Jack,' he said to himself out loud, looking to break the spell, his voice echoing eerily, amplified by the circular walls of the space, 'that's another thing to take out of your load of bollocks box.' Jack threw everything that he considered to be too far-fetched to be even remotely believable into what he called his 'load of bollocks box', which acted as his mental equivalent of a computer's recycle bin. Rarely did he have to restore any files from it. In fact, he mused, this might well be the first time ever.

It was time to go. The icy wave had settled into an uncomfortable creeping chill that was taking hold of every part of him, bit by bit. His instincts, which this time he was listening to, were telling him that he had outstayed his welcome here.

Swallowing a surge of inexplicable fear Jack stepped up to the shelf and lifted the blue skull, in spite of himself almost expecting something supernatural to happen. It didn't. He turned it over in his hands, looking more closely. It was heavy, life-sized, created from a sea-blue glassy material. How old it was he had no idea and wouldn't have believed it had he been told. It was strangely, eerily beautiful. As the lamplight caught the polished dome of the cranium, flashes of rainbow colour sparked. Instead of stowing it away in his pack as he had intended, the blue skull remained in Jack's hands, his eyes drawn constantly to her as he left the room to return to the surface and the welcome light of day.

*　　*　　*　　*　　*

The skull was Gal-Athiel. She had been created millennia upon millennia ago by the star beings of Theta from the purest blue obsidian, brought to Earth by those same star beings to aid in humankind's spiritual evolution and to guide it through its challenges. Over three hundred and fifty years previously, she had been brought to this cave, given up by the tribe who watched over her in order to protect her from those who would use her for their own power-hungry purposes. Here she would remain, hidden and undisturbed, until the day came for her existence to be revealed once more to the people of the Earth. That day had not yet arrived.

The warrior who had brought Gal-Athiel here in those distant times was that same empty shell who now rested before her on the sandy floor. He had sacrificed himself to ensure her safety. Would Jack's arrival now mean that his actions had been in vain?

*　　*　　*　　*　　*

It was the inescapable compulsion to keep his eyes locked onto Gal-Athiel that was Jack's undoing. His attention was no longer focussed on following the life line. Consequently he took a wrong turn at a fork in the path and walked for what he later thought was only several minutes before he forced his mind back to where he was and saw his error. By then though, he had lost all trace of his former route and the line was nowhere in sight. Throughout the time when his concentration was elsewhere, Jack's feet had continued to carry him through a myriad of passageways that his eyes had not registered. He was now wandering aimlessly adrift in this honeycomb of tunnels.

Jack felt the panic rise momentarily within him before his military training kicked in, pulling him back to rationality. He stopped and considered his position. He had an excellent sense of direction and trusted in it implicitly to guide him back. He reckoned he could only have lost his focus for a matter of a few minutes so couldn't be far from the main thoroughfare and safety. There was plenty of life left in the lamp batteries and he was carrying spares in his backpack, He would simply retrace his steps. It wouldn't be that difficult. It couldn't be far. The one thing he was certain of was that in all the time he had been daydreaming he hadn't made any sharp turns or negotiated any steep inclines.

What Jack was not aware of was the actual length of time his attention had been on the skull rather than the route. Far from lasting just a few minutes, as he believed, it had been over half an hour in all. Nor had he given due consideration to the complexity of the cave system. Every few metres the tunnel split in an array of forked junctions and side passages. Some he dismissed immediately – they were too narrow, too steep, too uneven underfoot to have passed through without noticing, even in his trance-like state. Others gave no clue at all. He was listening intently to his internal compass, but unnervingly its directions no longer seemed so clear.

The skull was now safely stored in his backpack – he would not risk being distracted again – but it was too late. Jack was facing an impossible task. Time after time he took a wrong route, having to backtrack to his starting point when the tunnel he had chosen ended in a blank wall, or a vertical shaft, or tapered away to nothing. He was becoming exhausted as the futility of his actions took its toll. Yet, slowly and steadily, Jack was making his way back to the main tunnel and the security of his guide line. His sense of direction was working. Unfortunately, and it would be his undoing, Jack was totally unaware of the fact.

Fear was rising ever more strongly in his belly now and he was unable to push it away entirely. 'Breathe, Jack,' he reminded himself over and over again. 'Breathe.' It would keep the first stirrings of true panic at bay, at least for now, though he could feel that it was ready to rise up and overwhelm him if he gave it half a chance. Surely he should have found the main artery by now and be heading for the joys of fresh air and sunlight. He must have come too far. Or taken a wrong turn again somewhere. He would have to retrace his steps once more.

So just fifty metres or so from the safety he was seeking so desperately, Jack made a one hundred and eighty degree turn and once more backtracked along the passageway. Within a few minutes he was hopelessly and irretrievably lost. Desperation finally claimed him, putting to flight all sense of reason and logic. In his panic, the last remnants of his sense of direction abandoned him completely, leaving him stumbling blindly as he headed deeper and deeper into the heart of the cave system and the bedrock of the hills. Slowly and inescapably he was descending, away from the surface and safety, down into the ensnaring bowels of the Earth.

* * * * *

At last Jack's exhausted legs forced him to a halt. His head was fuzzy and unclear. A warning voice in his mind, an automatic message, told him to eat and drink, that fatigue and dehydration were setting in. He hadn't refuelled since he'd left the campsite so despite his desperate need to escape this place, he forced down a few mouthfuls of water and a couple of energy bars. It made no difference. His head was getting thicker and more befuddled by the minute, his breathing more laboured. As he rose to his feet, he collapsed back down again to the floor, assaulted by dizziness. Jack forced himself to think as clearly as he could through the fog that was invading his brain, to assess the situation. For the first time in a couple of hours his long years of combat experience resurfaced.

The first thing he noticed was the staleness of the air. No through draughts washed these tunnels clean, as they had earlier. It was getting harder and harder to breathe. A final burst of rational thought filtered through. He was being poisoned, or suffocated, or both. Caves such as this, where there was no airflow, frequently trapped deadly gases such as sulphur dioxide, ammonia, methane and carbon monoxide. He must have stumbled into a pocket of foul air in these stale tunnels. He had to get out, and quickly. Jack forced himself clumsily to his feet, each tiny move costing him a monumental effort, and staggered back up the passageway at a shuffling run.

It was too late. He had lost the battle. The lethal cocktail of methane and carbon monoxide had done their job well. Jack tripped in the uneven floor and stumbled several feet before crashing headlong, sprawling full length on the cold, rough stone, smashing beyond repair the forehead light he still wore. He did not have the strength left to pull himself to his feet once more, was barely able to drag himself to a sitting position against a side wall. He had lost his grip on the flashlight as he fell. It lay on its side on the opposite side of the tunnel, its cheery yellow beam incongruous yet reassuring in this deadly place.

He was fighting for breath now, his chest heaving in great wheezing gasps as he battled to draw enough oxygen into his body to keep himself conscious. His heart fluttered like the wings of a trapped bird, beating a desperate SOS against the inside of his ribcage. Toxic gases were surging into his lungs, into his bloodstream, and his lungs were on fire as they worked to their limit. Bent double at the pain in his chest still Jack would not, could not, give in.

CHAPTER 49

I had become a bit more comfortable with being underground. Not happy, that would be too much of an exaggeration, but I could tolerate it, even if it still wasn't somewhere I really wanted to be. So far all the passageways we had explored were big enough to stand up in, and except for the initial squeeze through the rift at the back of the entrance cave, relatively spacious. Underfoot too, it was remarkably smooth.

The darkness was something else altogether. I have always had a fear of the dark, as far back as I could remember, and this place was pushing me to my limits. As long as I kept focussed on the lamps and the illuminated areas I was OK. If I looked beyond them into the wall of solid black that waited there though I could feel the panic bubbling away in my stomach. As for looking behind… I didn't dare turn round. My imagination was going into overdrive at it was. I breathed deeply and slowly in an attempt to hold it in check and fixed my eyes on the back on Frankie's head. Sensing my gaze she turned and gave me a welcome grin, winking her reassurance.

On and on we walked, following the line that had been set in place the previous day, retracing our route up to the point where the tunnel split and we had taken the passageway that had turned into a dead end. Today we would try one of the two other routes. There were so many passageways, leading off one another, so many junctions and forks. It was more than a needle in a haystack – we were looking for a needle in a whole field of haystacks. We could spend a lifetime exploring this system and not cover a fraction of it. How on earth did Callum think he could find one small chamber in this place, even if it really did exist? He was crazy. His fervour would not let him even consider that he wouldn't find it.

In my heart, though I knew he was right. We were in the place I had seen in my dreams. Knew too that however impossible it seemed, we would find that chamber today. After all, Gal-Athiel herself had told me so.

'Centre,' Callum decided. We had reached our start point. There were the three tunnels forking off the main route. The left hand one we had explored yesterday and it had been a long hike before we had come up against a wall of rock. Once, thousands, maybe tens of thousands of years ago, a waterfall had flowed there. Now it was dry, the vast cavern reaching out of sight above our heads to the upper channel with no way of accessing it. Disappointed, we had turned back.

We all stood and stared at the three yawning openings. Would any of them lead us on anything other than a wild goose chase?

'We'll try the centre one.' Even as he spoke, Callum was heading towards it.

I didn't move. 'No. That's the wrong way.' Callum was about to lead us in completely the wrong direction. 'Right, Callum. We have to go right.' How on earth did I know that? I did though. It was as clear to me as if someone had painted a large luminous arrow on the wall. The chamber we were looking for was somewhere down the right hand passageway.

Callum walked back and gave me a hard look. Whatever he saw in my eyes must have convinced him. 'OK, Gemma. It's your shout. We go right.' He gave my shoulder a squeeze. All at once thoughts of the previous evening flooded unbidden back into my mind and I felt my face burn. I was irritated at myself. Didn't I have enough to think about right now? Thankfully the shadows from the lights hid my blushes from the others. Not Callum though. He may have been impatient to continue the search but it didn't stop him taking a moment to wink at me and murmur in a voice so low only I could hear, 'You have no idea how much I am looking forward to the encore.' He turned away before I could reply. Which was a good thing, as his words had temporarily robbed me of any ability to speak.

*   *   *   *   *

Davey knelt to attach a new guide line to the one we had left the previous day. He gave out a long, low whistle. 'Looks like someone's been here before us, Callum.' He pointed to where the wall met the floor.

Concealed in the shadows a thin rope snaked down into the darkness of the right hand tunnel.

'Jack.' Callum almost spat the word out. He hoisted his pack higher onto his shoulders. 'Let's go. If he's still down there...' I hoped for Jack's sake that he wasn't.

We must have walked for at least another two or three hours. The tunnels here were less easy to negotiate. The ground was rough and uneven, and we frequently had to scramble over large boulders or through narrow crevices. This was not my idea of a fun day out, though to my infinite gratitude we didn't encounter any of those really tight gaps that involve turning yourself into a compressible contortionist. After everything that had happened, that would have been one step too far for me. Everywhere, side tunnels led on to more tunnels. But there was no sign of Jack. Could he have really made it all the way down here and then got back to the entrance and far enough away in such a short time?

How much further would Callum want to take us? Davey was getting openly restless and at least twice in the last half an hour had suggested that maybe we had gone far enough for one day. I moved up to him and asked why he thought we should perhaps turn back.

'Because it will take us just as long again to get back to the entrance, if not longer. We're all tired, you especially. You aren't used to this. It's too easy to trip and hurt yourself in this environment at any time. When you're tired it makes it all the more likely.'

I bridled at his comment. I didn't like being considered the weak link. He was right though, much as I hated to admit it even to myself. I was struggling. My physical fitness left a lot to be desired. As an author I spent a lot of time sitting on my backside and nowhere near enough time being active. This trek had been pretty strenuous from the beginning and here, now, I wasn't relishing the long trek back to daylight at all. Davey was the most experienced caver in the group. He knew his stuff. If he said we should turn back then it would be wise to listen to him. Somewhere deep within me however a little voice was protesting. We were close now, too close to give up. In any case, right at this moment, there was no way that Callum was prepared take notice of Davey's advice. We went on.

CHAPTER 50

I stopped and gaped, temporarily unable to believe the evidence of my eyes. I was standing on a level, sandy floor just inside the entrance of a small, circular chamber whose smoothly scoured walls glowed with eerie green luminescence. I had never been here before and yet I knew this place.

I took another step, glancing around. I recoiled, my skin crawling, screwing up my eyes so I didn't have to look. On the floor about five feet in front of me the body of a man was lying, curled up in the foetal position, his knees drawn tightly up against his chest. I had never before in my life seen a dead body and would rather have not done so now. My first thoughts were that it was Jack, even as I realised it couldn't be. This was not someone who had been here only hours at the most. The corpse was covered in a fine film of dust, and whereas Jack was short and stocky with short-cropped dark blond hair, even curled up it was obvious this had been a tall man. Long dark hair still draped over his shoulder.

I was absolutely not going to go in for a closer look. As scientists and archaeologists, Callum and his team did not share my squeamishness. I stood at the outer edge of the room, my back against the wall, watching with fascinated distaste as they approached the body, impressed at their restraint. They may have been mavericks working outside the accepted truths of their professions, but all three were consummate professionals. In spite of their excitement they were following strictly the scientific protocols and codes that were demanded on any archaeological site.

They tiptoed carefully through a circle of what were evidently deliberately paced small stones and crouched beside the body. Davey pulled a pair of latex examination gloves from his backpack and, putting them on, examined it more closely, disturbing it as little as possible.

'Definitely indigenous. Male. I'd guess about six feet tall though it's not easy to tell from the position of the body. Well built. Looking at his hair colour and build, I'd take a guess at him being in his late thirties or early forties. The body is well preserved. The atmosphere down here would have helped that. I would say he has been here a long time.' His professional first impression over, he sat back on his heels.

Callum let out a long, low breath, almost a whistle. 'Well, it seems we've found your Takuanaka, Gemma.'

My legs buckled beneath me and I sat down heavily on the hard stone floor. It had become impossible to deny the validations that were popping up all over the place, but this was something more again. This was hard, irrefutable evidence, in the form of the real body of a real man. Even now, that protesting bit of my mind wanted to claim simple coincidence. I couldn't.

I stared across at Callum in the green gloom in a silent plea for help in accepting all of this: the journal, the cave, the body. He simply winked, his usually grey eyes glowing emerald green in the unnatural light. 'Told you it was all real.'

This was not what I had hoped for, not what I was needing right now. What I needed, more than anything else, was a big reassuring hug. If Joe was here, he would have understood, given me a hug, sat down with me and let me talk until I had found some kind of balance once more. But Joe wasn't here, and I was learning quickly that Callum didn't act that way, had no concept that someone may have trouble accepting the reality of all this. In any case, I wasn't important right now. This room, and what was in it, was his sole focus.

'The skull? Where's the skull?' Callum's attention, temporarily distracted by the mummified corpse in the centre of the room, now flicked back to its main purpose. His eyes darted eagerly around the small space, settling on the natural shelf that ran at shoulder height almost the full circumference of the chamber. The excited anticipation on his face fell into deep dismay and disappointment. The shelf was empty. Like an automaton, Callum slowly stood and picked his way across to where the skull should have been. It wasn't. He looked again, as if doing so would miraculously rematerialize it.

'Shit!' Again he cursed, its harsh sound echoing in the acoustics of the chamber. 'The bastard got here first.' I scrambled to my feet and crossed carefully to him. Davey and Frankie were already at his shoulder. We could see it immediately. In the dust of centuries that coated the shelf, was a faint, almost circular outline. 'That's where it was.' The words were tight, clipped.

'How do you know it was Jack?' Davey asked carefully, wary of the angry frustration that Callum was barely holding in check.

'I just do.' He turned away.

I knew too. Jack had somehow found his way here and taken the skull for himself.

*   *   *   *   *

In that instant, all hell broke loose. For the second time that day, the world around me disappeared. This time I saw Jack. He was running desperately, lost, searching for a way out. The boundaries between us dissolved completely. I felt his distress, felt my – or was it his? I could no longer tell – hand clutching at his chest as he scrabbled for breath. I had been taken back there again, back to that place, back to his final moments. My body swayed, no longer able to remain upright. All at once I knew. This was it. This was that nightmarish dream. It was Jack…

Once more, my lungs were on fire. I couldn't breathe. Every intake of breath was a battle to suck in enough air. Fighting. Fighting to hold on, to find enough oxygen to feed my heart, my lungs, my brain. To keep me conscious. A dark mist was trying to force its way down over my eyes, swirling waves of red and black, the embers of my dying fire. I couldn't battle much longer, couldn't hold on. But I had to. Had to, because if I didn't it would engulf me, and I would be lost...

* * * * *

Hundreds of feet below and miles of tunnels away from the group in Takuakana's chamber Jack's head sagged as the last vestiges of consciousness ebbed from his body. He had lost. As he slipped into a black and eternal oblivion, his final thoughts were of his wife, Laura, and his two young daughters. They would never know now. Never know that he had found a treasure beyond value, or that because of it he had himself paid the ultimate price and now lay, cold and alone, entombed forever deep beneath the surface of the Earth, far from her warming sunshine and welcoming daylight. They would never know what had become of him, and would live the rest of their lives wondering.

* * * * *

I blinked in the glare of one of the head torches. Where was I? Beneath me the surface was hard and gritty. Bit by bit I remembered. I was in the chamber, lying on the floor, the others kneeling anxiously around me.

'Gemma?' I could hear concern in Callum's voice, 'Are you OK?' I struggled to a sitting position, the fog of confusion and disorientation slowly dissipating from my consciousness.

They must not know. I shook my head, trying to clear the thought, but it would not leave. *Gemma, they must not know.* 'But…' Surely if Jack was in trouble we should try to help him. *It is too late Gemma, no-one can help him now.*

In a blink I understood. Jack was already dead, or very soon would be, long before any help could reach him. He would not bring the skull out into the world, would never make it out of this cave system. In that moment I also understood with total clarity that the skull must not be recovered, must not be introduced to the world. Not by Jack, not by Callum, not by anyone. Not yet. The time was not right. Why? I didn't know, and maybe I never would. But I did recognise how important it was.

I had to hide what I was feeling. They couldn't know. Somehow I smiled reassuringly. 'Yes, I'm OK. Honestly. I don't know what happened but I'm OK now.'

Callum reached out a hand and pulled me to my feet. I stumbled, and for a moment his arms went round me and held me steady. Held also a promise I wanted him to keep. I stayed there a moment longer than necessary before pulling away from him. I was torn in two inside. Torn between knowing that I had to keep the secret of the blue skull and my desire to bring it to this maddening beautiful mixed-up man I was so crazy about.

*   *   *   *   *

I would not reveal what I had just experienced. If I did, Callum would go after Jack, resisting all efforts to hold him back, and he mustn't. Gal-Athiel, for it was her voice I had heard, had made it absolutely clear that she must not be found. If Callum or anyone else went off in search of her, I felt certain they would meet the same fate as Jack. I couldn't let that happen.

Moreover, in so few words, or maybe it was through something that came from beyond the words, the blue skull had convinced me of the necessity for her continuing isolation. The time was not yet right. If she was revealed to a world that was not yet advanced enough to handle her power and gifts, it could bring only destruction and pain. It was a secret I didn't want to have to keep, one I would rather I didn't know about at all, but it was too late for that. I deeply involved in this, whether I liked it or not.

I let them all think I'd fainted, which ruffled my ego a bit because I have never fainted in my life. Frankie and Davey were both so concerned for my wellbeing that I felt deeply touched and at the same time incredibly guilty for deceiving them. Callum, once he saw I was OK, dismissed it from his thoughts, which rankled in a different way. The needy woman in me wanted him to be concerned – a desire that was clearly not to be met.

What had happened had been caused by the vision I had lived and once it had passed I felt perfectly fine, physically. Emotionally however, I was shaken to the core. I had witnessed Jack's death throes and I couldn't tell anyone. No-one but me would ever know what had happened to him or where his body lay. My legs gave way once more as I thought about it all. I only stayed upright because of Davey's quick reactions. He threw an arm around my waist and kept me on my feet.

Callum threw another glance my way. 'Let's get you to the surface, Gemma. Davey, you take care of her. Frankie and I will go on ahead. I want to see if Ches can pick up the trail. I'm not letting him get away with this.' Callum's eyes were blazing with frustration as he scooped up his rucksack and flashlight. 'Wind up the life lines and ropes as you go Davey. If anyone snoops around I'd rather not advertise to anyone that we've been here or lead them to this cave. This guy Takuanaka deserves to be left in peace.' He cocked his head at the body, still curled on the floor where we had found him.

I was touched at Callum's unexpected sensitivity. Yet again he had surprised me. I looked across the chamber. Was that dried out corpse really Takuanaka? The others were clearly in no doubt. Taking into consideration everything that had happened over the last few hours, neither was I.

*   *   *   *   *

As Davey and I left the chamber I felt fear strike me in a way I had never experienced before. Images of the lifeless Jack assailed me, accompanied by a cold dread that we would suffer the same fate. Davey looked at me anxiously.

'Are you sure you're OK, Gemma? It's a long trek back.'

I forced a smile onto my face. 'Yes, I'm fine. A touch of claustrophobia. Just stay right behind me and don't lose sight of that line. I don't want to get lost down here.' I was making it into a joke but I was deadly serious. Jack's face would not budge from my mind.

'Don't worry, I've got it. We'll be topside in no time.' Davey was keeping his voice light, but he couldn't mask the concern in his eyes. The guilt I was feeling increased.

'I'm OK, Davey. Honestly. Come on, let's get out of here.' I was happier with Davey behind me than in front (after all, in the movies, it's always the guy at the back who gets jumped on). I quickly realised that acting as point man was not a lot of fun either. I was the one now forging a path into the leaden blackness of this subterranean world. Those horrible images of Jack had sent my imagination, always active, into overdrive. At times I could almost hear the fearsome bellow of a far off minotaur coming to claim its victims, or see the clawing hands of lost souls reaching out from the inky abyss of the side tunnels. Once, Davey's boot kicked a loose rock and I swear I almost hit my head on the roof, I jumped so high.

Davey could tell my nerves were wired to breaking point so he began to chat to me. It helped. To his amusement I tracked the lifeline with my hand all the way, holding on to it as if, should I let it go, I would vanish. I wasn't about to suffer the same fate as Jack. Davey teased me gently about it, making me laugh. It distracted me from my unwelcome thoughts. I had a suspicion he knew that, which is why he was doing it.

I have never been happier to see the sun. The shaft of daylight that cut into the entrance cave was as welcome to me as a banquet would be to a starving man. We had made it. I hugged Davey, taking him by surprise, and dashed out onto the hillside, raising my arms to the sun as if worshipping an ancient god. Below us, the campsite was pretty much struck and Callum was stalking up and down impatiently, cursing the lack of a signal for his cell phone. Within half an hour we were in the saddle and heading back for civilisation. Callum's focus may have been on tracking down Jack and the skull, but all that was on my mind was a hot bath and a comfortable bed where I could sleep until lunchtime. And something to take my mind off Jack.

GOR-KUAL: The Red Skull

Part V

THE CAMEL HERDER

CHAPTER 51

It was done. The old man, Hashu, sank heavily onto the low, roughly constructed stool that stood just inside the doorway of his simple home. Fatigue claimed every part of him. He was too old, too tired, for the journey he had just undertaken, but he had had to make it. Its importance could not permit anything else. Now that it was over, however, now that the precious object he had guarded for so many years was safely concealed once more, now that it would not be found except by those chosen ones who would be led to it when the day came, he could rest. His job was done. He no longer needed to be constantly vigilant against its discovery.

In his weariness Hashu leaned his back against the rough mud brick wall of his house and allowed his eyes to fall closed. As he drifted into the darkness of hard-earned sleep, memories of that long ago day when he had first come across his treasure flickered against his eyelids...

*   *   *   *   *

It was a hot day, so hot, and had been so for weeks. Even by the oven heat standards of the sun-scorched desert these temperatures were out of the ordinary. Yet life went on as normal. It had to. Existence here was hard and survival had to be earned. In these furnace days, this survival was that much harder and less certain.

At that time Hashu had been young, strong and, even if he said so himself – and as the recollection crossed his drowsing mind a smile touched his lips – handsome. His jet black hair, when not concealed beneath the flowing headdress that formed such effective protection against the sun's onslaught, rippled to below his shoulders, and eyes the colour of freshly mined coal watched intelligently from beneath heavy, dark eyebrows. Hashu may have been a mere camel herder but he bore both the looks and stance of a prince. In his semi-sleeping state the old man smiled again and slipped further into his remembering.

That day, so many years ago now, he had taken the camels out as usual. No matter about the heat, the camels had to be cared for, fed and watered. They were his sole livelihood and without them he would starve. As he followed his animals from the village, a grand name for the tiny cluster of rough mud-brick shacks, he allowed himself, as he usually did, to daydream. To imagine a life of riches and plenty; a life where as much sweet, fresh fruit and ice cold, clear, pure water as he could wish for was always available to him, and where he could dine daily on platefuls of delicious, meltingly tender meat; where he could sleep on silken sheets, and make love to his pick of luscious, firm-breasted young women with golden hair and soft skin, a different one every night if he chose; where he could spend his days learning, or hunting with his falcons, or sitting by a cool, splashing fountain surrounded by perfumed flowers and listening to poetry and stories.

All this he dreamed, yet none of it he knew, none of it he had ever seen. These fantasies came from the tales that the men of the village told as they staved off the chill of the desert nights around the fire pit. Could such a life ever exist? He didn't know. He felt sure that somewhere it did. Wouldn't the kings and princes of the palaces live in such an idyllic fashion? One day, he told himself constantly, one day he would discover a priceless treasure that would lift him to their ranks and make him the richest among the rich.

His wanderings took him to the pile of ancient ruins an hour's walk or so away from the village. No-one knew what they once had been although the older people told the legend of a lost city complete with magnificent palace, a city that one day had just suddenly ceased to be. Hashu was fascinated by the story and, ever since he had first come here as a young boy at his father's side, he had wondered. Could this be that city? It was hard for him to imagine it so, for this desolate, time-ravaged place had almost completely disappeared into the sand, only the remnants of walls visible through its shroud. He returned here often, drawn by a compulsion that he did not understand. He was fascinated by it, yet at the same time he felt a tremor of uncertainly and unease every time he approached what was left of its outer walls. Perhaps it was the ghosts of those long ago inhabitants who still wandered the bygone streets in an echo of their lives, or the memory of whatever disaster had befallen this place that remained forever locked in the fabric of its present.

He would normally roam the ruins, exploring, looking for he knew not what, but today the heat was too great. As the camels grazed on the coarse, sparse desert grass which grew on the bed of a former mighty watercourse, long vanished beneath the surface, Hashu lay in the shade of the tumbledown walls and tried to imagine what life here would have been like. Resting against the warm stone, the sand a soft mattress beneath his body, he dozed and dreamed as the camels munched and belched contentedly. When, from time to time, his eyes opened, their gaze lost itself in the vivid blue sky overhead.

CHAPTER 52

The sands here shifted constantly, carried at the whim of the wind. That which was uncovered one day could be buried under tons of soft golden grains the next. Two nights previously a severe sandstorm, the worst in a good many years, had hit the region. Word had reached the village that a whole family had perished in the storm, caught far from shelter and unable to reach safety in time. It was not an unusual occurrence, for these storms often came upon them out of the blue with only a few minutes warning as the air suddenly fell still and the heat increased moments before their ominous fast-moving clouds appeared over the horizon. In the village the inhabitants had rushed for their homes, sealing doors and windows as best they could against the choking dust that found its way through the tiniest gap, burning their eyes, rasping in their throats and lungs. The following days would be hard. Food would be in short supply. The camels could withstand the desert's fury but many of the goats and other livestock had not. Their bloated corpses still lay scattered where the wind had tossed them.

This morning the desert landscape was like a new country, the changes far in excess of anything Hashu had ever seen before. At the ruins the wind had scoured out deep hollows where it had spiralled within the walls of the buildings, its powerful vortices sucking up the sand and dropping it elsewhere in huge dunes. And although for a time he relished the luxury of doing nothing but laze in the cool shade, before long something deep inside of Hash kept poking at him. No matter how much he tried to ignore the unwelcome intrusions, they would not go away. It was his curiosity, bored with his idleness, urging him to get up and explore the transformed world inside these tumbledown walls. Hashu could not resist for long the call of this compelling place, which in its new found nakedness lay stretched out before him like a wanton lover, beckoning to him with the tantalising promise of secrets yet to be unveiled.

This morning everywhere was different, his familiar route barely recognisable. Deeper and deeper into the maze of buildings he wandered, exploring further than he had ever gone before, scrambling up and down the sides of steeply sloping dunes of sand that shifted beneath his feet. In places it was still piled high and he walked level with the tops of the walls. In others, as he walked, streets revealed themselves to him, still paved in smooth blocks of feet-worn stone now swept clean of their sand covering. Walls, which until now he had believed only a remnant of their former glory, showed themselves to be at what had to be nearly their full height. It was the former ground level that gave the mistaken impression that they had to have fallen. Now, inside many of these walls, a giant whirlwind had sucked up all of the sand and carried it off.

*   *   *   *   *

The floor was far below Hashu, five, maybe six times his height below, and in the newly re-exposed walls, protected for centuries by the dry desert sand, he could see intricate carvings of men and animals, flowers and strange symbols. Vividly painted murals covered other sections, their colours as bold and vibrant as the day they were buried, and in yet others the remains of richly decorated tapestries still hung. The floor itself was littered with debris and broken stone – shattered masonry from the roof that had once covered this great hall, perhaps?

For some minutes Hashu stood at the top of the wall, overlooking this wonder that had opened up before him. In all his imaginings he had never expected something like this. For Hashu saw now that beneath the desert surface with its scattered, unrecognisable ruins, the rest of this great city must still lie, hidden and forgotten. And surely this magnificent building had to be the great palace in which the king of this city lived?

What was that, over there? Hashu squinted against the fierce sunlight. In the far corner of the room, still half concealed where the wind had not completely cleared away the blanket of sand, a flash of dazzling white seared his eyes. Whatever it was, it was beckoning irresistibly. If he climbed down, would he be able to get out again? Yes, it would be relatively easy. Hashu was

328

agile and strong, and the carvings on the walls were deep and conveniently spaced. They would provide an easy foothold.

Cautiously Hashu lowered himself into the void. The walls were solid, the footholds secure, and he scrambled down easily. He cautiously approached the corner where the object still sparkled in the sunlight; it was a huge carved table or stand of some kind, formed from a pure white marble, a startling contrast to the dark brown sandstone and vivid decoration of the walls of the room. It was broken, smashed as it fell probably, the pieces jumbled together, one on top of the other. Hashu stretched out his hand and touched the largest of them. It was smooth, polished to a silky finish that the years had not touched. And what was that beneath it, that glimpse of dull red? He could just reach the object with his fingertips and succeeded in brushing away a bit more of the sand that hid it. It felt curved, polished smooth. Whatever it was, it was clear it had been shaped by someone's hand.

Intrigued by the mysterious find, his mind once more turning to thoughts of discovering some treasure that would bring him a fortune, Hashu began to move the heavy broken marble and sandstone blocks that covered it. He forgot totally about his camels, forgot about the sweltering heat that in the airless depths of the room was almost unbearable, forgot about the sweat that poured from his forehead and stung his eyes. This treasure was his. At last he reached out to lift the last chunk of broken marble that covered it.

'What in...?' He leapt back with a yell, his heart pounding. The piece of stone in his hands crashed to the floor. As he had lifted it, Hashu had come face to face with someone staring back at him, dull, sightless eyes meeting his own.

The body lay under the wreckage of the marble stand and had clearly been there since the stand had fallen, trapped by the massive weight of the stone. This though was no bare skeleton. The dry, desiccated desert air and the protective blanket of sand had preserved it to an incredible degree so that it seemed that he – and there was no doubt that it was a he – had died only yesterday.

With a curiosity that was strongly tempered by revulsion Hashu studied the body that sprawled at his feet. The man had been short and stocky, far different to the wiry build of Hashu's own people, and his hair, even in death, was thick and curly, the rich colour of saffron. His lower face was covered in an equally thick and curly beard of the same hue. Who was he? A visitor to this place yes, but had he entered here as friend or aggressor? Hashu forced himself to look into the frozen eyes and shivered. The passing of the centuries had done little to soften the cruelty and brutality that still emanated from them. No, this man had not come here with an open hand and heart. He had been intent on conquest.

Reluctantly, for while he was no stranger to death and its aftermath this dried out shell repelled him on all levels, Hashu prised the cadaver's rigid fingers from

330

their grip on the red object beneath and, shuddering, forced its arm away. Not wanting to damage this unknown treasure, he dug carefully with his fingertips into the soft, yielding sand that had settled around it around it until it was free. Gently he eased it out, surprised at its weight. As it came into view, Hashu drew in a sharp breath. Whatever he had been expecting, it certainly hadn't been this. In his hands sat a life-sized skull, carved from red rock. He recognised the stone; it was red jasper. He had seen it once before polished like this, in the hilt of a knife, and had even then been taken by its subtle beauty. It was not a vivid red, crimson or scarlet as blood is, but more subtle, muted, with a brownish tone. He believed he could almost feel the skull pulsing as he held it, the blood pounding more strongly through his veins. No, that throbbing had to be nothing but his imagination, and the powerful sensations in his own body due solely to his exertions in the sun and heat, and excitement at his discovery.

Nonetheless, as he held the skull in his hands under the searing sun it began to cast its spell over him. Pulling his water skin from his belt, Hashu sacrificed some of the precious contents to wash the film of desert dust from the surface of his still-pulsing brick red treasure. Where the water trickled, the ruddy surface, polished to a smooth flawless finish, gleamed in the bright sunlight. Hashu lifted it level with his eyes to look more closely, and the skull looked back at him, its blank eye sockets unsettling in their intensity, as if it was deliberately returning his gaze. It frightened him. Was this some demon come to steal his soul and condemn him to the torment of hell for eternity? Even as he held his gaze though, Hashu recognised that this was not the case. He could not understand it, did not know where the knowing came from, but the certainty filled him that this object was not an instrument of evil.

He could not draw his eyes from the skull in his hands. It was unusual, fascinating. Bewitching almost. It could be valuable. He would be able to exchange it for gold, of that he was certain, but it was not the priceless treasure he had so long dreamed of finding. Yet somewhere deep within him, Hashu knew that it didn't matter, that the true value of this skull was greater than any gold could buy. It was a conviction that rose up within him from his groin and settled firmly and immovably in his gut. In the same moment came the understanding that he had to keep it hidden, that no-one else must ever find out about it. That this skull was a source of immense power for good, but also one that could be misused and cause untold pain and suffering should it fall into the hands of those who sought power and domination. Just as clearly, Hashu suddenly saw that it was no accident that the skull had revealed itself to him this day. That he had been chosen for this. That perhaps it had always been his destiny.

It was a destiny that he did not welcome and he fought fiercely against it. Why should he worry about the skull? What was in it for him? Why should he be the one responsible for the safe-keeping of this mysterious object? It was only a carved piece of stone. If he couldn't profit from it, why bother with it at all? Holding onto it could cause him no end of trouble if it was discovered. He could be accused of theft, or be murdered by someone who wanted to steal it from him. Why didn't he just leave it here, down in this room, or rebury it in the sand for someone else to discover in times to come?

Even as, with a deep stab of anger and sorrow, he watched his anticipated fortune and the future it offered vanish before his eyes Hashu knew that he wouldn't do that. Neither would he sell the skull or share the secret of its discovery. The impulse to protect it was too strong, too powerful, to resist. As he stared down at it, heavy in his hands, a surge of strength and power enveloped him. Involuntarily he straightened his shoulders, ready to protect it from any threat. In some unfathomable way, this incredible object had drawn him here today, had chosen him as its guardian. He would keep it hidden, guard it, until the time came for it to move on. The question had been asked of him, unvoiced and unheard, and he had answered yes. Hashu dare not let his mind dwell on what that might entail, for doubt was already beginning to build within him. And yet, as he grasped the stone skull securely under his arm and prepared to climb back up the walls to ground level, an unexpected feeling of anticipation began to dawn in him alongside his fear and uncertainty.

The climb back to the surface was slow and laborious, burdened as he was with his treasure and, as a result, able to use only one arm to help himself. When he finally scrambled over the top of the wall, panting from his exertions, he saw that the sun had dropped low in the sky. He had spent far longer in the sunken room than he had realised. It was time to head home.

The camels were waiting patiently for him as he wrapped the red skull in the long, rough piece of cloth that was his headdress and set off for the village once more.

Little did Hashu realise, as he walked away from the newly uncovered temple chamber that day carrying his treasure, that his guardianship would last so many years, all his long life.

CHAPTER 53

What to do with it? That was the question that had preoccupied Hashu all the way home. He placed his bundle down on the woven mat that served as his bed and looked around his meagre home. He had to find somewhere safe to hide it before it was seen by anyone, but where? He had few possessions, nothing big enough to hold the life-sized skull. Moreover, it would have to be somewhere accessible, for Hashu understood clearly that he would want to take it in his hands, to sit with it, often. He could not think of anywhere.

Hashu sank heavily down onto his bed, a simple mat spread over the bare earth, laying the cloth bundle beside him. Where could he hide the red skull? He sat there for a long time thinking before he noticed his hand. He blinked, light dawning in his eyes. Lost in his thoughts, he had been idly scratching his fingers through the loose dirt of the floor, allowing it to trickle through his fingers...

The floor was earth and sand, hard-packed certainly, but he would be able to dig into it. Hashu scrambled to his feet, moved the cloth wrapped bundle and tore aside the thin, rough mattress. Grabbing the heavy stick he used to drive his camels, he sank to his knees and, with slow, deliberate blows, began to chip away at the floor.

It was not an easy task. The ground was hard and compacted, and his only tools were his knife and the stick. It took a long time. Eventually however Hashu straightened. It was done. He had chipped out a hole just large enough to conceal his find. He carefully unwrapped the skull from the cloth, laid it in the hollow and scooped the loosened sand back around it with his bare hands before replacing the mat once more.

It was very late by the time Hashu had finished. He did not light his lamp, simply lay down gratefully onto his bed, exhausted by the events of the day, and closed his eyes to sleep. Only to open them again immediately. A powerful swirling, rushing sensation was churning through his torso, and vivid colours were whirling across his closed eyelids. The physical sensation was so strong that it pinned him to the floor, unable to move or even cry out. Hashu was terrified and trembling. What was happening? Had he been wrong? Had he really disturbed some demon that was entering and possessing him? Even as these fears chased through his mind, somewhere deep inside himself he knew it was not so. In spite of the dizzying rushes of colour and energy his initial terror was fading away and he felt safe and calm.

The sensation lasted for what seemed hours but slowly he felt it ease. As it passed a wave of strength, courage and invincibility enveloped him the way it had all those hours earlier in the sunken chamber. The skull, that was the cause of all this. The words came into his mind like a whisper. As they did so, he realised that its hiding place was now directly underneath the base of his ribcage. He was lying directly on top of it with nothing but the mat and a few grains of sand between them.

An irresistible pull to set his eyes on the skull again, to touch it with his hands, overwhelmed Hashu. Ignoring his fatigue, he scrabbled to uncover the treasure he had so recently concealed. There in the darkness he sat, oblivious to the passage of time, tiredness forgotten, blind and deaf to everything but the object in his hands. Only stirring when the first rays of the morning sun tiptoed through his doorway, when he once more buried it beneath his bed.

Night after night this continued. Hashu would lay down to sleep, only to be called by the red skull, which he would dig up and sit with until daybreak, concealing it again as the sun rose. Yet despite his absence of sleep, he would be as refreshed and wide awake as if he had enjoyed a full night's deep rest. What happened in these hours, he would not later have been able to relate had anyone asked, only that he saw and heard things that were beyond wonder, that he travelled to places far beyond his small hut without leaving the place where he sat. And he learned that the skull's name was Gor-Kual, and that she came from a place far beyond the stars.

CHAPTER 54

Hashu would have to find a new and better hiding place for the red skull. An imminent change in his life was making it imperative. He was to be married. Hashu had lost track of the days and months since he had discovered the red skull, had not realised the date was almost upon him. A visit from his future father-in-law had been an unwelcome reminder. Within a month his new bride would be sharing his life and his home. He had to act, and act quickly, but what to do?

The answer came it him that night as he sat with the skull as usual. He would build a false wall at the back of his house where it abutted the large rock that formed the rear wall of the building. It would make the already tiny room even smaller but no matter. He only needed enough space to conceal it from prying eyes.

His mind raced. If he hollowed out some of the soft rock to form a flat-based niche just big enough, he would only need a thin layer of bricks to cover it. Of course, some of these bricks would have to be left loose so that he could remove them to gain access to Gor-Kual, but no-one else would know of this. As he contemplated the ideas, his spirits fell. With a wife in his home he would not be able to spend his nights with the skull as he had been doing. It would all have to come to an end.

'As all things must.' The thought came as a low voice, brushing through his mind. 'What had to be done has been done. The work is complete.' Hashu did not know what it meant. Still, he was strangely soothed by the words.

For the next week Hashu chipped away at the soft rear wall of his house. He dug clay from the river bed, forming it into rough square bricks which he dried in the sun. When anyone asked him what he was doing, he simply told them he was making his home more comfortable for the arrival of his new bride. He carried the bricks into his house and slowly, steadily, built them up into a wall, leaving the access to the hollowed out hiding place open. On the morning of his wedding day Hashu sadly and reverently placed the skull in the recess and pushed the final bricks into place. He stood back and looked. The loose bricks appeared identical to all the others. No-one would be able to tell that there was anything hidden behind them. When he was alone, he would be able to take down the bricks, retrieve Gor-Kual and sit with her, as he had been doing since the day he found her. There would be other opportunities too to spend time with the red skull. He would make sure of it.

* * * * *

His wife had been betrothed to him since she was a baby, an agreement between families that neither he nor she had had any say in. Even now she was barely more than a child, just thirteen years old, admiring and not a little afraid of her strong, handsome new husband. She was docile and obedient as she had been taught, and did not question whenever he left to head out into the desert, a strange bundle held tenderly under his arm. Hashu was a good, kind man whom she grew quickly to love and she did not wish to anger him with her curiosity. For despite his virtues she soon learned that he was quick to anger when she questioned his actions. So she did not, although, unlike as many of the other men did with their wives, he did not beat her for her questions, merely reprimanded her with a cold and cutting tongue. Hashu in his turn soon loved her deeply for her gentleness and willingness to care for his every need.

Sadly their union was not to last, her death coming soon after the birth of their second son. She was still only sixteen years of age. Afterwards, his sons had gone to live with their grandparents, his wife's parents, leaving Hashu alone in his grief, his own mother and father having died many years before. He turned back to the skull, spending more and more time in its presence, disappearing from the village sometimes for days on end. The villagers left him alone, understanding that he needed time and solitude to heal his sorrow. He found solace in the companionship of Gor-Kual, who always brought him the strength and courage he sought.

Until one day she no longer did. Or maybe it was simply that Hashu no longer needed her. He wrapped the skull in a cloth, put her back into her place behind the loose bricks, and more or less forgot about her. He did not remarry, did not feel the wish to, and there was certainly no need for he had two strong sons to carry on his name. He lived simply, for the most part content, his camels providing him with a meagre, though adequate living, and watching through the years as his sons grew up, married and had children of their own. Thoughts of the red skull rarely entered his head and there was no trace of the powerful energy that he had once felt fill his home and his body.

*   *   *   *   *

And that had been that.   Until the middle of the previous year. It had been the day when the sun was at its highest and daylight at its longest. It had also been exceptionally hot, a heat that transported him back to that day, so many years previously, when he had descended into a sunken room and discovered the red skull.   With the memory came a call, a distantly reawakened echo of what had been, a summons from Gor-Kual to take her in his hands once more and sit with her as he had used to do.

CHAPTER 55

It was a call he could not ignore. For the first time in over fifty years, Hashu crossed to the wall at the back of his home and with some difficulty prised out the once loose bricks. Dust and grit cascaded to the floor. He hesitated. Anything could be hiding in the folds of the cloth: a venomous spider or scorpion, even a small snake. Grabbing a short stick he poked around with it vigorously, hoping that if anything was lurking there it would be disturbed enough to flee, before he cautiously reached in and pulled out the dusty cloth-wrapped bundle.

Slowly he unwrapped the skull and gazed at it. Why now? After all this time, why now? The answer whispered unbidden into his mind

'Take me away. Hide me far from here where I cannot be found. They are coming in search of me. They know my power and want it for themselves. They cannot be allowed to find me. Take me away.'

Hashu did not know what the words meant. Who were coming? How could anyone else possibly know about the existence of the red skull? It had been lost, unseen, for centuries before he found it, and it had been hidden, unseen, ever since. What was this power that Gor-Kual spoke of holding within her? He had never felt any power – a sense of strength and courage yes, strange and wonderful visions certainly, but he had never considered it as power that a man could wield for good or evil. How *could* it be used in such a way? Had he not been compelled to keep her existence a secret though, to hide it from everyone, even his beloved wife? Why had it been so important that no-one knew of the skull? Where had that compulsion come from? Could that have been an expression of this same power? More thoughts filled into his head, this time of his own making, flooding him with trepidation. Where would he hide it? How would he find a safe place? He was old. How could he manage to do this thing that was being asked of him?

'You will know where.' The whispering returned. 'You will find the right place if you allow me to guide you.' With the words came an image, slowly forming in his mind: spires of dark, almost black rock. At their foot, an opening leading to a cave. No, more than a cave. A shrine, maybe? An image painted onto the wall – a lizard, but a strange looking lizard, the head and tail intact, the body merely a skeleton. Memories laughed at him from the edge of his mind. He had heard tell of this place but when? Where was it? Dim and far off, fragile fleeting recollections hovered like phantoms, little by little crystallising into clarity.

He had been a child, maybe ten years old, when a wandering storyteller had passed through the village. The storyteller had sat with the menfolk around their campfire deep into the night, captivating them all with his tales of adventure and mystery. He, Hashu, had sneaked from his bed without his mother noticing, to hide in the flickering shadows and listen to him speak. On that evening, the storyteller had told the tale of a sorcerer who had lived in this cave, the description, from what Hashu could recall, matching exactly the image he had just seen in his mind. The storyteller recounted how people travelled from far and wide seeking this sorcerer's wisdom, prophecies and healing. It was widely whispered that he was not of this world, that he wore a golden aura around him wherever he went, performed feats beyond the capability of any normal man, and was protected from all harm by a bodyguard of unseen forces. This cave lay far from Hashu's village, across the most desolate and forbidding of the desert lands, and legend told that since this magician's departure from this world – it was said by many that he rose up into the sky in a column of searing white light – it had been guarded by ghosts and malevolent spirits who threatened the sanity, and even the life, of anyone foolish enough to enter.

Hashu gave a wry laugh. This place was several weeks of arduous travel away across the heart of the barren desert. A younger man may make it. He could not. He had seen more than seventy years and was no longer strong or agile. His limbs had stiffened and weakened, and these days he was quick to weary. He could not do it. He could not succeed. It was too much to ask of him. He dismissed the thoughts from his mind.

Gor-Kual would not let him refuse however. Once more he began to spend each night in her company, as if with a lifelong friend. Slowly her influence touched him once more until, one night several months later, as he let his gaze settle on the gleaming brick red skull in his hands, a distantly familiar feeling began to pulse through his cells. It was a feeling he had forgotten, one he had not experienced for a very long time. Courage and strength were coursing through his body, touching every organ, every muscle, every cell, rejuvenating and awakening him. The skull's request leapt back into his mind, as clearly as the first time. All at once he was filled with an irresistible euphoria and excitement. Of course he could do it. He had never travelled more than a day's walk from his home, this would be the adventure of his lifetime. It was as if he had been taken over by someone else, someone who would not let him even consider refusing this mission.

Hashu set about his preparations, which in truth were few. Under the pretext that he could no longer cope with the work, he gave away his camels to his sons, keeping only the three best for his journey. Avoiding drawing attention to his actions he gathered what provisions he could, taking only food which the harsh desert sun would not spoil, and into a small pouch he tipped the few coins he had saved. They were pitifully few, a meagre reward for a lifetime's hard work, but it was all he had. He gathered and filled water-skins and tended well to his beasts' wellbeing, for it was they who would carry the greater part of the burden during this trek. Strangely, no-one seemed to notice anything untoward. If they did, it was not mentioned.

CHAPTER 56

Five days later, in the frigid darkness that preceded the dawn in these desert lands and before the rest of the village awoke, Hashu silently unhobbled his three remaining camels to lead them out into the starlit blackness of the desert. His mouth was dry, his stomach churning, fearful of the fate that may lie ahead. At the same time he was consumed with a joyful sense of anticipation and excitement at this adventure and filled with a sense of freedom the like of which he had never experienced before. He was stepping out of the comfortable and familiar into the unknown, and it was exciting. The red skull was safely stored in a small sack tied securely to the back of his favourite camel. These animals were his transport – it was too far to travel on foot – but so much more besides. They would provide milk for sustenance when his stores ran low, and guide him to water when his own instinct failed him.

Where he was heading, what he would find when he got there, he did not know. He was trusting the skull to guide him, was placing his life in her care. His rational mind kept repeating that this was lunacy in the extreme. He was heading into the desert without any clear direction, believing an inanimate carved object would guide him and keep him safe. And yet held firm in his heart, in his gut, in that ancient intuitive part of himself, he carried the instinctive knowing that it was all going to be alright.

*   *   *   *   *

It would be a long and arduous journey. Each of his camels carried a number of water-skins, which he replenished at every opportunity, some food, and a few items he hoped to trade for supplies in the few scattered villages and towns he was to pass through. Hashu also carried with him two long wooden poles and a length of thick cloth that would provide shelter from the hottest part of the day and warmth in the chill of the night.

As to the direction he should take, he had only his instinct and Gor-Kual to rely on. Every morning he started out trusting the skull to guide his footsteps, discovering that he knew, without knowing how he knew, which way to go, never straying from the path all day. Day after day he plodded on through the barren, featureless landscape in the inescapable heat. Rough stone strewn ground turned to shifting dunes and back again. Rocky hills and outcrops rose unexpectedly out of the sandy ocean. More than once he doubted his senses and the wisdom of his trek, especially the times when he left any trace of settlement behind him and started out alone across the desolate, empty desert lands. All the while his camels carried him steadily forward, their huge soft feet and inexhaustible stamina coping easily with it all.

At night Hashu lay wrapped in his thick woollen blanket, gazing up at the endless velvet inkiness of a night sky dusted with the shattered fragments of a million glittering diamonds, wondering where this journey was taking him – and if he would return. Once, and only once, he had taken the skull in his hands as he stared at the stars. He had felt such a strange connection to those far distant suns, a connection that was both so alien and familiar at the same time that it had unsettled and confused him intensely. He had not tried it a second time.

He counted the days, marking each one that passed with a notch onto one of his makeshift tent poles. Ten, twenty, forty, fifty days. Still he had not sighted his goal. He should have been exhausted, his strength drained, but he felt as young and vigorous as he had the day he had first found Gor-Kual, over fifty years previously. Something was feeding him strength and energy. Could it really be the red skull?

At last, late in the day of the morning when he had nicked the fifty-eighth notch onto the pole, he spotted the tall black shadow of a slender rock pinnacle rising above the desert dunes. Another appeared, then another. As he drew nearer they merged closer together, sinister and threatening, like the foul teeth of a desert dog, or the spires of a demonic castle that was waiting to draw him in and swallow him up. With a huge effort of will, the old man shrugged off dire thoughts of evil spirits and monsters.

Throughout the remainder of that day and the one that followed the peaks grew ever larger before him. The nearer he got however, the more he realised that their appearance was deceptive. The outcrop was not that big It was the angle and slenderness of the pinnacles that made them appear taller than they actually were, even though, when he reached their base, they still towered far above him into the deep blue afternoon sky. It was a black island rising out of the sand. The lower slopes were gentle, the spires rising sharply from their crest.

Once more, as if of their own accord, his feet knew the exact path to take. Hashu allowed himself to follow where they led. At the edge of a small flat stone platform, where the wall rose vertically to then divide into several dark columns of rock, he found the entrance he was looking for.

CHAPTER 57

The cave smelled musty. It was empty and long-abandoned. Who was this sorcerer who had lived here so long ago? What had he been like? Who would have made the long trek to consult him, or seek his blessing? How had he survived in this stark, unwelcoming land? If there had once been a water supply here, it had long ago dried up. Hashu's thoughts turned to the stories passed down through the ages in his own village and the nearby town; stories of how, long ago, the inhabitants there had tended fields and cultivated crops, with plentiful water supplies from a river that had sunk far below the surface of the Earth, and whose only legacies now were the wells that provided them with their water and the small oasis on which the town depended for its survival. Maybe in times long since passed by, this place had been part of a lush and fertile landscape too. Maybe it had not always been as isolated and desolate as it was this day.

Hashu blinked as he looked around the small chamber. Once his eyes had accustomed to the decrease in light, he could see easily. The sun streaming through the entrance provided more than enough illumination. It was a natural cavity, that was evident from its fundamental irregularity, but Hashu could also clearly see that it had been extended by human hand, though it must have been a long and laborious task to carve such a space from this hard rock. On one side, a bench or bed had been fashioned from the bedrock. Facing it was a small alcove that stretched in height from Hashu's waist to just above his shoulder. On either side of this niche... Hashu drew in his breath sharply. Painted on the rough wall were colourful images of a lizard, head and tail intact, the body merely a skeleton. One on each side of the recess. He was unquestionably in the right place. On the base of the alcove lay the remnants of long ago offerings: small pieces of jewellery, small pebbles and shards of stone etched with symbols and lettering, and... Hashu looked again in amazement. They were dried and withered certainly but still recognisable. Flowers. Where could they have come from in this arid wilderness?

A thick layer of dust covered everything. The last petition had been laid here a very long time ago. Maybe even centuries. Hashu wondered yet again who had lived and taught here. He explored further, revealing more and more secrets. The rear of the chamber, that at first sight he had thought solid rock, was in fact a clever illusion. A large upright stone had been positioned a stride's length in front of the back wall. Behind it a narrow passageway led deeper into the mountainside. The stone effectively hid the entrance to this passageway, which only became visible once he had walked behind it.

To go deeper into the chamber Hashu needed light, so he fetched the small oil lamp from his travelling bundle. Lighting it, he cautiously peered into the tunnel, apprehensive of what he might find there. It was empty. He crept further in. It ended a short way ahead of him in a wall of stone. At first glance he thought it a dead end until, as he moved his lamp to illuminate the sides of the passage, he noticed four small chambers leading off it, two on each side. He took a closer look in each of them. The ones on the left of the passageway were empty with blank featureless walls that again looked as if they had been hard won, chiselled from the hard bedrock. He turned his attention to the rooms on the right hand side.

As he entered the first one he stopped in amazement. It was filled with dozens of sealed oil jars, each of which stood higher than his knee. Most were upright but a couple had fallen – or had they been deliberately pushed over at some time long in the past? – and their contents, slender rolls of a fine, delicate material held closed with a wax seal, had spilled out onto the dusty rock floor. Hashu reached out for one, lifting it carefully. It was the colour of bleached bone, its fabric a little like the fine linens he had often seen for sale in the town market, but stiffer, holding its shape. Until he tried to unroll it.

He had been gentle, but the scroll was so fragile that it fell apart, crumbling into tiny, weightless fragments that floated gently to the floor. In the brief moment before it dissolved Hashu saw that it was covered in a script of some kind. The second scroll was a little stronger and withstood his handling better, so that he could take a closer look. It was the same, row after row of neat symbols covering the page. Hashu could not read or write so the symbols were meaningless and he puzzled over it for only a minute. This was not why he was here. His task lay elsewhere. He did not know what these objects meant, they had no value to him, so he simply left them where they lay.

The fourth chamber was different again. It too was empty. Unlike the blank bare stone of the other three rooms however, this one had numerous niches carved into the walls, six or more to each row, six rows to a wall. All were empty. Hashu suddenly knew without any doubt that this was the place he had been looking for. This was where he must leave the skull.

Carefully he unwrapped Gor-Kual from the rough length of cloth that had hidden and protected her for so many years, shuddering as she emerged from its folds. In the weak guttering light of his simple lamp she at all once appeared grotesque, her colour seeming to turn to the deep scarlet hue of fresh blood. A sudden icy chill of dark premonition trickled through his bones and a heavy understanding washed over him. The skull was not menacing him, she was giving him a warning. A warning that his now peaceful homeland would soon be torn apart by a violence and hatred that would last for many generations to come. Once more he shivered involuntarily, the images clear before his eyes. He did not want to know. Did not want to see this. Pray Allah he would be long gone from this world before such things came about. All he wanted to do now was to finish his task and get out of this place.

Quickly Hashu placed the red skull in the central niche of the wall that faced the door. As he stepped back and the lamp's light faded from that spot, she merged into the shadows and was lost from sight.

'Your job is done. You must leave now, and leave quickly.' As the thought whispered through his head Hashu did not need to be told twice. He hurried from the room back into the main chamber as quickly as his tired legs could move, still unsettled by the dark premonition that had touched him. He was possessed by a compelling and irresistible urge to leave this spirit-held place.

The bright sunshine that poured through the entrance was now illuminating the whole of the main chamber. The light calmed and soothed him a little and he hesitated for a moment. In that instant a far-off rumble, that he felt rather than heard, propelled him the final few steps out into the daylight once more. The rumbling grew louder and the rocky platform began to shake violently beneath him. Hashu stumbled, unbalanced, and fell to the ground. The tremor lasted only a few moments. As it faded, he raised himself onto his elbows and looked towards the cave entrance. A thick cloud of dust was billowing out of it, hanging in the still air.

Hashu remained where he was for a long time, fearful of a second tremor. None came. Eventually he cautiously approached the entrance and peered inside.

The dust was still choking but in the faint glow of his rekindled lamp, he was astounded to see that the entire rear section of the ceiling had collapsed, sealing forever the passageway and the room where the skull was concealed.

Slowly, wearily, he returned to where his camels waited for him patiently. In the few minutes since he had given up Gor-Kual, the last vestiges of his strength deserted him and he felt every one of his seventy three years. It was with little relish that he anticipated his long journey home.

CHAPTER 58

Once more Hashu set out into the emptiness of the desert sands. Now that his task had been accomplished, all he wanted was to be back in his home surrounded by people he knew and loved. He did not know the way back, had only a vague sense of the direction to take remembered from his outward trek. Once again he would have to trust, both in his own instinct and innate sense of direction, and that Gor-Kual would still be helping him, guiding his steps from a distance.

Day after day he travelled. Night after night he lay beneath the shimmering blackness of the sky, staring into its depths as if he could seek out its secrets. Trying to find some sense for the skull's presence in his life, why it had chosen him...with little success. Well, he no longer held her. she was no longer part of his life. Any danger she may have posed to him no longer existed. He was safe.

He was wrong.

*   *   *   *   *

Towards midday on what was, according to his rudimentary pole calendar, the eightieth day of his journey, Hashu spied a caravan cresting a distant sand dune. It was a large caravan, at least twenty five camels plus a good number of men on foot. At the same moment he spotted the travellers they must have seen him too because the caravan changed direction and headed directly towards him across the flat sands that separated them. As it drew nearer, Hashu's gut clenched in fear.

This was no merchant's train. These men were fighters, tough and strong, their faces mercilessly hard and battle scarred. They wore vicious curved bladed swords at their side and heavy duty pistols were tucked into their wide belts. Were they bandits? What could they want with him? Hashu had nothing of value but his camels, but that would not spare him. He was one against many, and he feared for his life.

He could not outrun them, could not fight them, so he drew to a halt and waited nervously for the men to approach. A strong hand reached up and yanked him unceremoniously from the back of his camel so that he fell heavily to the floor, knocking the breath from his lungs. The same hand dragged him roughly back to his feet where he stood, wheezing and gasping, his body desperately attempting to suck in the air it needed.

He forced himself to raise his head to take stock of his attacker, and found himself staring into a pair of pitiless, ice-pale blue eyes. Hashu pulled back startled, an chill rivulet of dread trickling down his spine. He had never seen eyes like that before. They seemed out of place in the creased, dark-skinned face of the man who stood in front of him. This man was no taller than Hashu, thin and wiry, and Hashu could sense an iron strength in those sinewy muscles. A hooked-nose, like the beak of a falcon, sat above thin, tight lips. And always those glacial eyes, in which all spark of mercy and compassion had long been extinguished, if it had ever existed. He waited for the man to speak, trying to still the trembling that shook his body.

'Where have you come from? What is your business out here?' As the questions barked out, the foul odour of his interrogator's breath choked Hashu's nose and throat.

He thought quickly. 'Kaddiq,' he stammered. It was a town he had passed through two or three days earlier. 'I – I – I have been visiting my family there.'

The frigid blue eyes bored deep into Hashu. 'You lie! You are the guardian of the treasure. Where is it?' Several of the men were already searching through Hashu's sparse belongings, not caring of the damage they were causing.

Hashu's legs were on the brink of collapsing beneath him. It was only through sheer willpower that he forced himself to stay upright and keep his face a mask of incomprehension. Instinctively, he knew that these men were searching for the red skull. 'I don't understand. Treasure? I am a camel herder. I have no treasure.'

'You lie,' the man repeated coldly, 'but you will tell us what we wish to know. You can tell us now, in which case we will kill you fairly quickly, or you can tell us from the depths of agony and hell that you will experience should you be foolish enough to choose that way.'

Hashu felt his bowels loosening in terror at the prospect of what those words signified. Still, somehow, he held firm. Where the courage came from to defy these brutes he did not know, but he could not, he would not, betray Gor-Kual's whereabouts. He clenched his buttocks, holding himself in. 'Please, no,' he begged, 'I don't know anything about any treasure. Look at me, how would I?'

The man merely shrugged. 'Take him,' he ordered.

'NO-O-O-O-O!' Hashu screamed in terror as rough hands forced him to the ground, gripping him painfully and spread-eagling his limbs.

'Release him.' The voice, soft but commanding, broke through Hashu's terror. A woman's voice.

'He knows and he *will* tell us. Stay out of this. It is not your business.' Hashu could hear the cold fury in his tormentor's words.

'It is my business, Moshar. The red skull is my business. I am here to find her, and you are here to assist me. Now release him.' Her words were calm and softly spoken, but the authority they carried was indisputable.

Moshar, Hashu's captor, scowled angrily but nodded in compliance and signalled to his men. The hands that held Hashu's limbs loosened. The old man struggled to his feet and looked at the woman who had spoken. She was tall, standing a head or more above his age-shrunken frame, dressed in robes of turquoise blue and gold. Unlike the custom of his people her head was bare and her face uncovered. Glossy dark gold hair, whose colour exactly matched the golden threads in her robe, tumbled over her shoulders and she stood proud and powerful. But it was her eyes that captivated Hashu. Eyes of the deepest, most vivid violet. Eyes that would entrance and bewitch. Eyes that, and Hashu sensed it rather than saw it, held within their depths a deep and inconsolable sadness.

'You are wrong, my lady. He knows. I have been charged to find the skull and I will make him tell us where it is.' Moshar's voice barely contained its fury.

'I am in command here, Moshar, and you will obey my orders. On pain of severe punishment by my lord you *will* do as I say.' Her words still calm and level, permitted no challenge.

Moshar was staring at her in open contempt and hatred. There was no doubt that it was she who held the power here, and it was equally evident that Moshar was sickened by it, that he despised having to bow to the orders of this woman. She paid no attention to his open hostility.

She was standing directly in front of Hashu, who was now on his feet though Moshar's men still held his arms wrenched firmly behind his back. He pulled himself up to his full height and stood as proudly as he could. It was an almost untenable effort. The events of the past few minutes had drained the last remnantss of his strength. Nonetheless, he straightened his shoulders, raised his chin and let pride shine in his eyes. For a brief moment he once more resembled the handsome prince of his youth.

'I am Saphira, queen, seer and sorceress. I have been charged by my lord with finding the red skull, Gor-Kual. I know the truth, spoken or unspoken. Always. I will know if you have spoken truthfully or if you have lied to us. Look at me now and do not try to deceive me, for you will not succeed.'

Hashu raised his gaze to hers and she stared into him, through his eyes and far into his soul. In that moment he had nowhere left to hide; before a heartbeat had passed he knew she had seen the truth. He braced himself for the worst. And then, a momentary flicker in those violet depths. It was brief, barely perceptible, but it was there. A flicker of reassurance, so slight it could not have been observed by anyone else. Sudden, bewildered understanding flashed through Hashu. She was on his side. Why was unimportant. What mattered was that she would not reveal what she had seen about him or the secret he carried. The questions would come later. Right now he was fighting to keep his legs from buckling beneath him at this unexpected deliverance.

'He speaks the truth. He knows nothing of that which you seek.' The lady Saphira turned away from Hashu dismissively.

'You are certain?' Moshar's words were loaded with suspicion, his own instinct telling him otherwise. He stared at her as if trying to see past her words, disbelief clear on his face. 'You are certain, my lady Saphira?'

'You dare to doubt my abilities? Or perhaps it is my word and my loyalty you doubt, Moshar?' Once more the words were level and smooth but the challenge was explicit in her voice, a challenge she knew would not be taken. He would not dare do so. 'I tell you, he knows nothing. Why would he? Look at him. He is an old man. Would the red skull have chosen a keeper who could not protect and defend her? Look at him, Moshar. You think he is one who could do that? Let him go.' Her words permitted no further argument. With an arrogant sweep of her robe she pushed past her questioner and disappeared from sight.

Hashu stood as upright as his tired, aged body would allow, doing his best to keep his face a blank canvas, the picture of an innocent man with nothing to hide. The strength and vigour that had accompanied him all his outward journey had deserted him totally. It was a withdrawal that had started from the moment he had left Gor-Kual in the belly of the mountain and started his return journey. Hashu realised that withdrawal was now complete.

Moshar thrust his cruel hook-nosed face up against Hashu's. The stench of this man's blackened, rotten teeth was unbearable and inescapable. Through sheer strength of will, the exhausted man stopped himself flinching or drawing back, forcing back down into his stomach the nausea that was rising up into his throat.

'Her word is inviolable. I cannot defy it. But I don't trust you, old man. You are hiding something from me, I feel it. If I had my way...' He let the menacing silence hang between them before he turned away abruptly. 'Let him go,' he told the men who still held the prisoner's arms in a vice-like grip. 'We will waste no more time here.'

Hashu found himself flung roughly to the ground, one of his guards unable to resist a well-targeted kick at Hashu's ribs that once more knocked the air from him, and left him gasping in agony for breath for several minutes.

Luckily, apart from some bruises no lasting damage had been done and within a short time he had recovered enough to be able to sit up and give thanks to the heavens for his lucky escape. How lucky had he really been though? The mysterious woman had known – he had seen it in those spell-binding violet eyes – and she had lied. If she had not done so... But why? Had it simply been to spare him? Hashu was in no doubt that his interrogators would have not hesitated for a moment to extract information from him in the most brutal of ways if they had been given the least cause to suspect he knew anything.

Or had it been for a deeper reason? An understanding of the skull and its importance? That it had to be kept from the clutches of men such as those he had just encountered? If that was the case, why was she with them? Though the question pricked his curiosity, in truth he did not really care. The skull was safe, and he had miraculously come through his ordeal unharmed and free to continue his journey.

*   *   *   *   *

An overwhelming sense of relief flooded Hashu's entire body when, after many more days' trek across the lonely desert, he at last saw the low square buildings of his village rising out of the desert sands far ahead of him. It had been a long, hard journey – much too long and much too hard for someone of his years. All he wanted to do now was rest. He had been travelling for more days than he cared to think about, over three months in all. Now, finally, his ordeal was almost at an end. The only thing that troubled him was how he would explain his abrupt and unheralded disappearance and his equally sudden return. He had left in secret, telling no-one he was going, had just vanished into the night. Now he was back again, after so many long days. His family, the whole village, they would all have believed him dead, that was certain.

To his disbelieving astonishment no-one treated his return as anything unusual, offering simply a cheery wave of a hand or a shouted 'hello'. It was as if his absence had not been noticed. Could Gor-Kual in some mysterious way still be helping him from inside the depths of the earth?

*   *   *   *   *

As Hashu roused himself from his dreams he smiled, satisfied. His work was done. He saw that it had grown dark. He must have been asleep for several hours. Slowly, stiffly, he got to his feet and walked outside to join his friends around the fire, to smoke, and share stories. But the biggest story of all – the story of the red skull – that would not be told. It would remain his secret, and his alone, a secret he would take with him unspoken to his grave.

CHAPTER 59

We were a very quiet and subdued group riding out of the camp that afternoon. It was late in the day to be leaving but common sense had taken a back seat. Callum was driven, determined not to waste any more time than necessary picking up Jack's trail. It has to be said that the rest of us were happy enough to go along with it. No-one was keen to hang around the cave now despite the difficulties of travelling in the darkness. Jack's actions had deeply affected each one of us in some way.

Davey and Frankie were fighting off the deep disappointment of having their goal snatched away from right under their noses, and Ches was unusually solemn and withdrawn, his habitual cheery smile nowhere to be seen. Maybe he was just picking up on the general atmosphere of anger and despondency, but I sensed it was something more, though what that might have been, I had no idea. Callum just fumed so silently and dangerously that no-one risked speaking to him.

As for me, the more distance I could put between myself and that horrible cave, the better. I was steeped in guilt over Jack, even though reason told me that any search would be unlikely to ever find him, and that even if by some miracle it did, it would be much too late. But still, abandoning him there, even as a lifeless body, seemed so callous and cold. I was in a totally unfamiliar situation, one I had never in a million years expected to find myself in. Then again, who would? Unsurprisingly I was finding it almost impossible to deal with. The vision of Jack's final moments replayed themselves over and over in my head until I thought I would go mad. Riding in silence in the darkness of the desert night gave little to distract me from these thoughts. I noticed Ches glancing at me curiously on a number of occasions as if trying to work out what was going on. I couldn't let anyone suspect I knew anything more than they did so I just threw him a fake smile. I could tell he wasn't fooled for one minute, but he let it go.

On top of all that, one question still puzzled me. Hour after hour as we rode I wracked my brains to come up with a plausible answer. It was no good. Whichever way I looked at it, I couldn't make any sense of it at all. Where was Jack's horse? If Jack was still down in the cave labyrinth somewhere – and I knew with every cell of my body that he was – why hadn't we found his horse?

He would have taken it up nearer the cave entrance so he could make a quick get-away once he had found the blue skull. But it hadn't been there, and the lie of the land was such that, unless he had left it a considerable distance away, we couldn't have missed seeing it as we climbed the slope. The others hadn't thought about it twice, believing Jack to be miles away by now. I was the only one who knew differently, that his body remained somewhere deep underground. It was a mystery to which I would never find an answer.

∗   ∗   ∗   ∗   ∗

Ches picked his way carefully over the rough ground beneath his feet, making his way back to the camp. He had hiked deep into the hills to perform his ceremony and only now, with the moon dipping back towards the horizon, was he returning. His route would take him right past the cave entrance. As he drew near to it he stopped and peered ahead, his night vision almost as sharp as during daytime. Fifty yards or so ahead of him, and about a hundred yards downhill from the cave entrance, something had moved in the shadows. As he focussed on the spot, he heard a hoof pawing the ground and a soft snicker. A horse. He moved a little closer. Jack's horse.

Ches had known the other members of the team – Callum, Frankie and Davey – for some years now and they were good friends. Jack on the other hand was a stranger and from their first meeting Ches had not trusted him. Jack had been pleasant and friendly enough, nothing in his manner would give cause for suspicion, but Ches possessed a latent psychic ability, the legacy of his shamanic ancestry. He had easily picked up that Jack had hidden motives and had decided to play a waiting game until the newcomer showed his hand.

When he saw the horse waiting patiently in the shadows, it was clear that Jack was making his move.

Ches had acted then. He had unsaddled the animal, stowing the saddle and bridle behind a large boulder, untethered it and sent it galloping off into the wilderness with a hefty slap to its flank. He had no concerns that he was sending the animal to a cruel lingering death in the harsh landscape. The horse was a mustang, strong and hardy, adapted to surviving in such terrain. It would find a herd to join, or maybe even find its way back eventually to the ranch where they had hired it. As Ches would later tell Callum, though no-one would pay much attention to his words, Jack would not be returning from the caves.

Ches was holding a secret. He knew about the blue skull, Gal-Athiel. It was a secret that had been passed down from his grandfather's father to his grandfather, from his grandfather to his father and most recently to him, a secret only the wisest of elders shared, one which all who held swore never to reveal. It was this tightly respected silence that had thwarted all Callum's attempts to unravel a lead from the native people, and because he had been able to find anything out about it, had assumed therefore that they had no knowledge. But keeping silent did not mean they did not know. Ches understood clearly the necessity of the skull remaining undiscovered, and that that continued concealment would be assured. Jack would not be needing his horse again.

It was with a heavy heart that Ches rode away from the campsite later that day carrying Jack's fate as a dark secret in his heart. He believed that he alone carried the burden of the truth, unaware that it was one another shared too.

*   *   *   *   *

'Found anything Ches?' Callum's voice, irritable and impatient, broke the stillness of the night.

Ches shook his head. He had been scouting since we had left the cave site, searching Jack's trail. 'Not a trace. Seems like he's disappeared off the face of the Earth.' Which, I reflected uncomfortably, wasn't too far off the truth. I still couldn't shake the feeling Ches was hiding something. He looked ill at ease and there was a tension in his voice. What was going on? None of the others had seemed to pick up on it, or if they did they weren't saying. Knowing what I did, there was no way I was going to either.

*   *   *   *   *

Four long – very long – days after leaving the cave, we checked back into the little motel in Page. Ches had stayed behind at the ranch saying he was going to visit his family nearby. Yet again I got the feeling he was hiding something though I would never find out what it was now. As soon as we had booked in, Callum disappeared into his room with only a brusque few words to inform us that he was going to contact the expedition backers and, in his words, 'find out what the fuck these slimy tossers are playing at'

After a quick, tense supper, the rest of us headed to our rooms as well. We were all exhausted by the last few days, drained by both the events that had overtaken us and the atmosphere that had hung over us like a shroud since. None of us felt like socialising.

CHAPTER 60

Once I had taken a very long, very hot shower to wash the desert dust out of my pores and, I hoped, clear away the cloying depression that was threatening to seize hold of me, I dug my laptop out of my bag. It was the first time I'd switched it on since leaving the UK, the first opportunity I'd had really. I was desperately tired and wanting to sleep but more compelling still was my need to get in touch with normality. To make contact with the real world that existed outside this bubble we had created around ourselves over the last ten days. Maybe I could Skype Cathy or Jamie and find out what had been going on in their lives while I had been in exile in the desert lands. Already those adventures seemed so dreamlike and far away…

First things first. I checked my emails. There were several waiting from Cathy, all more or less with the same content: *'Where are you? What are you doing? What's happening? Have you found it yet? EMAIL ME!'*

I fired off a long, newsy reply, telling her all about our discovery of the skull cave – knowing she'd be shrieking with excitement as she read it – and swearing her to secrecy. Callum would go ballistic if he found out but too bad. This was my story as much as his and Cathy had been in this with me every step of the way so far. She had a right to share in it. I left out the bit about

Jack though. I'd tell her some time, probably over a coffee or glass of wine when I got home, but right now it was a place I didn't want to go back to. Just as I hit the 'send' button, another email pinged into my Inbox.

Joe! It was from Joe. He was back – and coincidentally, in the US. Why now? Why, after four months of silence, had he got in touch now? It felt significant, though I confess I didn't have a clue why.

*　*　*　*　*

Callum... Joe... Joe... Callum. I tossed and turned, confusing, disturbing dreams roiling through my consciousness, restless and exhausting. Callum, whirling and swirling around me, one moment looming close, then fading away, only to appear again unexpectedly so that I never knew when or where. Catching me always off guard. Dizzying. Throwing me off balance...

Jack...

Gal-Athiel...

And always there, somewhere, Joe. Standing calmly on the side lines as if waiting for something. Patient. Safe. Reassuring in his presence, like a tranquil harbour. A rock to cling to in the storm.

Then, pouring in on me, waves of deep royal blue, sprinkled with the sparkling gold flecks of stars, cut through with the creamy glittering swathe of the Milky Way. An image, vague at first, growing clearer, slowly crystallising in my vision. Another skull, held in the hands of a strong, well-built, golden-skinned figure with flaming hair like a lion's mane. Reaching out, holding out the skull to me, placing it in my hands...

Callum, suddenly appearing there beside me, reaching out to grab it from me. I pull it away before he can take it. Joe, stepping in between us...

*　*　*　*　*

I woke, sweating and trembling, more exhausted than when I had fallen asleep seven hours earlier. I lay for some time in the warm sunlight that was streaming through the window and washing across the bed, letting it warm and soothe me. My heart was beating loudly, my thoughts were in turmoil. In the midst of this mental chaos, I seized upon the one thing I could understand: the skull. I had been shown another skull. Since arriving in America I hadn't dreamed about them at all. I'd just received the signal that this was all about to change.

As for the rest of it, all this stuff with Callum and Joe, I couldn't make any sense of it. The truth was that I didn't really try. I think somewhere inside me I understood exactly what it was telling me but I refused to look at it more closely. So I stuffed it to the back of my mind in a file called 'Too difficult and confusing'. And that was that, or so I thought. It wasn't though, was it? These things never are until we face them and deal with them.

When I arrived down to breakfast the next morning I found Frankie and Davey deep in conversation. They looked up as I joined them.

'No Callum?' I kept my voice as light as I could but I was deeply disappointed not to find him there. He had hardly spoken a word to me since we'd left Takuanaka's cave nearly five days earlier. His indifference was something I was finding hard, given what had taken place between us. I had been trying to ignore my feelings, and failing miserably. The truth was that his cold shoulder hurt. Hadn't our encounter meant anything to him? Of course it hadn't, I scolded myself time and time again. You knew what you were getting into, even if you wouldn't admit it. Frankie warned you too. So don't start whining about it like some lovesick teenager.

Despite the stern ticking off I was giving myself, however, I could tell my feelings were showing. Frankie and Davey were quick to pick up on it. They exchanged a quick glance before Frankie replied. 'He's left.'

'Left? Why? Where has he gone?'

'Boston. He's catching a plane out this morning. Said to tell you goodbye and that he'll see you when he gets back.'

'Well how long will that be?'

Frankie pulled a face. 'He told us he had a load of things to sort out and people to talk to and not to expect him back for at least two weeks, maybe more. I got the feeling he's going to see if he can pick up some sort of lead on Jack.'

I stared back at her, open-mouthed in disbelief. 'Boston? Two weeks?' I must have sounded like an idiot as I parroted her words, but my brain was refusing to take in what she was telling me. Two weeks? Callum had invited me over here, had even taken it upon himself to book my ticket without asking me first – and now he had simply abandoned me to my own devices without even taking the courtesy of telling me himself? I was getting angrier with Callum by the second. What was I going to do?

Davey looked embarrassed. 'We're really sorry about this, Gemma. It's not fair at all on you. But it's what Callum does. We should have warned you. Doesn't help you now though, does it?' he finished dejectedly.

'Well I'll just have to try and sort something out. Get a flight change if I can and head back to England. I'm not going to just hang round waiting for him to turn up if and when it suits him.'

'Look,' Frankie was thinking out loud. 'I've got an idea. I'm heading down to Sedona tomorrow. Why don't you come with me? I'll only be there a couple of days but it'll give you a chance to decide what you're going to do. It's so beautiful there, you'll love it. You may even decide to stay around for a bit. Take a trip out to the Grand Canyon maybe. It's only just up the road.'

While I doubted that I'd wait around in this Sedona place for another whole month or so, I liked the idea of seeing somewhere new. After all, I had travelled all this way, I might as well make the most of it. And the Grand Canyon has been top of my bucket list for years… I thought about it for a moment, then nodded. 'OK Frankie, you're on. Sedona it is.'

As soon as I got back to my room I answered Joe's email, telling him that I had been cut loose and was heading down to Sedona with Frankie. His reply pinged back almost immediately. *That's great. I've just about finished up here in Oregon, so why don't I fly down and meet you there? We'll spend a few days catching up and exploring. I can get there for the day after tomorrow, so let's meet up at 2pm outside the crystal shop that's down next to the creek.'*

'OK' It was a short one-word acceptance that shared nothing of the inexplicable warmth that had poured through me as I read his email, a feeling that everything would be alright now that Joe was coming. With it grew an equally strong feeling that right at that moment, Callum could go jump in the lake.

*   *   *   *   *

Last night another skull had been introduced to me. I counted – that was four I had met to date. If I understood correctly, there were thirteen skulls in total. Where was this adventure going to lead me next? Only time would tell. Only one thing was certain. It wasn't over yet…

THE SKULL CHRONICLES

Enter the world of the mysterious crystal skulls, and a story of loss, heartbreak, courage, sacrifice and love that spans millennia.

13 sacred crystal skulls, brought to Earth from distant worlds over 250,000 years ago. Their purpose: to guide humanity through its spiritual evolution.

Today they lie hidden, scattered across the world, their existence long forgotten. Waiting for the time when they will once more be reunited to lead humankind into a new golden age.

That time is approaching. The skulls are awakening, reaching out to make contact. They choose Gemma Mason, a 40-something year old Englishwoman, to bring knowledge of them to the world again, and to tell their stories: stories of courage, beauty and truth; of adventure, heartbreak and danger. Stories that bring into question everything Gemma had previously believed to be true, for she has been chosen to share a secret that will have repercussions for the whole of humankind.

OTHER BOOKS IN THE SKULL CHRONICLES SERIES

LOST LEGACY
The Skull Chronicles, Book I

13 powerful crystal skulls, brought to earth during humankind's infancy by ancient races from distant worlds. Now the skulls are preparing to reveal themselves once more, and they choose Gemma Mason to bring this knowledge to the world.

As Gemma starts to receive more and more enigmatic information in her dreams, she realises she is being asked to share a secret that has been hidden for thousands of years. A secret that that will change the entire history of the human race.

In Lost Legacy Gemma tells the story of two of these skulls, Gileada and Gal-Athiel, and of those who have been chosen as their guardians. As the tales unfold, and Gemma records them in the form of a novel, she finds herself forced to face her own doubts and fears as she is catapulted onto a voyage of ancient mysteries, adventure and self-discovery.

(ISBN 978-0957195233, Lyra Publishing, April 2012)

READERS COMMENTS
'completely believable, gripping and compelling'
'written with consummate skill'
'a compelling page turner'

PREVIEW: Book III
Provisional publication date, Dec 2013

'Lokar glanced up. Here the trees grew tall and strong, but taller still behind them, towering into the sky, dwarfing them and dominating the landscape for miles around, stood the massive stone built pyramid, the centre one of a row of three that partnered the nearby huge stone lion. The monument glistened like an iceberg in the shimmering heat of the mid-afternoon sun, its white limestone facade dazzling in the fierce rays. All three of these majestic pyramids were clad in this same stone, although he had heard stories that this had not always been the case. It was said that far in the distant past when they had first been built by peoples unknown, they had been covered in glass-like black obsidian, a covering that had long since disappeared. It was even whispered that the very apex, the point where the pyramids touched the sky, had once been clad in pure gold, in honour of the sun god who brought life to everything on the Earth.

Although he had grown up in the shadow of these vast buildings, Lokar never tired of them. They never ceased to fill him with a sense of awe and wonder, and reverence. There was something magical, something otherworldly about them, as if they had been planted here by some giant hand.'

MORE BOOKS BY THIS AUTHOR

FORGOTTEN WINGS
A handbook for spiritual growth and personal transformation

'When we remember our wings, we can begin to fly' 10 simple keys to opening up to the magical & limitless potential of life. It is knowledge that seems new but is as old as existence. Through the insights, wisdom and reawakened knowing that she has received on her own ongoing journey of spiritual discovery, Dawn reminds us of who we truly are and why we have chosen to play this game of life.

(ISBN 978-1846943539; O-Books, Sept 2010)

STARSPEAK
Messages of ascension, love, contact and more in the words of our star brothers and sisters

We are moving through a time of massive change, unprecedented in recorded memory, a time in which life as we know it is being turned upside down. But we do not have to travel through this often confusing and disorientating process alone, for from across the galaxies our star brothers and sisters have gathered to help us through this transformation.

Many people on Earth are now being contacted by these loving beings, receiving their words of guidance, encouragement and reassurance to share with those who as yet do not hear them. This book contains some of these messages, received by the author from the star beings of light, messages that are filled with the love and wisdom of the universe.

(ISBN 978-0957195240; Lyra Publishing, Dec 2012)

For more details, visit the websites at
www.dawnhenderson.co.uk
or
www.theskullchronicles.com

Dawn is available for book signings, talks and seminars. Please contact her via her websites.

BLOGS:
www.soulwhispering.wordpress.com
www.starspeak.wordpress.com